I0784027

BLOOM IN DARKNESS

AN ANTLER POINTE STORY

NOELLE UPTON

This is a work of fiction. Names, characters, places, and incidents are the product of the author's imagination or are used fictitiously. Any resemblance to actual persons living or dead, business establishments, events, or locales is entirely coincidental.

Copyright © 2024 Noelle Upton

All rights reserved.

No part of this publication may be reproduced or transmitted in any form or by any means, electronic or mechanical, including photocopying, recording, or by any information storage or retrieval system without the written permission of the copyright owner, except in the case of brief quotation embodied in critical reviews and certain other non-commercial uses permitted by copyright law.

No generative artificial intelligence (AI) was used in the writing of this work. The author expressly prohibits any entity from using this publication for purposes of training AI technologies to generate text, including, without limitation, technologies that are capable of generating works in the same style or genre of this publication. The author reserves all rights to license uses of this work for generative AI training and development of machine learning language models.

ISBN: 979-8-9917843-1-3

Revised Jan 2025

Cover art by Julia Saxton (Instagram: @j.sgrey)

This is a work of fiction. Names, characters, places, and incidents are the product of the author's imagination or are used fictitiously. Any resemblance to actual persons living or dead, business establishments, events, or locales is entirely coincidental.

Copyright © 2024 Noelle Upton

All rights reserved.

No part of this publication may be reproduced or transmitted in any form or by any means, electronic or mechanical, including photocopying, recording, or by any information storage or retrieval system without the written permission of the copyright owner, except in the case of brief quotation embodied in critical reviews and certain other non-commercial uses permitted by copyright law.

No generative artificial intelligence (AI) was used in the writing of this work. The author expressly prohibits any entity from using this publication for purposes of training AI technologies to generate text, including, without limitation, technologies that are capable of generating works in the same style or genre of this publication. The author reserves all rights to license uses of this work for generative AI training and development of machine learning language models.

ISBN: 979-8-9917843-8-2

Revised Jan 2025

Cover art by Julia Saxton (Instagram: @j.sgrey)

BEFORE YOU READ

Hello, Dear Reader!

Welcome back to Antler Pointe, our small New England town rife with shifters, vampires, and faeries!

While writing *Scars of the Sun*, I fell in love with two side characters and alluded to their romance that occurred largely behind the scenes. But, because my mind has a tendency to latch onto unexpected plans, I wasn't ready to let them go.

Though this *could* be read as a standalone, a major turning point for these two is also the major conflict in *Scars of the Sun*, and it occurs largely off-page in this book. For that reason, it's best you've read *SotS* before reading this one.

So! This is Tyler and Delaney's story. It's shorter than my other books, but it has no lack of romance, *spice*, and a bit of angst. Because of that, I have some topics and content that you might want to be aware of:

Tyler and Delaney are in the BDSM lifestyle, and this dynamic extends outside of the bedroom for them. Meaning, that their Dom and sub roles aren't just a bit of bedroom fun. Well, there's that too, but they both take comfort and care in truly living these roles. I know that this is quite different from my other books and couples, but as you'll see in their story, this type of relationship is perfect for them.

With that, you can find Daddy/boy kink, spankings, punishments, and lots of "good/sweet/perfect boy" being thrown around. Consent and communication remain a pillar throughout their interactions and relationship.

Also, you will find the following possible triggers in this book. Please take care of yourself in whatever way you see fit.

•Mature and explicit sexual content

•Explicit language

•Violence and gore

•Morally gray-ness

•Substance abuse struggle (neither of the MCs)

•Mention of child abuse (sexual, verbal, and neglect)

•Mention of trafficking (these moments are not gratuitous or explicit, but they are not shied away from)

•Slut shaming statements made toward one of the MCs

•Depictions of PTSD symptoms

•Mention of the US HIV/AIDS crisis

•Mention of the death of parents

I believe that's everything. Really, this book is a romance with a HEA, but there is some heavy stuff that Tyler and Delaney have gone through to get to it—separately and as a couple.

I hope you enjoy these two boys that I love so much. It is my most grumpy/sunshine pairing yet, but they complement each other so beautifully. And writing Delaney's dialogue and inner thoughts were just so fun and precious!

Happy reading!

To all those that have read my stories and encouraged me thus far.

CHAPTER ONE

DELANEY

"**C**ome on! We go way back!" The harsh edge to his voice was slicing against my ears and my heart. Didn't he realize that this was hurting me too?

My clothes were already on for the show, but Charlie's long stream of texts and then phone calls just kept on coming. "I'm already having to keep my summer job and juggle school, internship, and—"

"Oh, yeah, poor Delaney with his fancy school. You got a job, so you *can* help me out. After all the shit we been through, you *owe* me."

And I did. I knew that I did. We'd been the only two, and I didn't know where I'd be if he hadn't been there to lean on. He'd also forced me to toughen up. Well, as much as I could manage with the personality I'd been given.

I picked up my phone, giving in and sending him the two hundred that I really couldn't afford to give. *Lauren will give me the shifts. It'll be okay,* I reassured myself.

"Thanks." Charlie confirmed that he'd received the money and got off the phone. My lungs expanded, and I tried my best to focus on putting the finishing touches on my face. The sink that I shared with my roommate, Alex, was cramped with our various toiletries and cosmetics. The old bulb above the mirror wasn't the best lighting for this, but I knew how to manage with less.

Far less.

I set my phone on my favorite getting ready playlist, though the pop music was a far cry from the type of songs I'd be hearing later tonight.

Honestly, last evening had been terrible, and that feeling was persisting into today, no matter how hard I tried. Sure, I'd been lucky to find an attractive guy to take me home, but that was never my issue.

I hummed along to the pretty song while watching myself in the mirror. The eyeliner was tricky, the brown color doing nothing to hide how red and tear-swollen my eyes were. Black felt too harsh for my skin tone when I'd rustled through my sparse makeup bag, even with the clothes I'd meticulously picked out for the show tonight.

My hookup's cold look this morning flashed in my mind, like it had been since I walked out of his apartment while it was still dark out. A nice cuddle and some breakfast weren't meant for me, and that was okay. I sniffed and ran product through my hair, getting the blond waves to settle.

No, when Ma was alive, she'd always said to look on the bright side of things, even when everything else was dark. And, wow, there was a lot of bright in my life now.

As I drove into town, I worked through the tightness in my chest and the itchiness in my eyes. Little ol' me, going to college, in a car that I owned and hopefully on my way to be voted into a new pack. And—

"Well, there's a spot!" I muttered to myself and parked right in front of the bar Alex had instructed me to go to. They still hadn't told me why they decided not to go to the show, but I'd already bought stuff for my outfit. And on my tight budget, it just didn't seem reasonable to let it all go to waste. With all the black and gray, there weren't many places I'd wear this to.

Eyeing myself in the mirror, I patted my hair once again, and I remembered how that man had run his hands against my scalp in the bar last night, grabbed it while we had sex. It was somehow overwhelming and not enough.

As much as I tried to shake the desire, my body still craved a harder touch, maybe some harsh words. But I also wanted to be caressed and praised, instead of looked at like I should've known to leave the minute he collapsed back onto his bed.

I arched my neck and cast my face to the roof of the car, forcing my tears to go back in. That was fine.

After I paid for parking, I pushed my way inside the bar, and —wow! It was so lively inside, people dressed in a rainbow of dark colors and makeup. But as I said 'hi' and waved at those that met my eyes, most of them returned it kindly. Alex had been right —there really wasn't anything to be afraid of.

I didn't much like the taste of alcohol, and my nerves were still going on enough that I didn't want anything in my stomach. So, I walked through the crowd, trying to remember what Alex told me about finding the best place to stand.

I was about to give up when a familiar wintery scent made me perk up. Well, now, that was lucky!

"Hey, Ramona!" I tried to get her attention and made my way over. I excused myself past the nice people here to watch the show too, and my arms were already opening to pull her into a hug.

I knew that I had to get better about my boundaries with people—though I'd been working on that since I was a little boy, so maybe this was just how I was. Touch made me feel better, and having my favorite people against my skin made me feel safe.

Not everyone liked that, my best friend included, but I must've been special, because she squeezed me back and mushed her face into my chest. Friends were mighty hard to come by, and now I had more than I knew what to do with! Ramona was a tough nut to crack, but when we separated from the hug, she smiled up at me and asked if I wanted to sit with her. She really didn't have to ask, because I was gonna request anyway.

She was probably the prettiest person I knew. Her sun-kissed brown skin went so well with the black hoodie she wore, and her gorgeous curly hair framed her usually-serious face. But she smiled at me, amber eyes shining as she asked me how I was. Not much ever changed with me these days, for that I was grateful, and I was elated to hear that she was doing well.

I knew that she'd been in a bad way for a while, but she was like the smartest and kindest person I'd met. She deserved all good things.

Ramona pointed to my chest. "Didn't take you for a metal fan," she said, and I blushed. It still felt odd, listening to such harsh and screamy music. But when I was in the right mood for it, I found that the songs could go pretty well with how I was feeling. Before, I'd thought that all these songs sounded the same, almost always scary. But Alex played it exclusively in our apartment, and when I packed up and moved to Antler Pointe to follow the best scholarship I managed to get, I'd made a promise to myself to try new things.

Focus on my studies. Get a job. Join a new pack. Now, I was at a heavy metal show!

I explained a little bit to Ramona about how my strict Southern upbringing frowned upon this sort of thing. To save myself from the memories, though, I didn't go into detail about just how controlling things had been in Howl's Fury. What being one of only two non-shifters had been like.

No, instead, I focused us back on her as the lights began to dim. I leaned closer to Ramona so that we could hear each other, and her blush was visible on her skin.

"My mate is one of the guitarists," she shared. Like it wasn't the most amazing thing.

A few moments after, a striking-looking jaguar shifter sauntered onto the stage, guitar already at his front and ready to go. He started the show, strumming a booming rhythm, and I had to give it to her—his fingers were sure and nimble on his instrument. His long, black hair looked soft, and when he glanced over at Ramona, he grinned and winked.

Joy for my friend bubbled up my throat, and I shook her shoulder. "Oh my lord, is *that* your mate?" His cocky smirk was definitely befitting of a lead guitarist, and I knew from what she'd already told me that he was quite extroverted compared to her. Even though she told me their story, I asked for it again, the hopeless romantic in me never one to deny myself a good love story.

He was sweet to her, sounded like, and it made me think of her family. Who, going beyond the obligations of pack, welcomed me to their garden. Befriended me when they didn't have to.

My own had died with Ma, then exploded with the destruction of Howl's Fury. Charlie and I had been among the handful that got away before it was too late.

I sighed when my friend finished her story. "You're so lucky, Ramona. A great family and a new mate. Maybe your good luck will rub off on me."

Her mate's band finished their set, and a new one was about to start. Silently, I hoped that she was going to stay for the whole thing, because I was enjoying the music more than I thought I would!

"Ah, I guess. It's still new, but—"

"Hey, beautiful," someone interrupted, and Ramona and I both turned to the owner of the deep voice. I had to look down, right into the brown and silver eyes of the lead singer that'd just left the stage.

They were like darkness and the churning clouds of a thunderstorm, wreathed by smudged black eyeliner and matching perfectly with his cool scent of rain. But the kind that came after months of dry days, carrying the hours into night.

With that, too, were distinct notes of *male* and... expansiveness. Something that transcended life and death, crossing between the two just by its very nature.

A vampire.

And he was trying to hit on my friend who had a mate.

I knew firsthand what it was like to feel pressured by unwanted advances, and I couldn't bear anything souring my friend's happiness. Really, it made me mad. Vampires were strong, powerful, and I wouldn't tolerate him trying to wield that against her. Especially when her mate was somewhere around here.

So, I turned and let my irritation show. My pa and uncles always used to give me a hard time for not using my size for 'something good' like boxing or playing football. But the first time I got tackled in the kiddie league, I'd sobbed until Ma scooped me up on the field and let me go home.

To stand up for my friend, though, I had no problem using what I was born with. "She's taken." I let the timbre of my voice come through as well before turning my back on the vamp. Ramona looked fine, but I was spittin' mad. Who did this guy think he was—

A firm, undeniable hand grasped my face and turned me around. My heart and lower belly lurched as I was forced to look at him.

My wide eyes took in the pale skin and tousled black hair. His lip ring pulled upward as he smirked at me. "Not talking to her. Let me buy *you* a drink."

Now, hold on. Buy… what?

I blinked and swallowed. "You want to buy *me* a drink?" My voice came out way higher than it'd been a second ago.

He moved his thumb on my cheek, storm-cloud eyes watching the way he pet me. I felt frozen and melting all at once. "That's right, baby boy."

My heart began to truly race now, those gently intense words doing something to my insides. "Um…" I couldn't really think. Not with this scarily attractive vampire so close, and not even when Ramona gave me a thumbs up and left the table with her mate pulling her somewhere else.

The vampire trailed his touch to my jaw, giving me shivers all the way until he cupped the back of my head and caressed the edge of my ear. I couldn't even keep myself from whimpering, but hopefully the noise of the bar swallowed it.

With the way his lips twitched again, though, probably not.

His ears were pierced with small silver hoops, and though he was quite a bit shorter than me, his confidence made him seem eight feet tall. "So, what'll it be?"

"Ah." I blinked rapidly a few more times, trying to get my tongue to form a coherent answer. Ramona hadn't said where she was going, but she would be fine, right? I was here to try new things, and though I was familiar enough with getting hit on, this vampire's sort of commanding air was definitely something new. "Sure."

He gave me one last pet on the ear then plucked at my shirt. "Follow me," he said and started walking away without looking back. The sleeves of his shirt were cut off, like mine, but where my jeans were looser, his were a slimmer cut that highlighted his legs. The black boots on his feet thumped against the bar floor, and after ogling for a minute, I scrambled off my seat and did what he said.

Though a lot of the people congregated at the bar were taller than him, he had no trouble getting them to move. And when he leaned against the counter, the bartender walked quickly towards him.

"Hey, Tyler. Jameson?" Tyler, his name was. It was a nice name. A *really* nice name.

He nodded and glanced at me behind his shoulder. Well, he actually swept his eyes from the top of my head to my shoes, devouring me where I stood. Nervous and excited at the same time, I clasped my hands at my front, which made his eyes flash with a look I knew all too well. Lust. "What would you like, …?"

I gaped a moment before shaking myself. He was asking my name too, maybe? "D-Delaney. And a Coke is fine." Alcohol did nothing for me—my metabolism was way too fast.

"Delaney." The vampire smirked and gave me another appreciative once-over before repeating my order to the bartender.

While we waited, Tyler didn't turn around, and when he took both of our drinks and started toward a more secluded area, I followed.

"Sit." He nodded at a sofa that was pushed up in a far corner of the room. Not many were back this way since it was the furthest seat from the stage, and with most people standing, we were in our own little world.

I sank into the cushions and tracked Tyler's descent into the seat right beside me. He handed me my soda, which I took with both hands, and I started sipping from the straw.

Tyler ran a hand through his hair, never taking his eyes off of me as he drank from his whiskey. It was like we were in a vacuum or an invisible bubble. Commotion rang around us, but I couldn't hear anything besides my own nervous breaths and the unnaturally slow beating of his heart.

When he rested his arm on the back of the couch, he went a step further and twined his fingers in my hair. His blunt nails scratched my scalp, and I had to clench my eyes shut and breathe. Or else I'd roll over and show him my belly.

That was another problem I was still working on. I didn't know him, just that he sang for a band and that his name was Tyler. But his fingers and stare were doing something to me.

"Are you enjoying the show, Delaney?"

My eyes flew open, and I moaned again. He shouldn't say my name like that. With so much sin that my cock was rapidly stiffening in my jeans, and I just wanted to let him do whatever he wanted to me. As long as he kept touching me like this. But that was how I got in trouble last night.

"Um, yes. I am." My eyes kept fluttering closed as he kept his hands in my hair. It just felt so nice, making me tingly all over. I'd never been caressed like this, let alone by a vampire. Though his scent was cool impending wind, his fingers were warm. So warm.

"And your Coke?" He leaned closer, breath fanning against

my cheek. I could see even better the silver specks in his eyes, the slight shimmer in the black liner that made them sparkle.

My tongue felt dry in my mouth, to the point that licking at my lips did nothing. "Y-yeah. Thank you."

Tyler smirked again and took another sip from his whiskey. Usually, I disliked the smell of liquor, but on his breath, it just deepened how he was making me feel. Intoxicated, sinful.

I was no innocent virgin, not by *far*, but he almost reverted me to that. Oh, what did he want to do to me?

My eyes rolled back into my head when he closed the last few inches between us and brushed his nose against the curve of my neck, just over my pulse, and inhaled. "Oh," I exhaled.

He chuckled against my skin, breathing me in, and when he started *kissing* me, I was lost. Everything that wasn't Tyler ceased to exist. My world narrowed to the soft skin of his lips, the warm and spicy caramel of his breath, and the coolness of his scent.

Wet and sharp teased my pulse point, his tongue and teeth—fangs. A small part of me marveled at how brazen he was. Surely, no one could see close enough that he'd let them out to tease me, but I didn't think either of us cared.

Tyler pulled the skin of my earlobe between his teeth and licked away the sting. "You smell like the best part of summer."

I curled further into him, let myself rejoice in the attention from this stranger. The frustrating thing was, I knew how this went. That my own constant search for validating touch, something I'd been conditioned to crave for as long as I could remember, would only set me up for heartbreak at worst. An uncomfortable goodbye or ghosting at best. And at the end, I'd be alone. Always alone.

But with his lips on me, now his hands massaging my thigh to the point of feeling like homemade jam, I was weak.

Tyler maneuvered my head again, our lips almost touching. My lashes fluttered in the presence of that smooth, pale skin and those thundercloud eyes. "Are you going to let me fuck you, Delaney?"

I squeaked, all rational words leaving my brain. The directness wasn't the problem—or maybe it was. Though he was smaller than me in stature, I didn't have any doubts that one night, or even just a few minutes, with Tyler might be the intense touch that I'd been craving. Would he feed from me while he did it?

"Okay," I whispered.

Tyler gave me another nip at my throat, speaking into the skin. "I would say that we could go to the green room, but I can hear my guitarist fucking his mate as we speak. So. Are you going to come home with me, baby boy?"

And he kissed me. Hard and demanding, but that just made it better.

The car ride to his house was a blur. One with more metal music pounding the speakers while his hand moved back and forth over my lap.

"Oh, god," I whimpered when he first moved his palm from my thigh to right over my hard cock. And he barely said anything, nor did he look at me as I was already coming apart at the seams. As much as I could move in the seat of his car, I squirmed and humped his hand, taking and taking what he was giving me. If I was going to get kicked out as soon as this was over, I'd rather enjoy it now.

But, of course, when I got close to coming, warning him that it was too much, Tyler let off. Just removed his hand and placed it on the steering wheel.

I never claimed to be a prideful person, and that was evident in how I began fiddling with my belt buckle, the need for release my priority. Maybe then I could think this through, thank him for the drink and ride in his fancy car then ask for him to drop me off. Or just stand outside and order myself a ride. Call Ramona to come pick me up.

My hand snaked beneath the fabric of my briefs, but as soon as my fingers met the hot skin of my shaft, a low, calm voice made me freeze.

"Don't you dare."

I gasped, mind a scramble of need while trying to process his words. The car lurched to the side as he turned, and I looked out of the window for the first time in a while.

Darkness, trees, and the glow of his headlights.

My heart picked up for other reasons. We weren't in town anymore, nor were we anywhere I'd been before. How could I have been so stupid? I hadn't told anyone where I was going, and I was in the car with a vampire that could surely drain me dry.

With wolf shifter blood running through my veins, I was raised to believe I was superior. Even though I couldn't shift, I was stronger than a human, and with my appearance, most people didn't even try. They never got to see how confrontation-avoidant I truly was.

A vampire, on the other hand? I was aware what kind of destruction they could cause. But I let some pretty eyes and a soft touch lure me into the belly of a beast anyway. And it was looking like I'd die without an orgasm, too.

"Calm, pet. I've already fed today. I won't eat you." He'd kept his eyes on the road, but now he flicked them toward me as we approached the lights of a house up ahead. "Well. Maybe a little bit."

Slowly, I removed my hand from my pants and pulled up the zipper. Somehow, the pacifying words felt more reassuring than they actually were.

And when he parked, pulling up to a big, modern home, the sleek and expensive sight was enough to distract me. Growing up in rural Alabama, I'd never been exposed to luxury. My idea of wealth was having a space of your own to call home, but it seemed that this vampire had a different standard. Even his garage was gigantic. And instead of using it as another storage space or workshop, there were two other cars—all sleek and expensive—and a fridge.

I was gaping out of the window, nose nearly pressed against the glass, when he slowly opened my door. When had he slipped outside?

His hand, smaller than mine and dressed in a few chunky black rings, extended my way. It was sturdy, the flesh warm. Someone being this gentlemanly wouldn't murder me, right? As I accepted his offer with my palm resting in his, I realized that he'd never really promised not to kill me.

But his thumb rubbed the back of my hand that was encased in his, and it gave me another boost of assurance. I unfolded out of the car, letting him lead me through a door that opened to his kitchen. I didn't have time to truly take in the black marble countertops, but I ate up as much as I could. The polished wood floors beneath my feet. The dark walls with large paintings.

When we finally came upon a room with a sunken space in the middle, I felt my nerves return in full-force. Was I making a mistake? Was I just setting myself up for failure again?

My hand still in his, Tyler stepped us down where there was a set of expensive sofas and a glass coffee table. Instead of guiding me to sit, however, he plopped down on the leather seat while I watched.

Watched him lean back, spread his arms against the back cushions, and run his eyes up and down my body. I felt myself blush, no matter how many times I'd been in this position. He hadn't told me what to do now, so I didn't budge. Just clasped my hands at my front again.

He hummed and licked at his bottom lip, tickling the ring there. "We should discuss boundaries. Is anything off-limits for you?"

I kept my eyes downcast at his feet with my fingers still held low and polite. Like I'd been taught. Oh, goodness, I was such a mess, because there should've been no reason for me to fall back on these ways like I did.

"Um, don't kill me?"

He chuckled in a way that went straight to my insides, making them all melty and tingly. I wasn't the smartest, something I was also trying to make peace with, but I would've been stupid to not have this confirmation up front.

But if he went back on it?

"I won't be killing you, pet. You're too delicious for that. What else."

My eyes scanned the floor, tentatively prying open the lid I kept on all of the memories from back home—no, Antler Pointe was my home now. Howl's Fury was gone and erased. Even if my experiences—good, bad, and otherwise—would always be with me.

Without thinking too deeply on everything, because I would certainly start crying, I mumbled in response. "No spitting on me. Or saying hateful things."

There was a pause, a silence that made me think he'd hear my hard limits and decide it wasn't worth it. He was intense, so maybe he needed that sort of thing to get off? I wasn't going to blame him if that was the case. I just knew that I couldn't be part of it. That, at least, I would protect myself from.

"All right. That's no problem. Safe word?"

My face scrunched, thoughts trying to find one but coming up with nothing. Starting to panic, I lifted my gaze a little, only to collide with his stare that was dark and light at the same time. "I don't have one."

He didn't make it a thing. Just sat, with his arms wide and legs slightly spread. The only thing that moved were his lids that gave a blink to let me know that he was alive. Then, his lips. "Traffic light system then. Red, stop. Yellow, slow down. Green, keep going."

That was simple. I could remember that. I nodded.

"Tell me that you understand."

Oh, Jesus. My mouth went dry as I squeezed my hands again. As nervous as I was, I was even more excited. Tyler was already going to surpass my hookup last night. He already had with the sinfully innocent kisses and petting my hair at the bar. Those hands of his were strong, I could tell. Not that I would resist them, though. Not at all.

I nodded again. "I understand. Red means stop, yellow is 'slow down', and green is 'keep going.' I'll remember."

"Good. Now, take off your clothes."

Just like that. Maybe for someone else, the hard edge of his command, which was now solidified even more than it had been, would be scary. But for me, it was soothing. I didn't have to think. Didn't have to worry about doing the right thing or about how my mind could get jumbled up sometimes.

I grasped the hem of my cropped shirt. I said, "Yes, sir," and pulled it up and over my head. The coffee table was right beside me, so I loosely folded my shirt and dropped it there.

When I straightened, Tyler's gaze was stuck on my chest, and by the sight of those fangs of his, I supposed he liked what he saw. How could I not preen a little bit? Sometimes it felt like I didn't get any benefit of being born into a Wolf pack, but the muscle definition wasn't always a curse. Being active was fun, but I preferred nice walks compared to the gym. Thankfully, I didn't need to try at all to bring out that look from the sexy vampire.

My jeans came next, my fingers growing steadier and steadier as I unbuckled, unbuttoned, and unzipped. After crouching to pull them down and step out of my shoes, I stood back up to find Tyler with one of his hands on his own crotch.

My cock had grown rock-hard again, precum seeping through the white fabric of my briefs. They really didn't leave anything up to the imagination.

With my clothes on the coffee table, shoes lined up on the floor just below them, I hooked my thumbs in my briefs but looked to him with the question in my eyes.

"Those too, boy."

I whimpered, whole body flushing at the way he said that. I obeyed, pulling down my underwear. My hard cock slapped against my stomach, and a little moan slipped out of my lips. But I knew not to give into my urge to start touching myself. With the way his eyes were burning right now, I knew that it would come with a harsh punishment. Maybe me truly leaving here without coming. That might be the thing to kill me instead of his fangs.

I just needed him to touch me, and his refusal to do it, just sitting there and looking at me, was making it worse. My dick was so hard, turning so red that the crown was almost purple.

"P-please, Tyler, I—"

All of a sudden, he was standing. Nostrils flaring, fangs out, and though he was at least a foot shorter than me, I knew without a doubt that he was the one in charge. He'd do with me what he wanted, and oh goodness, that sounded like just what I needed.

"You'll call me 'Sir' while you're here, or get out. Now, kneel."

My heart stuttered for a second, and more of my precum dripped onto the nice rug beneath my feet. I'd never scrambled to my knees faster, but I didn't even feel the hardness of the floor or the fiber of the rug scratching my skin. Eyes wide, I looked up at him while resting my hands on my thighs.

He stepped forward, and like this, I was at a perfect height to suck him down my throat. That was, in a way, better than him doing the same to me. To be a vehicle for his pleasure.

Where had he been all my life? I would remember this night forever, and we hadn't even done anything yet.

"Yes, Sir," I gasped as he started to undo his own tight jeans. The dickprint had been promising, but watching him pull out the real thing was nearly enough to make me come untouched. I whined through my nose, wanting that thick length stretching my lips and sending me into that hard-to-reach place of true mental bliss. He might've been on the short side, but there was nothing small about that cock. Oh, god.

All these types of decisions I'd made, going home with strangers that took things way too far or just gave a few hair pulls and called it a day, were in search of *that*. Could he really give it to me?

He didn't bother pulling his pants any further down than he needed to, and it was even better this way. Me completely naked and him fully clothed apart from his dick that was just a few inches away from my mouth.

His fist held it steady at the base, facing me, and his other hand shot around to grab the back of my head. A sharp flash of pain and quick tug had me gazing up at him. My fingers dug into my thighs, committed to be good and not desperately jerk off. My chest heaved as I fought to take deep breaths and not pant with my tongue out.

"How are you going to tell me you need me to stop?"

I was almost drooling at this point, mind already slipping away, but I managed. "Red, stop. Yellow, slow down. Green, keep going."

"Good boy." His voice had taken on a new roughness, too. And his cock had been just as flushed as mine. This was doing something for him too—*I* was doing this for him. "Now, with your mouth full, you tap twice on my thigh if you want me to stop. Do it now." With shaky hand, I did and reluctantly returned it to my lap. "Good. Now, open." His dark hair had been messily slicked back for the show, but now, a few locks framed his temples, matching the smudged liner around his lashes. The silver in his eyes was catching in the dim light of the room, and my own rolled back in my head as I opened and felt the warmth and salt of his tip on my tongue.

His fingers tightened in my hair, creating a sweet, dull burning while I swept my tongue over him, exploring his length. I groaned with his cock in my mouth, loving the weight of it, the musk of his scent. And when his shaft was good and slick, he shoved himself to the back of my throat.

I was gone. My gag reflex was something I'd lost long ago, and Sir moaned, growled, as he held my head with both of his hands and fucked my face. Drool trailed down my chin, onto my neck. My lashes fluttered as I fought to look at him but also riding that current of pleasure. I could do this forever, and maybe I'd finally found the right guy. Could I even dare to hope?

I'd been enjoying, all clear thoughts gone, but then his cock was ripped from my throat. With nothing to swallow around anymore, my worries came crashing in.

"Did I say you could touch me?" Oh. *Oh*, my hands had wandered to hold onto his legs—when had that happened?

I bit at my swollen lip. "I'm sorry, Sir. I didn't mean to."

He grabbed my neck, squeezing a little but not cutting off any air. I felt owned. "Do it again, and you'll be punished, pet. I'd rather fuck you after this, but I'll decide against it if you make me. Am I clear?"

In that second, 'Sir' wasn't the word I wanted to use for him, but I managed to fight that one back. "Yes, Sir. I understand. Please, I'll be good, I wanna be good," I babbled.

With the one hand still holding my hair taut, he brought the other to caress my lip. The difference in both touches made tears spring in my eyes so fast that I wasn't able to hold them back.

It was hard to explain, but the tightness in his face softened, even though his expression didn't really change. He spoke around his long, sharp fangs that looked like they'd split my skin like butter. Would I taste good to him?

"I know you do, sweet boy."

And then he was back in my mouth. I kept my hands on my thighs, squeezing to make absolutely sure that they stayed there, and after some time, where I really was in danger of coming and about to tell him to give me a moment, he pulled out again.

This time, though, he pumped his cock before my face. I whined again, sticking out my tongue.

He gasped then groaned while the veins on his neck strained. Ropes of warm cum, salty and bitter and amazing, splattered all over my face. "Fuck, boy. *Fuck*," he gritted while he pumped the last of it out for me.

I swiped my tongue through all that I could reach without using my hands and swallowed it with a hum. "Thank you, Sir."

For the first time since entering his house, he smirked a little, and I saved away that moment in my mind for later.

He took off his own shirt and used it as a rag to clean my face.

The gentle swipes were almost enough to steal my attention away from the tattoos on his chest. Writing along one of his slim but defined pecs that I couldn't get myself to focus fully on and decipher.

"Get up," he commanded, and I did. He placed his hand on the back of my neck and pushed me out of the room and further into his house. "Let's see if that ass is as perfect as your mouth." I ducked my head, but I didn't know how successful I was at hiding my blush and grin. Yes, trying new things could be good sometimes.

CHAPTER TWO
ONE MONTH LATER

TYLER

I released the man below me, letting his body slump into the back seat of my car. The hum of life, pulsing in my veins now that I'd drunk my fill, was heady. The resolution of a hunt and kill was always satisfying—never mind the shadow that was now there, too.

This one had been… what was his name again? I shifted in my seat, trailed a finger over him. Forgettable face, forgettable hair. Even the thrill of picking him out, pursuing him all night, and giving him death instead of a rough fuck was quickly abating.

"Shit." I sighed and dragged my hands over my face. It was a clean kill—the only blood left was the few drops on my lips and surrounding my fang marks. But, as I got behind the wheel, I was already planning the rest of the mundanities of my evening.

Well—the sun was rising with a few shades of gold and orange lighting the black of the night—morning, now. And I had to go to work.

Pulling up at the funeral home, procuring a gurney from inside, and lifting the cooling body onto it were routine and automatic movements. It was the least picturesque way of disposing of a kill, but it was certainly the most effective I'd utilized in these years of immortality.

I sat on the counter, staring at nothing while I waited for the cremator to warm. The kill had been unplanned, but when the urge struck while I was out downtown, I gave into it.

Wasn't like I had anything—or anyone—better to do, anyway.

Some hours, a quick shower and change back at home later, I was walking down the streets of downtown Antler Pointe. My nephew prattled on as we walked past cheery shopfronts and restaurants. The sunlight was only mildly irritating with a cover of milky clouds covering its rays.

Contrary to popular belief and media lore, I did *not* burst into flames or sparkle or turn into dust, even under the brightest and hottest sunlight. No, it pissed me off, offending my senses on a cellular level.

Nearly forty years of this, and I'd made it a point to at least learn a decent amount about my kind. Maybe thousands of years ago, sunlight was an issue. Just as other creatures evolved, so did we, and the sun just left me slightly weakened.

And less tolerant of my nephew chatting up every fucking person he bumped into on the street. When I'd decided to go down the path of immortality, I never really intended to be back in my hometown, forced to take him under my wing. But, what could you do?

Addiction was a beast, and when my little brother got swept up with it once again, I couldn't deny my elderly parents' call, all the way from Jeju-si where they'd always dreamed of retiring.

"Did you take care of marking everything we need to restock?" I interrupted Robin as he pushed open the door to the coffee shop he kept raving over. The service today had been harder for him, so when he'd asked if I wanted to take a longer walk to get some coffee, I agreed.

My nephew pushed up the sleeves of his shirt, a sign that no, he did not check inventory. "Um, I forgot. I'll get to it when we get back, I swear."

I sighed and nodded, letting it slide while we took our place at the back of the line. He'd had a tough go of it when his father had to go to rehab for the second time since I'd moved back to town. And even though William was out now, everyone was still walking on eggshells, uncertain if he'd relapse again.

I faced forward to look at the menu, knowing damn well that I'd just order a black coffee. The flavor was strong enough to taste like something, even if having to piss was annoying and a waste of time. The things I did for my family. "All right. What do—"

A deep, sunny voice made my eyes snap to the register and my body straighten and tingle at the same time.

"Yes, ma'am, we'll have your order right there at the end of the counter once it's ready." That southern drawl fucking did something to me. The sweet and innocent scent of summertime that was floating through the air, as if knowing that just a whiff would make me want to peel off my suit jacket, drag him into a back room, and bend him over.

Whatever Robin was saying was of no use to me. We made our way toward the front of the line, and I saw the moment Delaney noticed me.

The way his back purposefully stiffened and his Adam's apple bobbed with a nervous swallow. His blond waves were tamed by a chocolate brown hat that matched his eyes and the freckles dusted across the bridge of his nose and tops of his cheeks.

"Hey, Delaney, how's your day going?" Robin said absently while scanning the menu above him.

"Uh—" The boy who saved my life shook his head as if to clear his thoughts and directed his attention to the tablet in front of him. "It's good. Thanks. What can I get y'all?"

"Hm, I'll just do my usual, and whatever my uncle wants." Robin waved a hand toward me, and I saw the confusion flit across Delaney's face. No, I'd never mentioned that I had family in Antler Pointe, and if one wasn't privy to small town gossip or hadn't attended a funeral with us in recent years, they wouldn't know that I wasn't just a member of the Lee family.

I didn't broadcast that I was actually the oldest of the Lee brothers, what with William looking every year of his fifty-six. And my body was still frozen at its twenty-seven-year-old state. No, if someone asked, I explained that I was a cousin that'd come to work at the family business. Those that would've remembered me from when I was a child were either gone or few and far between. No slip-ups had happened yet.

"Just a medium black coffee, no room." I pulled out my phone to pay for our drinks while trying to catch Delaney's eyes that he kept on the screen. His heart was beating so fast, like a rabbit being chased through the forest. That surely meant he wasn't happy to see me. Right?

According to Río's mate, I'd royally fucked up with this non-shifter Wolf. But it was for the best. He was becoming too attached after making sure I didn't die.

No other reasons.

He still wasn't looking at me when he turned around the tablet for me to sign, which was making me even more irritated. His wariness of me left me clenching my jaw, and I gave double the cost of our order as a tip.

While my nephew went off to wait at the end of the counter for our order, Delaney spun the tablet back around and sucked in a breath. And as I was turning to follow Robin and put some distance between me and the soft scent of this boy, his mumbled words made me still.

"Thank you, Sir." It was quiet, as if he barely lost the battle to hold back the words. A million responses formed in my chest, threatening to bubble out. All called back to the short amount of time we'd spent together before I'd gotten shot. The hazy memories of him keeping me fed so that I didn't succumb to whatever poisonous coating was on the bullet meant for the sister of the Wolf Pack Leader.

How I'd expressed my thanks before telling him that whatever was between us wouldn't continue.

I couldn't think of anything appropriate to say. Nothing that wouldn't give mixed signals. So, I joined Robin and tried my best to focus in on his recounting of his mortuary science classes. And when we grabbed our coffees and left, I did my best to not let the boy's presence draw me back in.

The surly female wouldn't look at me.

We were hanging out in my rehearsal room after practicing for our upcoming show, her mate and I passing a blunt back and forth now that our human bandmates had left. The weed we smoked was way too strong for them, and Brody was fucking relentless. There was no way we would've been able to smoke without him bitching and whining that we weren't sharing with him. But I really didn't want to perform CPR on my bassist or rush him to the ER.

"So, whatcha been up to, man?" My guitarist extended the blunt to me after taking a hit, bloodshot eyes in good spirits. There was a new life that shone in them now that he had a mate.

She was typically fine around me, but ever since this business with the boy, she'd been acting particularly frosty. Which was her prerogative.

And to think, I'd almost died because I made a split-decision to save her life and jeopardize mine. But I couldn't have the best guitarist we'd had in the band quit due to overwhelming grief.

I shrugged and kept my attention on him and not the Wolf in his lap. "Work. This."

He nodded. "Cool, cool." When I gave the blunt back to him, he nudged his mate. "Want a hit, baby?"

She eyed it and set her amber eyes on me for the first time in weeks before looking at her mate. "I'm not sharing spit with him."

"Aw, come on, Princess. You gonna be like this forever?"

Her expression remained unchanged as she settled further into his lap. "Yup. I can keep a grudge for an eternity. Be glad that you're one of the few people I love." He laughed and kissed her nose, totally enchanted by her shitty attitude and insistence on meddling in my affairs.

Río took another drag from the blunt, but instead of exhaling into surrounding air, he pulled Ramona's head toward his, and she opened her lips. He exhaled smoke into her mouth, and she inhaled, chest expanding.

It was annoying.

He took another hit before passing it back to me. I rolled my eyes. "The Wolf needs to stay sober so you both can go home. You aren't allowed to sleep over anymore." Last time, they'd fucked for *hours*. Each time I walked into that guest room now, I swore that I could still smell it. No matter how many times I changed the sheets.

"You're still mad about that? Maybe you should just apologize to little dude instead of stalking him at his job. Getting laid might do you some good." I glared at Ramona while she smacked her mate on his chest, though that didn't stop him from giggling.

I wasn't *stalking*. I didn't stalk. My nephew liked the place, and he'd taken up walking there often when things were slow. He was having a rough time because of his dad, so it'd seemed like a nice gesture to join him when he asked. And maybe sometimes when he didn't.

Now, Robin just waited outside of my office when it was time to go. And maybe once or twice, I went by myself on the way in when I wasn't working from home.

"What is Delaney saying to you?" I asked with my inhibitions almost on the floor.

Ramona wrapped her arms around her mate who was purring like a fool. "That this ungrateful ass keeps showing up at his job, and he doesn't understand why when said asshole *doesn't even like coffee*."

Delaney's words during those days I'd been injured had been petal-soft. Encouraging me to drink from him while I lay bleeding on the Pack Leader's land with a bullet in my chest. Then again in my bed as he held me close. He'd bathed me and been eating around the clock so that he'd be ready and able every time I rolled over in my stupor and latched onto his neck.

But that'd all been too much. The intimacy brought the wrong ideas for what we were. Why was I the villain for seeing that?

I sneered. "I thanked him, didn't I? And I do like coffee." But my retort sounded weak, even to my ears. No, I tolerated coffee because it was one of the few things other than blood that didn't taste like nothing. After that day with Robin, I just happened to grow a taste for the particular brew they used at the place.

She glared at me. "That's bullshit. And you know it. If you wanna live in this big house by yourself, haunting it with your misery, don't bring other people into it. You fucked up a good thing and hurt my friend. The least you could do is leave him space to heal. You're confusing him."

Río whistled and looked at me with sympathy before rising to stand. I followed the two of them to my feet, taking the last hit and stubbing the blunt out in the ashtray. He smacked a kiss on his mate's forehead while she still looked at me like I'd pissed in her cereal. "Come on, baby. Let's go home so I can work that anger outta you."

Even the blush on her face as they walked out of the rehearsal room and left didn't dull her disdain. But she didn't know what the fuck she was talking about.

Finally alone, I blared the newest songs for the EP we were working on and went to warm up some blood from my stash. When I'd built my house, the kitchen received the least consideration, obviously, so it was small for a home this size. Really, I didn't even need to do this in the kitchen, but we all clung to relics from our human lives.

Retrieving the medical-grade fluid warmer from the cabinets and using it to bring my dinner to the right temperature seemed less clinical when I was standing beside a stove. But to do that, I had to reach past the jar of peanut butter he'd left. Being a consistent food source for two weeks took a lot of energy, and signs of his presence still filled the usually empty spaces in this room.

Now, at least, I had something in case my bandmates whined about needing a snack.

My fingers drummed on the counter while I waited for my dinner to heat to body temperature. Going out and finding an actual person to drink from was normally far more appealing, but I was just fine staying home sometimes, too.

Fuck what Ramona said.

It was for the best that the boy and I didn't continue. The way his big, innocent eyes would glaze with pleasured tears as I thrust into him. The way he nuzzled against me while I fed from him and healed.

The boy was too earnest, and though I'd long ago made peace with my decision those decades ago, there couldn't be a future with him. He was young—too young—but that didn't last.

And I would stay this way.

Death was a constant in my life. Essentially growing up in a funeral home probably informed most of my life choices. Even when I'd gone to New York City to 'find myself', I'd gone to school, become a physician, and used my free time to party and do everything I never could in Antler Pointe.

But watching droves of my friends go during the HIV and AIDS crisis, just like that, had broken something in me. No matter how many hours I had worked, how much we tried to get the powers that'd been to do something, my friends died. And it was curiosity and self-preservation that pushed me to enter this new era of immortality.

Scared for my own life and wanting to be alive to continue helping were a constant storm darkening my days. Stumbling upon a flippant vampire at a club in New York City was just dumb luck. He was the owner, turned out, and had an air of danger that drew me in, along with his ice blue and silver eyes.

When he'd started to drink from me, I wasn't stupid—I knew that my life hung in the balance. And if that were to be the end, I would shoot my shot and ask for my human life to end for one of immortality to begin.

"All right," he'd drawled and drained me nearly dry before forcing drips of his own blood into my mouth.

What I didn't realize then was that turning was a toss up—he'd probably expected me to not survive.

And when I woke up the next evening with a burning hunger in my stomach, fangs that ripped through my lips as I tried to breathe, and limbs that moved disorientingly fast, my life had been forever changed. And he was gone.

What kind of vampire was named Boone, anyway?

Now, I settled by my pool, mug clutched in my hands as I reminisced on the old days. It was almost funny that I and those I lost were all frozen at how we'd looked in the eighties.

The blood I was now drinking came from someone in their middle age, the flavor a bit deeper. And with a hint of juniper berries, like they grew up somewhere surrounded by the trees.

The boy tasted just as sweet as he smelled and with a layer of summer citrus, like an excitement for life.

I wasn't a martyr—in my most selfish of hours, like tonight, I coveted him. I wanted that softness and innocence for myself, but being tied to me, either turning or mating him, would dim that light. Even I wasn't that much of a dick.

No, flowers like him didn't bloom in darkness.

CHAPTER THREE

DELANEY

Charlie gulped down the coffee I brought over from work. Employees got all the free drinks we wanted, and I still remembered what my cousin preferred to drink at Howl's Fury when we got a moment to ourselves.

We sipped, watching the patrons of downtown Antler Pointe walk by in the summer afternoon. I'd found a bench in the shade, waiting and people watching for an hour before he'd scampered up, huffing about the town that I'd already come to love so much.

Juno and Josie were walking out of a witchy shop, hand in hand, and their waving caught my eye. Normally, I'd run over to chat, but my old friend's presence kept me rooted in my seat. He'd made the journey all the way up North when he found out I moved here after we parted ways.

So, I waved back at the witch and wolf shifter I'd become pretty good buddies with, smiling and hollering that I'd see them later. They did the same while continuing into the coffee shop.

"So, do you have it or not?"

Charlie's voice cut through the moment, and I twisted my body to face him. I was bigger than him, but not by much. Where

I was a bit bulkier, he was lean. Back when we were trying to go unnoticed and clean in peace or servicing whoever, I'd envied his size.

I learned early on that people could be especially cruel when they saw you as some trophy they'd been able to abuse into submission.

Not that my instinct wasn't to submit, anyway. Or would that be different had Ma lived? Had I had a better upbringing. Looking around at the bright, smiling faces around me, knowing that I had a pack meeting tonight with my new family, I let the what-if's trail away in my mind.

"How much do you need?" The two hundred I'd given him those weeks ago was certainly long gone, but it'd taken me until now to almost make that back, once all my expenses were taken care of. My scholarship and grants only paid my tuition, so rent, car insurance, my phone, and everything else to just live were on me. With twenty hours of my week set aside for my internship, I worked as much as I could, but I had to keep my grades up too.

At least I had more than enough to keep me busy when things went belly-up emotionally. I was good, now, at keeping a good cry to thirty minutes max. And boy, had I taken full advantage of those weepy breaks.

"Three hundred. Four would be better."

I gasped, searching his face and hoping that he was joking. What in god's name made him think that I had that kind of money?

"I don't have that, Charlie. I didn't even really have the two that I gave you last time." Discreetly, I took a sniff in his direction, even if it made me feel lower than dirt. I wasn't the best at scenting, but substances like drugs and alcohol had a distinct aroma. Neither were on him, so that wasn't it. Why did he need so much money, and why on god's green earth did he think I had it?

He passed a hand over his short hair that was the same color as mine and narrowed his dark blue eyes. "You don't have it. I find that hard as hell to believe." He raised his brows expectantly, like he was waiting for me to spill some secret, but I still didn't know what he was talking about.

At a loss, I opened my free hand helplessly. "Wha-what about the job you got last month? You said that you were just waiting for your first paychecks to hit."

After taking an angry pull from his straw, he set the empty plastic cup on the pavement beneath our feet. "You think I make enough bussing tables? Not all of us slept their way into fucking college."

I felt that hit like a punch to my stomach. My gaze became watery, but there was no way I was sneaking off to give into the urge to sob right now. If I made it out of Howl's Fury by some stroke of luck from the universe, Charlie did by force of will and a whole lot of spite.

After our old pack imploded, I stayed in shelters, took up the social workers' offers of GED classes to get the diploma I'd been refused when my 'pack duties' forced me to drop out years prior. I bussed tables, like Charlie did now, studying like a fiend during my off hours.

That woulda been it, but I met some other kind, kind folks that saw something in me. Helped me get into community college, and when an advisor *there* caught me on an off day, venting how much I wanted a fresh start somewhere *far* away from Alabama, they helped me apply for any and every opportunity.

Antler Pointe College had been the only one to offer me enough money where I could manage to attend. Federal grants took care of the rest, and here I was. My wages bought me an ancient yet reliable car for a GED present to myself, and I drove hours and hours with a grin on my face and straight up fear in my stomach.

Sure, I wasn't a saint—I'd never been given the chance to be— but sex hadn't been involved in my long, winding path here.

"I didn't sleep with anybody to get here, Char," I whispered, head ducking and eyes on my lap. And even if I had, could he really blame me? If the roles were reversed, I certainly wouldn't.

"Well if you didn't, makes ya wonder how you got the money to do it. You sure your old man didn't leave something for you?"

My mouth twisted, and my brows lowered. What was he going on about? Pa was long dead and, far as I knew, hadn't a penny to his name. Just the clout of being a brother of the Leader of Howl's Fury, a house that'd been in the family for generations, and more than a few of us under his thumb.

"Wha—I'm sure. And even if he did, I don't want it." Anything to connect me to the male that offered me up once my mama died was better off rotting in the grave next to him, if you asked me. "You'd know better than me," I grumbled, but then felt like garbage after it left my mouth.

Charlie's sneer was enough to make my tail go between my legs. Well, if I had one.

"Which is why I'm fuckin' *asking*." At a certain point, Charlie stopped bopping from bed to bed like me, and got hogged up by my pa. Not a mate, but he started sleeping in his house, in his room, and it made me feel better that one of us got out. At least a little bit.

He'd been with pa when everything went to hell, the pack members turnin' on each other, the mobsters seeing them as more a liability than an asset to run their drugs and guns. Though, they really hadn't needed to give more than a little nudge. Members started turning up dead after simple squabbles, some lesser members left early on when they could smell trouble. The rest had been executed when it threatened the Serafim business.

I was too unimportant and was spared—for that I'd learned to be grateful.

I shook my head and finished my lemonade. "I don't know what Pa told you, but he didn't leave me anything. Someone at the homeless shelter had to help me open my first bank account after everything happened. I just got lucky to be where I'm at, and I can help, but I don't have much. Best I can do is another two-hundred, Charlie. *I'm sorry*." My voice got choked up at the end, and as best as I tried to hide my tears from him, they spilled.

His lip curled even more, and I shrank back. "Whatever. Send it to me, and I'll see you around."

And he was gone. Getting up and joining the foot traffic until I lost sight and scent of him.

The bonfire on Leader's land was crackling and popping, and everyone was relaxing into the post-meeting fun. The sun was already down, and most everyone was on their third or fourth slice of cake by now.

I was still making it through mine, balancing the paper plate on my lap and swallowing the rich frosting. My best friend was across the grassy area, sitting with her niece and nephew while her mate was telling them some story with his hands waving and claws out for dramatic effect.

But my body felt a little heavy. Not near the type of depression I'd felt in the past, but it was like there was film between me and them. Thin enough for me to see and hear and enjoy watching them have fun. But thick enough for me not to be able to take part.

Even Harrison's excited hollers, hopped up on sugar and his eighteenth birthday glee, wasn't truly reaching me.

So, I hummed in my seat, watching and just grateful to be in their vicinity. If this was the worst I'd feel around this pack, I'd more than gladly spend each and every day like this.

The heat of summer was slowly giving out, and the slight breeze felt nice on my skin. *Something* on my skin.

"Is the cake all right?"

I startled and looked over to my right. A few camping chairs down was Leader and his mate, who was watching me from her perch on his lap.

I blushed at the attention and the envy twisting up my spine. That she had someone strong and safe that held her with so much love that I could scent it all over them. Sweet and decadent like Ma's pecan pie.

My plate was only half-finished, but that wasn't her fault. It was tasty, but my stomach felt like a rock and an empty shell at the same time. I made sure to take a bite while she was watching me, though. "It's great. Really."

I almost requested she give me her calming touch again. That witchy boost she blessed me with during my first meeting when I was so scared her mate was like every other Leader I'd met.

But she looked so happy to be sitting and enjoying the night with Leader, so I held it back.

"Okay." Sylvie eyed me a second longer, probably seeing more than I knew myself, but she eventually nodded and turned back to her mate. His pale skin and hair was almost the exact opposite of her brown coloring and black, bouncing strands. "Delaney's the one who helped me harvest those greens you loved this week, baby."

Even though I knew what she was doing, I perked up a little bit, knowing that I might've pleased Leader Orion. He confirmed with a quick nod while Sylvie was caressing the edges of his bearded jaw. "I'm getting more into French cooking, and we have slices of quiche left that we will send home with you."

"That's a great idea, baby." She kissed his cheek, and color spread across his face from the attention.

"Thank you," I said thickly. It wasn't like I was special—they were kind and helpful to everyone. But that again was far from what I'd grown up with. A Leader who never really asked anything of me, and a role model like Sylvie who had already taught me so much. Their sister Ramona who spent time with me and was my voice of reason when I got mixed up or scared. Even her mate who always jumped at the chance to cheer me up, despite being Tyler's friend.

Tyler.

A rush of tears threatened to spill over, but I blinked them back. Maybe being on this land, sitting not far at all from where he'd been shot, was having more of an effect on me that I'd realized. The beginning of the pack meeting had been a bit awkward, but everyone, including myself, was determined to not let the bad memories outweigh the good.

And Tyler had lived. I'd been so scared, and although his popping up at the coffee shop had me really confused, it reminded me every single time that he'd survived.

I finished my cake in a rush, not wanting Sylvie to feel bad after probably baking for hours to accommodate the appetite of an entire Wolf pack. Harrison alone had eaten almost a whole cake himself.

I shook my head again, trying to erase the not so great times floating to the front of my mind. When I focused back in on the world around me, my ears were again filled with excited pack chatter, the yips of the pups that were running around with frosting-smeared cheeks. But I couldn't help pick up on the hot whispers between Leader and Sylvie.

Instead of perched, she was straddling Leader's lap with her bare arms wrapped around his neck. She nuzzled into the side of his face. "What are you going to do about it, Dr. Gealach?"

He grasped the side of her neck and brushed a clawed finger against her skin. "Behave, mo ghrá." The rumble of his voice was low but filled with everything I'd thought I once had in Tyler.

No, actually, he'd given me more than that. A stern voice to clear out the noise while giving me all the touches and skin contact that I needed. The mixture of hard and soft, pain and pleasure that I'd never had with anyone before.

Sylvie and Leader Orion continued to go back and forth, this time too quiet for me to hear, and I really tried my best not to glance their way anymore. But it sure was hard when Leader rose to his feet with a growl and held Sylvie close. She wrapped her legs around his waist and continued to plant kisses and whisper in his ear while he walked them toward the forest.

I glanced over my shoulder, catching Ramona and Río cuddled up while they continued to entertain the little ones. Vera and my boss at the coffee shop, Lauren, were holding hands while they chatted with a few elder pack members, and everywhere I looked, I saw couples or clusters of people so happy and carefree.

A lightning bug glowed out of the corner of my eye before landing on the back of my hand. I kept still, and another one did the same. I smiled weakly as they lit up my skin a few more times before taking off and bobbing away.

CHAPTER FOUR

TYLER

I sat in the private office we used for speaking with families, Robin at my side while we both faced the crying adult children of the deceased.

Really, I was shadowing Robin since he was now in the last semester of his mortuary science program. We both preferred other roles to *this* part of the job, but he needed to know how to do it. Not that I was very good at comforting or caring for others.

My father was the one with the magic touch. Being able to calm the most emotional of people while having an eye for detail that made the services and business thrive. Decades ago, he'd opened other homes across the region, and I thanked the universe that those mostly ran themselves. Aside from the odd call here or there, most of my attention went to ensuring William was staying in his program and that the Lee Funeral Home in Antler Pointe was running smoothly until Robin could take over.

Not sure what we would've done if Robin hadn't taken an interest in the business, because I sure as shit wasn't going to do this longer than I needed to.

"You have our cards, should you have any concerns between

now and the service. Do you have any other questions for us at this moment?" Robin softened his voice, slowed it down and made sure to lean a bit forward, staying engaged.

He was doing well, thank goodness. He took a special interest in the body preparation, embalming and reconstruction and such, but he was far from abysmal at this part of the job.

My nephew must've gotten that bone of compassion from his mother. I'd always been pissed at Will for not being able to make it work with Melanie, but it was better that she'd seen William's unwillingness to accept help early on.

The family thanked Robin and I both with watery smiles, and we walked them out to the lobby. I held the door for the family, reciting my rehearsed words that I gave to everyone. Over and over and over, taking the template from my father who I'd watched do this all throughout my childhood.

Once they were well into the parking lot, Robin gave a last wave, and we ambled back inside. He unbuttoned the top of his shirt, and I nodded at Beverly, who was our administrative assistant and bookkeeper. She'd been here since I left for New York, freshly out of the closet and determined to put this life behind me. She never said anything about the fact that I looked essentially the same, even with thirty-eight years passed.

If there was any good thing about Antler Pointe, it was that the people here were either blissfully unaware or knew how to keep their fucking mouths shut.

It'd really piss off my parents and may destroy the family business if I had to start killing people left and right.

Robin ran a hand across the bangs of his hair, then down to the longer strands at the back of his neck. It was a look that William had worn once, when it was in fashion decades ago. But the kid had a tough relationship with his father, so I never mentioned it.

"All right, Samchon." Robin slipped into speaking Korean now that we were alone and headed back to my real office. "*How was that? We're working on communication techniques at school, and I tried some new stuff there.*"

He took a seat on the sofa while I claimed one of the armchairs on the other side of the coffee table. *"Good. Not really any notes aside from redirecting when people start cycling through saying the same things over and over. Sometimes you have to be more directive."*

Robin pulled out his phone and started tapping with his thumbs, making notes. *"Yeah, sometimes I get caught up and don't want to interrupt. Got it. What are you up to now?"*

I thought for a moment, running over the day's tasks before I could change and meet my guitarist at the skatepark.

"Settling the schedules, coordinating an interview for a new attendant. Ordering supplies and meeting with Bev to go over the books." All that would certainly take me well into the late afternoon hours, but I enjoyed these duties more than dealing with people who were emotional more often than not.

Robin pursed his lips and looked up from his phone. *"I can take some of that off your hands. I finished my homework for the week yesterday, and all my stuff is almost done for the day."*

We continued to go back and forth, deciding on what tasks he'd take off my hands, and soon, he returned to his office to get started. I worked away at my desk, feeling the day tick by and the constriction of the business. Where before I'd spend my immortal days writing and doing what I damned well pleased.

At least the workload kept my mind off of William, wondering if he was being truthful in our last check-in, reporting that he was still clean and adjusting to life at the sober living home.

And my mind barely wandered to the boy.

How I didn't mind his tears one bit. How every time I went to get coffee, I got closer and closer to saying something to him. It didn't help that I saw a glimmer of hope in his eyes each time, but then Ramona's scathing assessment would run through my thoughts. Or my own hesitation to bring him into a life of death and biding time.

Both things I had no shortage of.

After a few hours, Robin popped up in my doorway just as

Beverly left my office. "You down to get some coffee? I could use the boost."

I looked at the time on my computer screen, finding the working day almost done. But, I still had more to do, and Delaney's freckled face, pinked with a blush, gave my heart a little jolt. Maybe a quick coffee run would give enough *something* to tide me over.

Maybe I'd finally talk to him.

I clenched my jaw and shook that thought right out of my head. Sometimes he wasn't working, and if he was there and I said anything, what would it even be? That I wanted him in my bed again?

That I wanted to apologize?

The sex had been amazing, but that was only part of it, and if he accepted any apology from my lips, what then?

I followed Robin out as Beverly shook her head at us from her post behind the front desk. "I still don't understand what's wrong with what's in the pot in the kitchen, but spend your money how you please." She waved us off.

Robin laughed, but I was focused on the knots in my gut and the excitement buzzing under my skin.

DELANEY

Today was so slow, I was doing everything extra that I could find to keep busy. Dust the merchandise displays, clean and restock the register area. Spruce up the chalkboard sign for the specials. I'd been told that my handwriting was nice—it had to be if I wanted to be a teacher to younger children—and making it all pretty was fun!

I was just an hour away from the end of my shift, but I had no real plans tonight. So I was content with wiping down the tables again when the bell on the door chimed for the first time in the past twenty minutes. I straightened with a smile on my face, but I caught his scent just before I turned around. My lips threatened to fall, wobbling a bit, as I walked to the register.

Robin gave me a polite nod while he perused the menu like he was going to get something new. And I kept my eyes off of Si—his uncle. That was still a weird thing to reconcile, but I could see the resemblance, even with the difference in height.

"Hey, Delaney, how's it going?"

"Fine. A bit slow, but that's normal for this time. Did you wanna just do your usual?" Maybe if I just ushered them along a little. I didn't even bother asking Tyler what he wanted. That, I knew, would stay the same.

Because it was always like this. He'd come in with Robin or on his own, order a black coffee, leave a ginormous tip, and go without any explanation or reassurance. No matter how much I got my hopes up.

Ramona and Sylvie said that I hadn't done anything wrong, that it was his problem, not mine, and I was trying real hard to remember that. I chanted it to myself every time he left without smiling or saying much of anything.

Robin sighed. "Yeah, yeah. I'll just get my usual. Thanks."

I gave them their total and turned around the tablet for Tyler to fill out as I stepped away to make their drinks. Just a few more minutes, and I could go home. Or maybe see if Ramona was free to talk again. Lord knew that she was probably getting tired of me, but I'd never been through something like this. What was I supposed to do?

"We'll drink these here, actually." My hands stilled, and my head snapped up.

Robin grinned and nudged his uncle with his elbow. "Thanks, man. I could use the break." And Tyler shrugged while staring right at me. What did that mean?

"Uh-um, yeah. If y'all wanna sit, I can bring these to you?" Maybe if he wasn't right in front of me, I'd be able to think for a second. Or text someone for their advice.

My heart was beating something fierce the whole time I rustled up Robin's frozen mocha with whipped cream and dispensed Tyler's plain drip coffee, no room.

I forced steady breaths as I walked over, keeping my shoulders down and back. "Here ya go." I deposited them on the tabletop between them.

"Thanks! I'm going to go to the restroom, be right back," Robin stood and left, and I should've done the same, going back to the register.

But Tyler was still looking at me, and I got caught again. "Um, is there—is there anything else you needed?"

His hair was combed back, his white button-down shirt crisp and far from how he'd dressed when we met. I bit my lip, trying so hard to forget what it was like to have his fangs in my neck, or what the tattoos on his chest looked like.

"Sit with me."

I almost choked, and I waited to realize that I'd misheard or for him to take it back. But that never happened. He sat still, leaning back in his chair and looking at me without blinking.

Unlike some of the other things he'd said to me, this wasn't a command. It felt like enough was open at the end of it—not quite a question, but I didn't feel scared for what he'd do if I didn't take a seat.

No, I was scared that if I turned away, I would miss some sort of chance to better understand what happened. So, I sat down, my fingers twisting together in my lap, and I focused my ears on the slow beating of his heart.

"I'd like to see you again."

Was this a joke? Wha—why? Just three days after he was healed, he'd sat me down, thanked me for taking care of him, and told me that he'd prefer not to continue seeing each other. We were never together, even I knew that. Him getting shot came only two days after the night I went home with him.

"You deserve better, Delaney. Tyler's a fucking asshole, so don't you

dare think you did something wrong. If he wants to get you back, he needs to work for it."

With my best friend's advice in my mind, I took a bracing exhale and forced back my excitement for this moment I'd been dreaming of. "You weren't very nice to me before."

Tyler nodded once, something else I wasn't expecting, and the light from the sun reflected in the silver of his dark eyes. "You're right." He cleared his throat. "I apologize. It wasn't fair of me to treat you that way."

I searched his face, the soft curve of his pink lips and the short black bend of his lashes. Try as I did to scent emotions like my friend was teaching me to, I couldn't figure out what his intentions were behind showing up at my job, saying these things. "Okay," was all I could think to respond with.

"So, would you consider it?"

I started to say 'yes', so much wanting to have his hands on me again, his words of praise when I did what he said. But I was supposed to be growing. To not let this type of stuff happen to me again.

Apologies were good though, right?

"Consider what?"

A second passed. "Come over tonight." Again, it wasn't quite a question, but it wasn't quite a command either.

I opened my mouth, still about to agree to anything and everything he'd give me, but my friend's particular frown when she caught me 'making excuses for other people' flashed through my mind. I snapped my mouth shut, breathed, and thought through the events that'd occurred thus far. Would going to his house to continue hooking up be enough for me? What did I really want from this?

Then my mind went down a spiral of things I knew I couldn't have. But there was one thing—maybe.

"I want a date. A real one."

Tyler had been waiting patiently for me to think things

through, but now, his lips parted. Like it was the last thing he expected. He sputtered for a second, then, "I don't date."

My heart sank. Right there, all the way down next to my stomach. *He's not the one, and that's okay,* I chanted to myself and began to stand. "It was nice to see you again. Let me know if you need anything." Hopefully no one else came in, because a good cry in the back sounded perfect for a time like this. But I also didn't feel that particular clenching in my chest that I was so used to. This was me growing. Standing up for myself.

I turned to go lick my wounds, but that strong, firm grip wrapped around my wrist. His hand was just as warm, and my body automatically halted.

"Wait," he exhaled, but I was too scared to look at him. "Okay. A date. Tonight."

Eyes bulging out of my head, I felt my heart rise again, this time thumping almost out of my chest. "Okay." His brown and silver eyes were pleading, as much as they could, anyway. And it was the first time it ever occurred to me that he could be yearning for what he had as much as I was.

The bell on the door chimed, and Robin's footsteps started toward us. "I'll pick you up at seven o'clock."

What could I say when all I wanted to do was squeal and do a happy dance? With customers coming in and his nephew walking back over, Tyler released my wrist, and I just gave him a smile—a real one this time—and headed back to the register.

I was grinning for the rest of my shift, so excited that I could barely keep my focus on my job. It didn't even really matter what we did. Maybe I should've been concerned about that, but with what little I knew about Tyler, I trusted him to be intentional about whatever it was.

I'd walked to work today, trying to save on gas and enjoy the pleasant weather, and I danced with each step on the way home to get ready.

My first date!

"Okay, which shirt do you think?" I stood far enough back so that my outfit options were visible. On the other end of the video call was Ramona, brow furrowed as I went back and forth on the two shirts I was stuck between.

We'd already settled on my nicest pair of jeans, Tyler's text notifying me that we were going to dinner and drinks after. I unfortunately didn't have much in the way of *nice* clothes, and I didn't wanna be in my student-teacher attire tonight.

The first was a more tasteful button-down, but the floral pattern was fun! The other was pink and a bit more daring. "Well, *that* one shows off your assets more. How much do you want him drooling over you tonight?"

I laughed—she could be so blunt and funny. "I think a lot. I'll pick this one." The crochet fabric revealed enough of my bare skin underneath to tease, but that's what people wore on dates, right? It wasn't like he hadn't seen every part of me already. But, wait. This was a first date. "Or do you think I should be more conservative? Is this too suggestive?"

Ramona huffed. "I think it matters more what *you* feel comfortable wearing. If he has any sense, he'll think you're sexy no matter what you wear. And other people don't matter. So." She shrugged, and I felt so much better.

"Okay, okay, last question!" I flung the rejected option onto my bed and began changing into the new shirt. "What do you think ab—"

"Woah!" A new voice sounded over the phone, and when I stuck my head through the shirt, I saw Ramona's mate covering her eyes. "You tryna steal my mate, little dude?"

I chuckled and situated the fabric over my torso. He'd started calling me that after Ramona formally introduced us, and it was funnier that he thought it was hilarious. "I'd never! Plus, she's not my type." She scoffed and crossed her arms while we both laughed. "But quick, I want your advice too! Do you think Tyler will like this?" Río was his best friend, after all. Even if neither would use those words.

I did a little twirl for the camera. Río tapped a finger on his chin, and his and Ramona's faces were now smushed together so they could both give their opinion. "Think so. He was really nervous and shit. Wait—where'd you get it and did they have it in red?" He cut his eyes to my friend. "Think I could pull that off, Princess?"

A new heat took over her now unfocused gaze, but I was stuck on the other thing he said. "Wait!" I picked up the phone and held it in front of my face. "He was nervous?"

Río did the same, even though Ramona was grumbling in the background. "Oh yeah, basically shitting his pants, if vamps can even do that. Don't tell him I told you."

"He should be! Delaney, if he acts funny, just call me."

"Did he tell you where he was taking me?" He said it was a surprise when I'd texted, trying to figure out what outfit to put on. Hopefully this wasn't too fancy. My makeup was light, just some brown mascara and a little bit of blush. I'd been told that the combination made my freckles pop.

Suddenly, her phone was held up high, and I saw Ramona trying to reach for it while her mate looked like he was having the time of his life. Though he sometimes made me nervous with his flips from lighthearted to intense, he really was good for her. "Nah, I've already said too much. Just know that your fit is fine for what he's got planned."

I pouted but let it go. As nervous as it made me, I also really liked surprises. "Okay. Thank you both!" One-handed, I put my phone and keys in my pocket, though it was a bit of a fight with the tight fabric.

"I mean it." There was an outraged yelp, and Río disappeared from the screen to be replaced by Ramona. "You deserve someone treating you like royalty. If he makes you feel badly *at all*, you call me. I'll fuck him up."

And that made me tear up a little. I walked out of my room,

passing Alex's on the way. I really was the luckiest to have a friend like Ramona, and by extension, her mate. "I know. Thank you so much. Love y'all!" She always got a little flustered when I said that, but it was true!

She sighed. "Love you, too. Have fun." I could tell that she wanted me to give Tyler a harder time, but her support and readiness to defend me meant more than she probably knew.

I sat on the beaten up sofa in the living space, leg jumping while I waited for the time to tick down. TV and my phone couldn't keep my attention, and my chest was fluttering with anticipation for what was going to happen. Would we kiss? Had he slept with anyone else? Though the thought hurt, I supposed I couldn't be mad at him for that.

My new roommate was walking his dishes to the kitchen when a resounding knock rang through the apartment. I froze, Tyler's scent on the other side suddenly making me so nervous that my brain stalled for a second.

"I got it," Alex called and walked to the door.

By the time I actually got to my feet, they were both looking at me with very different expressions. Alex's was more confusing, looking quickly over my face and body before he retreated back toward his room in a rush so fast that I didn't have a chance to ask him what was wrong.

And, with the way Tyler was staring, my focus was pulled much more strongly in his direction. I'd make sure to check in with Alex later.

"Hi." I stepped closer. Tyler's black hair was nicely tousled, somewhere between the professional style he wore for work and the messy one for his metal shows, and his silky shirt was the color of dried blood. The top few buttons were undone, showing off his chest and draping off his shoulders in a way that had my mouth watering. His black pants looked equally as nice, fitting him perfectly.

Tyler's gaze landed on my chest, then my legs, before returning to my face. He blinked a few more times. "Hey."

"A-are those for me?" I pointed to the bouquet he held at his side.

"Oh." He looked down at them, almost as if he'd forgotten they were in his hand. "Yes," he extended a paper-wrapped bouquet of red roses to me, "for you."

They were beautiful, artfully arranged to the point that I knew they weren't just from the grocery store. I took them and bent to sniff the delicate perfume. After spending many hours with Sylvie and her gardens, I found that I liked the flowers the most.

For a split moment, I almost started crying. For the expanse of flowers that'd burned down with the witch house, for the thought I could already tell Tyler put into this small, traditional gesture. For the happiness that was making it hard to think.

I laughed at my silliness, shaking my head and blinking the wetness in my eyes away. "Can I put these in water before we go? Or will we be late?"

Tyler's hands were in his pockets, and despite our height difference of at least a foot, he never seemed to look up at me. Instead, his stance was even, confident. The brown and silver in his eyes held so much, though. What was he thinking?

"We'll be fine. Take your time." The low register of his voice curled around my spine, and I tried my best to calm the beating of my heart. He could most certainly hear it.

I turned to the kitchen and waved him to follow. Then I thought about one of the sillier legends I'd heard about vampires. Did waving him over the threshold count as an invitation?

After rifling through the cabinets, I found an old plastic vase that would have to do for the time being. I straightened, but I also didn't miss Tyler flicking his eyes away from my butt.

As I filled it with water, he leaned against the counter, crossed his arms. "What's so funny?"

I started unwrapping the roses and retrieved my spare gardening shears I kept in the junk drawer. My lips were still pulled back, the aftermath of my giggles shaking my chest. "Well, I started thinking about the silly legends about you needing an invitation inside." Didn't have to tell him that I caught him checking me out.

When he didn't respond, I frowned in thought. "Wait—*do* you need one?"

He raised a brow, but the little smirk that made his lip piercing twitch made me relax a bit. "No. I always thought that particular one was absurd."

A beat of silence passed between us, but it was kind of nice, too. Inside, I was still buzzing, but the anticipation of having him in front of me was gone. He was here, and I hadn't messed anything up yet. *We even joked a little,* I reasoned as I placed the flowers just so.

"I'll just put these…" I stood in the living area for a second, contemplating the best place before deciding on the end table near the window. I'd try to keep them alive for as long as possible, and then, maybe Sylvie would know about drying and saving them? Yes, that would be so nice. "Okay! I'm ready…" I spun back around, only to find Tyler way closer to me than I thought he'd been. Close enough for him to take my hand in his.

He brought the back of it to his lips, and I gasped at the soft contact. "You look beautiful, Delaney."

"Oh." I chuckled and used my other hand to fiddle at my semi-sheer shirt. "Well, I was hoping that this wasn't too much. I had a dressier shirt that's a little more conservative if you don't like this one or feel like I'd make us look out of place. It's just that it's new, and I wanted to be…" I clamped my mouth shut. Darn it, his eyes just made me feel so fidgety, and this was my last chance, so I needed to make sure—

While keeping my hand in his, Tyler used his other to cup my cheek. I swallowed. "You don't need to explain yourself. You look amazing. You always do." Oh, goodness. Did he really think that?

"Usually I just have a hat on and smell like coffee beans." The words escaped with his steady stare holding me upright and still.

The serious expression on his face broke a little, cracking an even bigger smirk that was almost a smile. "And you're always beautiful. I have a car waiting for us downstairs if you have everything you need?"

Wha—like his car was downstairs? Well, I expected as much. Or I would've been fine if I were driving. Really, if he kept touching me, I would be more than happy with a walk around the block.

I nodded, and Tyler took charge again, leading me out of my apartment and down the stairs to the small parking lot of my apartment building. But the large and expensive-looking black car that he led us to wasn't one I'd recognized from our brief time together. Had he gotten a new one?

He opened the door—to the back seat and not the passenger— and gently nudged my lower back. The scent of new, clean leather flooded my nostrils. Confused, I leaned into Tyler's reassuring touch still on my back and slid in. What a change it was to be in a car big enough that I didn't have to fold myself like one of those origami cranes.

Tyler climbed in after me, and once he shut the door, the car moved away from the curb.

"What happened to your car?" I couldn't help but ask.

The way he sprawled in the seat, legs parted and shoulders back with ease, was so different than my crossed legs and clasped hands. "I figured it'd be nice to be driven for our date."

My mouth went dry, and I looked frantically to the front seat but couldn't see anything. The fancy SUV had one of those privacy things so that we could talk without the person driving being privy to what we said. Or what we were doing.

Had Río said that Tyler was nervous? It surely didn't seem like it. Meanwhile, I was starting to feel like I was lost at sea with only his touches as a life raft. My own nervous stammering was going to make me sink and drown if he kept on.

"Does it make you uncomfortable?" His question made the anxious thoughts screech to a halt. Did it?

After a moment, wheels turning in my brain, I shook my head.

"No, it's just…I don't know what's expected of me, I guess. This is already more than I anticipated."

His brow wrinkled, the frown pulling at his smooth cheeks. "I don't expect anything. Just for us to spend time together and for you to be honest with me."

Oh. Oh, I could do that. I nodded so hard that my hair shuffled against the leather of my seat. "Okay. Yes, I can do that. Thank you."

Tyler's face pulled in the other direction, landing in an approving smile. But this time, it didn't have to do with sex. If something as simple as agreeing to be honest, which was what I was going to do anyway, was all he was telling me to do, I would. And relax into our time together.

CHAPTER FIVE

TYLER

Delaney was barely containing himself. The emotions on his face flitting quickly from giddy to curious to shy, creating a mixture that was so precious and enticing, I was barely keeping myself from pulling him into my lap. To pet and kiss and taste.

Antler Pointe didn't have much in the way of fine dining, and when I had hastily planned our evening, I decided against taking him to a bigger city to enjoy what they had there. After waffling back and forth, I finally settled on this place that was casual enough for a first outing but nice enough to be special. He deserved it.

Delaney sipped from his mocktail, long brown lashes fluttering as he observed the dark curtains of the restaurant and the abstract shape of the chandelier above our heads.

As soon as Robin and I left the coffee shop, I'd holed up in my office, researching and planning because I didn't know what the fuck to do on a date. Well, the basics, sure. But Delaney's and my circumstances were quite unique. Also, there was the fact that I didn't eat food.

He didn't seem bothered that I barely perused my menu, though. He did, however, run his gaze over his for a long period of time. Chewing at his fingernail while he squirmed in his seat, as if he was weighing so many possibilities that he couldn't decide.

Our server came over, and I saw the pause of panic before he schooled his face into a sunny smile. I stepped in before Delaney could order. "Another round of drinks, please. And he'll have the crusted snapper. Thank you." Both of them gaped at me for a moment, but the server quickly collected themself, took our menus, and flitted away.

Delaney lowered his eyes to the table, but my eyesight was honed well enough to watch a bright blush suffuse his cheeks. His tan skin was so sensitive, and I knew just how soft the height of his cheekbones were. How sweetly the flesh of his neck yielded against my fangs.

I cleared my throat and mind of that track of thought. "How is your internship?"

The boy was naturally submissive, his big shoulders leaning inward now. And then his face would break in summery glee. The pop of his dimples was genuine this time as he recounted his assignment at the Montessori school in town for the second semester in a row. How much he loved working with the children there, though writing his papers and doing assignments were a bit trickier for him.

It'd been decades since I was in school, but I was able to follow his excited chatter just fine. It was infectious, his gentle kindness. The pink of his shirt and the blond of his hair glowed in the light of the candle on our table, but that had nothing on the air of *goodness* around him.

Fuck, what was I doing here?

Getting pulled into this boy that was a walking billboard of all that was good in the world. What the hell was he doing here with me?

"What about you? How's work?" He waited, sipping on his

bright purple drink.

I threw back the rest of my bourbon and picked up the new one that was dropped off a few moments ago. "People are always dying, so business is fine." I shrugged. "I just oversee that things stay running smoothly, but it's been a fairly well-oiled machine for most of my life. But," I paused while his entree appeared, and we both thanked our server before they left again, "we shouldn't talk about it while you eat."

"Why not?" he asked while digging right in. He blinked at me while he chewed, waiting.

"Because most people don't like thinking of dead bodies while they're enjoying their meal."

Delaney shrugged and made a humming noise of approval that went straight to my cock while a thick rise of pride filled my chest. I made the right choice of his meal. "It doesn't bother me. And it seems like an interesting job. Do you enjoy it?"

Before I could stop myself, I gave him the truth. His presence drew it out of me. "My brother was supposed to take over from my parents, but he's got his own issues to work through. Robin is his son and is getting his mortuary science degree right now, so hopefully, he'll be the one in my position when he's ready."

Delaney was already halfway through his plate, and after a giant bite and swallow, he put down his fork and rested his hands in his lap. "It sounds like you're a good brother and son. But do you dislike being here, then?"

I pondered that a moment, took another sip of my drink. I'd told him to be honest with me, and if I was doing this—*dating* the boy just for an excuse to get close to him, I could at least do what I was asking of him. "At times. It's like a betrayal to my younger self who felt like he was beyond all of this. And, yet, here I am working in my father's old office."

Delaney frowned a bit and resumed eating. Shit—I knew it would be too much. Why the fuck did people do this shit anyway? And why did I agree to it?

He took the last few bites of his food, scraping as much of the pan sauce as possible until his plate was completely clean. "I think it's noble of you to sacrifice some time to help them. I hope they appreciate you."

He smiled kindly, like the sweet boy he'd been through all the bullshit that occurred between us. The traumatic events of the night I got shot, him having to care for and feed me, then me breaking things off in a hasty move of self-preservation.

Did my parents appreciate what I was doing? Who the fuck knew. Maybe it was out of a sense of guilt, what with my leaving putting the responsibility of family legacy on William. Not that it caused his addiction struggles, but still.

"Are you ready to go?" I asked while signing the receipt for his meal and our drinks.

He rolled his lips between his teeth, eyes on the table. "Are you taking me back home now?" He sounded... disappointed.

"Not unless you want me to. There's a bar not far from here that I planned on taking us to."

Delaney's face lit up, and he scrambled out of his seat. "Yes!"

Really, what could I do but stand and guide him out of the restaurant? We received a few curious looks, but they obviously didn't matter. This dating thing wasn't so bad.

I'd been wrong. So very wrong because as soon as we entered one of the two suitable places to go dancing in Antler Pointe, Delaney was inundated with hungry eyes. No, he wasn't *my* boy anymore, not truly, anyways. But all the lustful gazes made me want to slaughter every person here. What would he think about that? Me giving into those baser urges that leaned toward blood and carnage?

He, on the other hand, took it all in stride. He kept his arm hooked in mine, and I followed his eyes which were innocently and excitedly staring at the dance floor. By now, the bar was quite full, and multiple bodies writhed suggestively to the pumping music.

I didn't fucking dance, much preferring for my food to come to me.

But this was a date, and something about the way he'd been so ready to deny me earlier today told me that this was my last chance. And, I glanced up at him, I wanted him to be happy. To have fun.

"Would you like to dance?"

It was all the permission he needed. With his bubbly nod in answer, I pulled us to a corner of the dance floor where I could better ensure that no one put their fucking hands on him.

At first, I basically stood there while his large body started moving, finding the rhythm of the loud music until his hips started rolling. I swayed stiffly with the same cadence, but I couldn't focus on anything besides the hot fluidity of his movements. His eyes were closed, the corners of his lips pulled up. Like the pleasant way he would sleep when he was having a nice dream.

Delaney twisted around, wiggling to the music. He never strayed far from me, but it was as if we were in two different worlds. His filled with bubblegum and sunny days, while mine was unfeeling, dark. Despondently clinging to him and stifling a gasp each time my fingers on his waist brushed against the bare skin that peeked out from beneath his shirt.

He turned around again, but this time, he curled his arms around my neck. His skin was always so damn warm, like I was standing under the rays of the sun. I looked up at him, now that we were so close, and he was staring back. He fluttered his lashes, but not in flirtation. Like he was thinking of what to say but couldn't quite decide.

While we watched each other, the song changed to an even more upbeat number that clanged against the slow bobbing we'd descended into. His cock was straining in his jeans—I could feel it pressed against me, and surely, he felt mine.

Making another decision for us, I dragged the boy to a dark corner of the club. The lights and music still pounded in my ears and vibrated my teeth, but Delaney's trusting hand in mine was more than enough incentive to ignore it all.

We sat on the hard fabric, my breaths heavy as I tried to control the urge to take him right there. What kind of person did that make me? All I did was take and take from this boy, and here I was again, doing the bare minimum of taking him out to eat and for five minutes of dancing.

And he was looking at me like I hung the moon. Large frame leaning toward me, his breaths were heavy with his excitement from the dance floor still lingering.

I put my arm on the back of the booth seat—I couldn't help myself—and the boy scooted even closer. Even more, he fisted the front of my shirt, crushing the silk in his hand like how he did my sheets when I would take him to bed.

"This is so nice," he said reverently and smushed his cheek against my temple. The movement was fucking up my hair, his hand wrinkling my shirt, but he could have everything I owned, chain me up in his bedroom, and I'd still ask him if there was anything else he needed.

I rested a palm on his thigh, giving him more of the body contact that I knew he craved, and almost immediately, he whimpered into my hair. Like a puppy forever starved for affection. Could I be that life source?

Pushing away the inevitable question of what we could even be past these few moments, I pulled my head back from his and returned with a kiss.

Delaney's sigh brushed against my face, and when I threaded my fingers through the hair at the back of his neck, he let me take control. His lips were soft and responsive, but their movements were always in reaction to mine. The slip of his tongue always after the guiding push I gave first.

My gums itched with my fangs begging to drop, so I pulled

back from him. It was dark enough here for me to let them out, but this evening was about him.

"I'm sorry, Delaney. For everything," I whispered between us. The music was bumping against the air around us, and maybe that's what gave me enough courage to admit again that I'd fucked up.

I could almost feel his eyelashes brush against my skin. He swallowed and squeezed my shirt a little tighter. "Th-thank you. I forgive you. I was never really mad. Just confused."

I groaned. This sweet boy—I was taking my filth-caked hands and raking them through the pristine pastel petals of his soul. Helping my family and my bygone career of saving lives didn't override the fact that I wasn't remorseful nor apathetic when I killed. It was thrilling. A game sometimes, a way to also get my dick wet at others.

He'd never asked, but I'd give up all of that for him. "I messed up, Delaney. You've been nothing but perfect. Truly."

His chuckle was watery, and when I sat back another inch or so, I saw the glistening path of a tear that'd escaped and was running through the cloud of blush on his cheek. I would've started panicking, but his crying, this time, came with his smile growing wider. "Does this mean we're gonna go on more dates?"

I swept my thumb through the teardrop before it could fall off of his jaw. I popped it into my mouth, and while the delectable taste wasn't as sweet and rich as his blood, it was just as delicious.

"Of course we will, sweet boy."

I hadn't wanted to pressure him by using the endearment, but once the words left my mouth, he gasped and pled to me with his wide stare. His heart started pounding, a true, resonant thud that I'd be able to pick out of any crowd. "And…you still want to be my Sir?"

Oh, good lord. I groaned and smashed my lips to his. This boy was too pure for me—for this entire fucking world—but if I had to be the demon to protect him, I'd sure as shit do it. I'd tell him to keep his eyes closed while I slaughtered all that threatened his happiness. I'd be the one to trudge through hell if it meant that it'd leave a clear path for him to heaven.

He curled into me, clinging and moaning while I devoured him.

I released his lips for a moment, to let him breathe, but he whimpered in protest like he didn't even want it. "That's right, baby boy."

CHAPTER SIX

DELANEY

A boyfriend! I had a boyfriend, and he was so incredibly sweet that I just went about my days smiling for no reason. Or, wait, I kind of already did that. But maybe the difference now was that every moment of my days were filled with the memory of his hands or lips on me. Or the real thing once we reunited.

And Tyler said before we got back together that he didn't date, but boy, could he plan a heck of an evening! We'd been to a museum, restaurants fancy and casual, beautiful walks in the park, and we had another evening planned after I was done with school for the day.

The only thing that ever gave me pause was his putting on the breaks whenever things got too steamy. It'd been two weeks, but we had yet to have sex. When I asked him about it, taking his command for honesty to heart, he'd startled for a moment while we sat on the park bench and watched a few ducks splash in the pretty pond. His arm was around my back while I finished the ice cream he'd bought me. "I didn't want to rush you. I wanted to do this right."

He'd wiped at the corner of my mouth and pushed his thumb against my lips. I'd licked at his skin way longer than it took to clean it of the chocolate ice cream, and his jaw clenched as heat swept his face. "It wouldn't be rushing. I love it when you're inside of me."

Tyler had groaned and pulled back his hand. "Okay, boy. After today, no more waiting." So he *did* still want me!

He'd walked me to my shift that afternoon at the coffee shop with his promise heavy between us. And now, that moment was almost here.

I barely contained myself during my classes, constantly looking at the clock to count down the minutes. And when my professor finally dismissed us, I shoved my bulky laptop into my backpack and made a beeline for the door like I had a fire in my britches.

Trying my best to avoid any collisions as I scampered up the hall, I pulled out my phone to text Tyler that I was heading outside to meet him. Again, he'd kept the details secret from me, but that just added to the anticipation.

My classmates chittered on about their weekend plans, the dreaded late Friday afternoon classes done, but I barely took it in. With my hip, I pushed open the door, and blinked past the dying sun rays that shined right in my eyes. The warmth was a nice addition to the hint of chill that was settling over Antler Pointe in the evenings and mornings. Where I was from, fall was pretty much a pipe dream. But here, it was its own season.

Would Tyler like to cuddle in front of a fire? Blow across the top of my apple cider until it was cool enough for me to drink?

I was lost in the fantasy of his puckered lips and a cozy evening, so I initially walked past the rumbly Challenger while staring at my phone and wishing he'd reply already!

But as soon as his scent met my nostrils, I stopped and back-tracked my steps like someone pressed rewind.

When my feet scraped to a stop on the curb, my jaw dropped as the window rolled down. Tyler had dark sunglasses on, and he rested his arm on the door, leaning toward me. "Get in, baby boy."

We were drawing stares. In the back of my mind, I noticed that, but what was in the forefront was how sexy he looked with his black dress shirt unbuttoned at the top, his hair of the same color messy like he'd run his hands through it.

I struggled to move for a second, struck with how handsome he was and the fact that he wanted *me*, but his raised brow over the rim of his glasses got my little butt into action. And would he be mad at me that I'd already prepped right before classes this afternoon? Even the prospect of punishment had me giddy.

Once I settled into the passenger seat, he peeled away into the parking lot of Antler Pointe College's education department and started toward his house.

For this date, he told me, I wouldn't need anything but myself and an overnight bag. "How was your day?" he asked over the bubbly music playing over the speakers.

I stuffed my hands between my thighs, not wanting to fidget too much. That would shift the plug I'd put in as a surprise to him.

"Good, but I'm glad school is done!" I blushed over at him. "I missed you! How was yours?"

He rested his hand on the top of my thigh. "I missed you too, pet." I beamed. "And work was fine. The usual. Tell me about what you learned today in class," he said and turned down the music a little bit.

"Oh, well…" I launched into all that I could remember from my classes, and that in turn caused me to reminisce about the situations I'd encountered at the Montessori school. Some children that made me exercise every single thing I'd learned thus far, while others were more easygoing. I loved it all, feeling like I was making a positive influence that set them up for greatness.

To not have that wasn't impossible to overcome, but I knew firsthand that it was more than difficult to claw yourself up out of that hole. It would've been unattainable for me without the kind people I'd met along the way.

I was still talking away when we drove up to his house and eventually into his garage. He cut the car off and shifted in his seat toward me. Tyler set his sunglasses in the compartment overhead, and the settling of his brown and silver eyes on my face had me holding my breath. "We're having dinner by the pool tonight. Do you need to freshen up before then?"

He coupled the question with a hand on my neck, stroking his fingertips through my hair that hung in wavy, messy strands. I cut my hair myself to save money, so it was nowhere as nice as his, but he seemed fascinated by it all the same. Maybe because the color of it was so different from his? Whatever the reason, I could stay sitting in the car with him all night if I weren't already wanting so badly what all was to come.

"Um, I-I'm okay. Unless you feel like I need to?"

Tyler pulled me into a hard kiss. One that was its own answer to my question. And when his tongue made its way into my mouth, I welcomed him in greedily. Only a few seconds of kissing, and he'd reduced me to a panting, needy mess. His hard hand against my face locked me in place, while his lips were soft against mine.

When he pulled away from taking all the air from my lungs, he didn't go too far. "You're perfect the way you are. You can put your things in the bedroom and meet me outside? Do you remember where it is?"

I swallowed. Memories of him reducing me to a crying, coming wreck flashed through my mind. His harsh slaps on my behind while he pounded into me. A movie playing as I snuggled him, and he fed from me before falling asleep against my chest.

My nod was a little unsteady, and by the time he kissed me again and pulled me out of the car, I was trying my hardest to keep my legs from trembling. The bustling of some people while they cooked in his kitchen didn't make it easy, though.

Especially when I pushed open the door to Tyler's bedroom

and was almost overtaken by his masculine scent. Steady, controlled. Safe.

He was safe, and he wanted *me*. While I was by myself, faced with Tyler's giant bed dressed in fancy black sheets and his dark, decadent wallpaper, I did a little jig.

Then, I set my bag at the side of the bed that'd been mine when I slept over and scampered back through the hallways, letting his scent guide me. In this state of mind, I couldn't be bothered to rely on my memory of the way.

By the time I made it outside, the sun was already gearing up to set, and Tyler was lounged back in one of the pool chairs, hands rested beneath his head as he stared up at the sky. When I approached, he shifted his legs off of the wooden pool lounge, planting his bare feet on the stone.

Tyler nodded to between his legs. "Come here, Delaney."

He sure as sugar didn't have to tell me twice. I shot forward and around the pristine blue pool until I was standing between his legs. His strong hands rested on my hips, providing a steady force that I leaned into off instinct.

My jeans were worn, holes in the knees surely to come with a few more washes, but my Sir was looking at me as if I was dressed in the designer wardrobe he preferred for himself.

Without a word, he flipped open the button on my pants and pulled down the zipper that would get caught sometimes. In Tyler's hands, though, it glided easily, and if that wasn't the darnedest thing.

He sucked in a breath, jaw clenching, when he saw what I had waiting for him underneath. Heat flooded my cheeks, but I didn't pull away. The white lace was something of a treat that was usually for my eyes only. It made me feel nice to have the soft fabric against my skin, and if today was the day he'd finally *touch* me, I wanted to give this to him when he already gave *me* so much.

"Look at you, pet," he whispered roughly and pushed up my t-shirt to expose my belly button. Tyler kissed in the ridge of my muscles, and big ol' swarms of butterflies fluttered against my heart.

Well, until he snuck his tongue out and licked my skin. Then, a desperate moan seeped out of me, and my hips bucked toward his face. My cock pressed against the panties, and suddenly my present for him was a prison.

He kept on kissing and licking but only made it so far as the edge of the white lace. Teasing me. "Please, Sir," I whined. My hands were behind my back, clenching and trying my darnedest to be good.

Tyler hummed against my skin, giving a cruel vibration that reached the base of my cock. The front of the underwear was wet with my precum, now, and the weight of the plug inside of me wasn't helping in the slightest. Luckily it wasn't the kind to press on my prostate, just to keep me ready for later, but there were way too many sensations happening right now.

His tongue snaked beneath the waistband of the panties before he looked up at me. "Keep your hands behind your back, boy. Or else I stop. Do you understand?"

I almost broke my neck with how forcefully I nodded, and he gave me one of his handsome-as-sin smirks. "I understand, Sir. I'll be good."

And he rewarded me. He pulled down my panties just enough to free my straining dick and heavy balls. That alone was a relief, but then he swallowed me down in one go, and my eyes crossed.

"Oh, *Jesus!*" I cried and just barely remembered to keep my hands clasped. It was almost painful, how good his mouth felt. Sir's nose nuzzled against my crotch, and he swallowed around my cock that was buried in his throat. He didn't say that I wasn't allowed to move my hips, right?

I panted, sweat already beading on my temples as Tyler pulled back, only to take all of me again. Again and again and again, while I dared to give little thrusts.

It didn't take long. Some might say I lasted for an embarrass-ingly short amount of time, but I couldn't bring myself to be ashamed. Not with the way my Sir moaned around my cock, enjoying taking care of me in this way too.

And when I came, unloading myself into his mouth, Tyler's eyes locked with mine.

He pushed my hips away once I was done and tugged at my shirt. My body was trembling, and my mind was fuzzy, but I was still able to follow his command. I sank down next to him, let him grab the back of my head and bring his lips to mine.

I opened my mouth and took in the cum that he fed me while we kissed. My hands fisted the front of his shirt as an anchor. My Sir. My boyfriend.

Once I swallowed it all, Tyler gave me a small peck on my top lip, the tip of my nose, and finally one on my cheek that was surely a flaming pink.

He put his arm around me while I cuddled up to him. "You were so good for your Sir. Sweet, perfect boy." I lapped up Tyler's praises, and they calmed me into a warm, peaceful state. I nuzzled beneath the collar of his dress shirt while the sun continued to set.

After a while, a gentle nudge on my shoulder startled me, but not enough to shoot up from where I was being held so nicely. I hadn't even realized I dozed off!

I blinked through the disorientation, finding the sky only a few shades darker. It couldn't have been more than thirty minutes, but there was already a little wet spot of drool on Tyler's neck. I swiped at it with my hand and looked up at him sheepishly. "Sorry." I blushed.

But he just kissed my forehead before jutting his chin toward the house. "Don't be sorry. I know that you get tired from school. But your dinner is ready. Are you hungry?"

I turned over my shoulder to look where he'd gestured, and what had been a bare patio table before was now dressed in a white tablecloth, candle, bouquet of flowers, and a plate covered by one of those silver dome thingies.

My eyes grew wet, and I squeezed into Tyler even tighter. "You're the best boyfriend in the world."

His chuckle shook the both of us. "Well, it's my first time being a boyfriend, so I'm glad that I'm not totally fucking it up."

"Oh, *no*, Sir, you've been perfect."

Tyler kissed me again on the top of my head and gave me a good squeeze before pushing to the edge of the lounge. "I didn't start that way with you. So, thank you for letting me try to make up for it." He stood and extended a hand to me. I felt almost shy as I took it, and we walked over to the candlelit dinner he had prepared.

Tyler pulled out my chair for me, and I smiled unsteadily while I sat. Soft music was playing from somewhere, and the glow from the pool and sky above made this all so romantic.

He removed the covering from my plate and revealed an elegantly plated steak and vegetables. My stomach rumbled as I picked up my fork and knife.

Tyler was leaned back in his seat opposite me, and he lifted a wine glass that was definitely not filled with wine. Did those people he hired know what they were pouring in there?

He caught my confused look while I started eating. "A friend of mine who's also a vampire knows a chef who is discreet. Did she do okay with your food?"

I smiled around a big bite of my rare steak. "It's so good!" Tyler nodded in satisfaction and took a sip from his glass. The blood stained the edge of his lips, and that got me wondering again. He raised his brows, seeing the question on my face. "Um, Sir, why don't you...why don't you want to feed from me anymore?"

He coughed on the sip of blood going down his throat, and it took a second for him to be able to swallow it. I started panicking that I asked the wrong thing—maybe he didn't want to because we were together now? Or he only had in the past because he needed to and that I actually didn't taste very good. That would make me sad, but I'd tasted my blood once after cutting my finger on accident, and it just tasted like pennies, so—

"Delaney. It's not that I don't want to. I just don't want to use you for that. It's not why I'm with you."

"Oh," I breathed. "Why are you with me?" Our first hookups were fun, then he did need my help, so now… what was the reason? Not that I was complaining, but he'd never said. Already, I was learning that Tyler didn't talk about his feelings much.

He frowned, and I was getting ready to apologize when he set his glass down and placed his arms on the table. His palms faced upward in silent command, and I dropped my fork so that I could hold onto him. The body contact settled my last bit of nerves. "Pet. I'm with you because of how kind and sweet and curious and fun you are. Not to mention the fact that you're absolutely beautiful and the perfect boy." Tyler's brown and silver eyes held mine, making sure that I heard every single word. Tears were falling down my face. "Do you understand?"

Did I? The words he used to describe me were simple, but the intensity behind them wasn't. I mostly just saw myself as a mess.

He told me to be honest, so I shook my head. "Not really. I mean, I understand the words, but I guess I don't see myself like that."

He pursed his lips. "That's okay, pet. I'll be sure to try and change your mind." He let go of my left hand but kept the right. "Now, finish your dinner." That was said with finality and command, so I continued eating like he told me to.

While I finished my meal, I asked him about his band, and he told me about their upcoming show in a few weeks. How he'd started writing songs when he went to college and that forming the Concrete Executioners made the move back home a little less miserable.

Soon, my plate was clean, and the crisp glass of Coke was drained. The same was true for Tyler's dinner.

"What does that taste like?" I pointed to the empty wine glass.

He slowly smacked his lips, as if tasting the last bit that lingered so that he could better describe it to me. "Every person is different. This particular one was like coffee, then a bite of sunset."

How did something taste like a sunset? "And what does mine taste like?"

Instead of answering right away, Tyler pulled on our joined hands.

I followed him to my feet and continued to let him lead me back inside the house. Those people were still here, wiping down his kitchen, and we both thanked them as we passed. My dinner was fantastic, and I told them so.

And as Tyler kept going, the fluttering in my belly started back up again. There was no question that we were moving toward his bedroom to do what he promised me.

The dark hallways passed in a blur while my thoughts were going and going and going. Should I not have eaten that whole meal? What would he think of the surprise I had waiting for him? Was he going to end up uninterested with me after this?

Was I going to be any good?

Tyler pushed open the door to his room, and I squawked in surprise. I'd just *been* in here. But instead of how it was before, there were… rose petals.

Lots and *lots* of pink petals were scattered on the floor in a trail that led to the bed, and the candles that he usually kept as decoration were lit. The curtains in front of the large windows were closed, keeping the room and us in our own little world.

With tiny steps, I crossed the threshold behind Tyler, and for the first time in what felt like forever, he untangled our hands. I immediately started fiddling with the hem of my t-shirt while he closed the door, sealing us inside.

CHAPTER SEVEN

DELANEY

I was crying again. The tears shouldn't have even surprised me anymore, but I was startled by my own reaction all the same.

No one... no one had done this for me before. Taking the time to plan all of these things. Paying attention to the temperature I liked my steak or taking an interest in the stories I shared about my day.

"Um, I...I need to go to the bathroom," I whispered and scampered into the connected room. The cold water I splashed did nothing to settle the redness on my face and neck. Actually, all it did was mess up the locks of hair at my temples. "Shoot," I muttered and tried to fix it as best I could, but nothing was working. And then I caught a whiff of my armpit that still smelled fine, but would *Tyler* think I smelled nice?

I stared at myself in the mirror, eyes wide with panic, so I raced into the large shower. I chucked my clothes off as quickly as I could while turning on the shower at the same time.

It was one of those with the multiple shower heads, but I remembered how to work it from before. At least enough that it only took a few moments of fumbling with the controls to get a steady stream from the water above.

With Tyler's fancy soap and shampoo, I scrubbed myself down and breathed. This was what I wanted. This was my boyfriend making our second first time special, and here I was, crying in the shower.

All the times I'd showered before walking out to meet a male or group of them in the other room. I wasn't always told to do it—sometimes it was my idea. But none of them had treated me like this. Like I was something special.

My next deep breath was more of a shiver, even with the hot water still coming down on me. After Ma died, it'd felt like the only way to survive and be touched at all. When you couldn't shift, what other use to the pack were you? That was what I'd been taught, and for a long, long time, I believed them. Charlie and I were the only non-shifters in Howl's Fury, passed back and forth or even loaned out to other packs. My family. Their friends.

I fumbled through turning off the shower and braced a hand on the tiles. Breathed. They were gone. We'd made it out, and I had a male that cared about me—

And I just ran away from him without saying anything! I jolted, realizing too late what I'd just done while I got swept up in my thoughts again. I plucked a towel off of the fancy warmer thing and swiped it harshly over my body, rubbed in messy globs of his unscented lotion over my skin.

I stopped in the middle of the bathroom again—what was I supposed to wear? My dirty clothes were folded in a heap on top of the toilet, and there was no way that I was putting those back on. Did I... should I just go out there naked?

But a black robe that hung on the back of the door caught my eye. That was definitely new, and when I pulled it off the hanger, felt the soft and warm fabric between my fingers, I realized that it was my size.

I sucked in more air through my nose, pulling back the tears that threatened to rush out, and shoved my arms into it.

When I finally stepped out with wet hair and bare feet, I found Tyler still dressed, though his black hair was messier. Like he'd been running his hands through it. He sat on the edge of his bed, arms propped on his thighs, and when our eyes met, I could see that I'd done wrong. His brow was pulled low, the corners of his lips turned down.

I held my hands at my front and hung my head. "I'm sorry, Sir. I-I just got o-overwhelmed and worried."

He glanced around the room, at the candles that were now noticeably shorter than they'd been before. He looked down at the petals beside his thighs before returning to me.

"This was too much. I'm sorry, Delaney. I thought this would be nice, but I see now that—"

"No no no." I jerked forward and fell to my knees in front of him. Clenching my hands under my chin, I begged him to understand. "Sir, no, this is beautiful and perfect, and I just—I got all mixed up and worried, but you didn't do anything wrong."

Tyler watched me seriously, waiting for my bumbling words to run and dry. How could I ruin our night so easily? He put so much thought into this so that all I had to do was shut up and enjoy it. I couldn't even do *that*.

"Shh, pet." He took my face with both hands and swept my cheekbones with his thumbs. "I want you to be honest with me. Remember? That means telling me how you feel."

"I know, Sir." My lip trembled. I did know, and I'd been doing so *well*.

"So, tell me."

I opened my mouth but closed it before any words came out. How did I feel?

Scattered in my head, my throat a little tight. My chest was the same, but in my belly, those flutters were still there. With him in front of me, with his hands on me. My thighs felt the stretch of my position, but that felt good, too. To be kneeling for him.

Now, it only had to be him.

I followed Tyler's order and told him all of it, not wanting to miss anything important. He treated me like everything was important.

Tyler bent and kissed my forehead. That was a good sign, right? He didn't pull back all the way, keeping his face close. The silver clouds within his irises had hints of blue that complemented the chocolate color surrounding them.

"Stand up, boy."

I gasped at those simple words, the shift in his tone that made my spine straighten.

It was the thing to cling to. My Sir in front of me, his commands, his touch. He'd shown me that he was safe, so it was natural to do as he said. More than that, it was comforting.

I straightened, suddenly very aware of the robe against my skin. The soft rug beneath my toes. Tyler looking at me with hard, hungry eyes. He knew what I needed.

"You remember your safe words?"

"Yes, Sir."

"Tell me."

"Red means stop, yellow means slow down, and green means keep going."

"Good," he rumbled. "What's your color right now?"

I didn't even need to think. Just a few seconds, and he'd emptied all thoughts from my mind that weren't about us. "Green. Green."

"All right. Show me what's under that robe, boy."

I groaned a little but did as he said. How quickly my skin became ultra-sensitive, to the point that the brush of the robe against it left goosebumps. The warm air of the room was somehow better and worse at the same time.

My cock was fully on board, hard and jutting out toward him, and my nipples were hard peaks the same color as the flower petals around us.

My Sir's nostrils flared as he inhaled and took me in. I hoped like hell that I was pleasing to him—maybe I should've put the panties back on.

I stood, hands behind my back, and waited while he rose. He walked slowly around me, appraising my naked body without a word. Or a touch. The contact of his eyes only left me trembling with anticipation.

Until his hand snatched the back of my hair, pulling it taut. His voice was even deeper than before as my body arched, and a groan shot from my lips.

"Color."

"Green," I gasped. The agony was so sweet, the touch quenching and further igniting my thirst. Sir bit my earlobe and tightened his hand, bringing on another flash and roll of sensation.

And then he was gone. Dropping his touch and stepping away from me while my scalp and ear were throbbing. "On the bed, pet. Crawl to the middle." My cock jumped a little at the command, but I managed to hold back my moan that time.

I walked on unsteady feet until the mattress hit the front of my shins. Under my lashes, I glanced at my Sir beside me and dropped to my hands and knees. The plush flower petals and comforter cushioned my way across the firm mattress.

"*Fuck*," Tyler cursed under his breath when I got far enough up the bed for him to fully see my backside and what I had waiting for him.

The plug was pink, too, and I'd ordered it online just for tonight.

Before I could turn around and sit, a stinging crash smacked against my right butt cheek. "Color," he demanded, but I was already pressing back for more.

"Green," I whined and was rewarded with four more quick slaps that stung so sweetly. My behind was throbbing, the skin hot from the force of his hand.

"Turn around, pet," he breathed, and I did that, too, pressing into the bed to deepen the slight burning from his spanks.

My hard cock flopped against my stomach, and I squeezed the covers between my fingers to keep them away from where I wanted so badly. Because I wanted to be good for him even more.

Tyler was now at the foot of the bed, working the buttons loose on his shirt slowly. "Look at you, boy. You belong in my bed."

"Yes," I groaned as he undressed. That in of itself was torture. Watching him shed the funeral home director suit and reveal the male underneath. He was always intense, always dark, but without the pressed shirt that he now dropped to the floor, he was more.

His pale skin was tight with lean muscle that I knew held much more power than met the eye. The black and red markings of his tattoos that I now knew were his favorite poems. After the turning process erased them, he got them redone so that they'd remain, always.

"Did you come when you were prepping yourself earlier today?" He started on his slacks, unbuckling his belt.

I'd never been so thankful to have denied myself an orgasm as I was in that moment. "No, Sir. I just cleaned and prepped, and that's it."

He hummed a second while unbuttoning and unzipping his pants. "Good boy. You don't come unless I give you permission. Ever."

I sucked my lips between my teeth, scared and so turned on at the same time. That was going to be a hard promise to keep. "And if I mess up…" My words trailed off as he pulled down his pants and underwear, stepping out of them and rounding the bed in all of his naked glory. That fat cock was hard and dripping, and I just wanted it inside of me. Somewhere. Didn't really matter.

But he kept on torturing me, fisting it when I wasn't allowed to touch anything. My mouth watered, and I couldn't keep my tongue in my mouth as I watched.

"If you mess up, you'll be punished."

That got me pausing. A trill of excitement ran down my spine, but that lick of fear was also there. "What kind of punishment?"

A hard hand closed around my throat, and I shot my gaze up to his face. My cock jumped again, and I was realizing that I was dangerously close to being in real trouble. The constriction on my throat didn't affect my breathing—at least physically. Mentally, though? If he'd let me, I would've flipped over and presented myself for him to destroy me.

Tyler continued to jerk his cock right in front of me, letting his own precum slick the way, and some trailed onto the sheets, when it was supposed to be *mine*. "I don't tolerate brats. I'll punish you as I see fit so that you learn your lesson. Do you understand?"

My Adam's apple bumped against the palm of his hand as I struggled to swallow. He wasn't cutting off any of my air, but I still had to fight to find my words. "Y-yes, Sir. I do. I'm sorry."

"Good." He released me, and just when I was about to beg for him to put his hand back on me, Tyler climbed onto the bed and knelt between my parted thighs. I set my feet flat on the mattress, opening up for him to do what he wanted, and I choked when he brought our cocks together.

I bit on my lip as hard as I could to fight off the pleasure that the contact caused. The sight of it made it even worse. They were about the same length, but where mine was slimmer and curved slightly to the left, his was thicker.

Tyler brought both of us in hand, and I cried out, so incredibly here for it but also quickly coming apart.

Our precum mixed, casting the pumps of his fist in a loud, slick noise that joined with our groans and panting. I was probably tearing holes into the covers with how hard I was holding onto them, but it was the only way I was going to be good. Especially when he bent and started kissing on my cheek, nibbling on my jaw with hard snaps of his teeth. With my quick healing, the marks would be gone before the morning.

If only I could keep them on me always. To be reminded of the glorious pain.

My hips were moving with little thrusts, the sensation of

Tyler's cock against mine just making me want more and more and more.

"You like that, pet?"

I blew out a gust of air and nodded with his face against mine, but my cry filled the room when he bit down hard on my earlobe again. It felt too good. Too much.

"Words. Use your words."

"Oh, god, S-Sir I'm trying not to come. *Please.*" It was a good thing he'd let me earlier tonight, or else I would probably already be receiving my punishment.

Tyler pulled back his face and cock and pushed me onto the mattress. I fell to the pillows beneath me and released a gust of his petrichor scent. "You're not coming until I'm inside of you, pet."

Tears. Tears were falling from my eyes now, wetting the pillowcase underneath me. I wanted to come so bad, and my poor cock was so stiff that it hurt and was missing his.

"But you're a good boy, I know." Tyler reached for the plug, and I sobbed in relief. Finally.

He didn't just take it out, though. No, he pulled on it, causing me to cry out again while he leaned over me. Owning me.

Tyler pulled on the plug a few times, always pushing it back in. Just adding to the sensations and continuing to tease me. Through my watery vision, I saw him watching, his fangs now visible.

"Bite me. *Fuck* me. Please," I begged, and he slammed his gaze to mine. There had to be some relief soon or else I might die. In that hazy moment, it didn't feel like an exaggeration at all.

He hummed again that rumbling noise that I felt all the way in my bones. After another teasing pull and push, he took mercy on me and slowly pulled the plug all of the way out, leaving me open.

I was so past self-consciousness now, and his heated look between my legs just made me squirm with need. I panted through clenched teeth, my eyes squeezed shut because the visual of him looking at me with his thick cock jutting out from between his legs was too darn much.

The mattress dipped a little with his movements, and beneath my breathing, I heard the shuffling of a drawer opening and closing and the snick of a bottle.

And then, *then*, I finally felt the unmistakable touch of his cock against my hole. "Oh *god*."

Tyler pushed against me as I bore down, and the slip of his cockhead into me left my back arching with an electric zip that raced up my spine and back down. He kept on until I'd taken all of him, slowly bottoming out. My cheeks rounded as I blew out another breath. I'd forgotten how full his girth made me.

Tyler planted his hands either side of my chest, and I finally cracked open my eyes to see him staring down at me.

My Sir was so beautiful and sexy with his hair wild and his muscles bulging with strain and pleasure. "You're so tight, pet," he gritted. "The perfect hole for my cock. The perfect boy for your Sir." He pulled back and thrust in to emphasize his point before bending down to give me a hard kiss.

We swallowed each other's moans, tongues tangling until he cupped the backs of my thighs and pressed my legs into my chest.

Tyler nearly pulled all of the way out of me, gave me a moment to let out a little mewl of anticipation, then plunged back in. He picked up his pace then, fucking me into the mattress while my mind teetered on the edge of becoming completely lost and trying to hold off my release for as long as possible.

"Fuh—S-Si—" I tried, but each word just ended in another gasp, another moan. My vision was crossing, and there was a long stream of precum pooling on my stomach now.

"That's it. Such a good pet. " His words didn't sound that steady either, and when he bent down, his rhythm slowed enough for me to rest my legs on his shoulders. Tyler propped up on his elbows beside my head and kissed me far more gently than I would've expected. "You can come after I do. Not a second before."

He sank his fangs into my neck at the same moment he started fucking even harder than before. I screamed, rejoicing in the twin sensations of pain and pleasure.

Tyler didn't say I couldn't do it, so I clutched him to me, holding him close as he sucked my blood and pounded into me. Feathery, swoopy sensations swept across my chest, all the way down to my cock, and with my Sir nailing my prostate dead on with every thrust, there was no way. Absolutely no way I was going to be able to hold on. My body was bent completely in half, and there was no fisting my dick to carry me into an orgasm like I'd normally need.

Him drilling inside of me and the friction between our stomachs was enough, though.

Maybe it was just perfect timing, or maybe he sensed it and took mercy on me, because Tyler's hips lost their steady rhythm, and he gave one last thrust before coming in me.

That was all the fireworks under my skin needed before they went off. I arched into his embrace and my vision blacked out. Another wave of tears fell from my eyes, and my cum filled the space between our bellies.

It took a while for me to come down from that fuzzy, pleasant place, and even when I did, the shadow of it was still cast over me. Over the both of us.

Meanwhile, Tyler was still at my throat, no longer sucking but lazily licking and kissing. At some point, my hands had buried in his hair. Did he like me scratching at his scalp?

"Thank you, Sir," I said on the end of a content sigh. My thoughts were calm. Just filled with happiness and him.

Tyler gave one last kiss on my neck before he propped up on his hands. How stunning was he? In the glow of the candlelight, my blood made his lips as red as cherries, and his black lashes were lowered halfway over his eyes. "You taste like summertime. Like oranges and lemons and vanilla. Like ice cream and sunny days."

Oh.

That was way better than pennies.

I grinned a sleepy smile at him and hummed, happy as a clam. "Thank you, Sir," I said again.

"You're welcome, sweet boy." Tyler removed my legs from his shoulders. Slowly, he began to pull out of me, and that cut through the haze a little bit.

"Wait!" I gasped. "Get the plug. Please." I tried my best to feel around for it in the covers but was coming up empty.

Tyler let loose a breath like a chuckle, and joined in my search. "Trying to keep your reward?" He was teasing. I knew he was, but it was actually the truth. Eventually, he was able to find the plug somewhere near my left foot. "I'm going to clean it off, but I'll come right back, okay?"

"Okay," I croaked and watched him pull his softening cock out of me. As soon as the contact was gone, I clenched my legs together.

Like he promised, Tyler used his vampire speed to rush into the bathroom in a blur. I heard the sink running and the shuffle of a towel before he was on the bed with me once more. He slicked it up with some lube, and I opened my thighs for him.

Tyler gently situated the plug back inside of me and used a warm washcloth to wipe up my own cum that was drying on my belly. When he was done, he kissed my bellybutton, and I truly relaxed into the bed. The covers were so soft, and all the tension in my body was gone.

CHAPTER EIGHT

TYLER

I hand-fed Delaney while he showed me one of his favorite TV shows. It was some cartoon that he would watch as a child, and even as an adult, he came back to it frequently.

I leaned against a mountain of pillows while he lay curled on his side, head in my lap. After I'd retrieved the snacks I bought for him and a bottle of water, he was easily coaxed away from falling asleep by the strawberries and pretzels.

With one hand in his hair and one holding the leafy end of the fruit, I made sure that my boy got the proper comedown he deserved. He'd started pouting that he wasn't thirsty when I first tried to prop him up to drink some water, but the now-empty bottle was evidence to how right I'd been.

"Okay, so it may not seem like much, but that's going to keep coming back later! It's important!" he somehow exclaimed and yawned at the same time before munching the last good bite of strawberry.

I was just managing to split my attention between taking care of him and keeping up with the episode. "That pai sho game? I missed what tile the uncle just played."

Delaney twisted to look up at me with a wide, grateful grin. He was still naked, all thick muscles and tanned skin. "What?" I asked and brushed my finger over his brows.

When he'd said he wanted to watch cartoons, I hyped myself up to trudge through something stupid, but the story was actually pretty good. Perhaps it was also finally fucking and feeding from him that was leaving me in a good mood. Feeling him come around me while drinking his blood.

I'd agreed to a date and gotten myself a boy in the process. Had to admit, seeing him light up every time I planned something excited me more than I'd ever imagined.

Having him on my lap, in my arms, gave me a sense of content that I'd never known before. Would it be so bad if I kept him?

"Oh, Sir, we're gonna start this from the very beginning and watch the whole thing. I'm so glad you like it! It's my favorite, *favorite* show."

His eyes sparkled as he wiggled on the bed. The movement of his head had my cock taking notice, but I ignored it to kiss him and scratch his scalp. "All right, boy. Why don't you start us at episode one, and we'll fall asleep to it."

"But I don't want to miss anything!" He yawned again while I started gathering the leftover snacks to take back to the kitchen. I hated to tear myself away, but I didn't want fucking ants or something in my bedroom.

I left and came back quickly, but somehow he was already losing the battle with his drooping eyelids. *This boy*, my chest warmed.

I blew out all the candles and pulled back the covers as much as I could. His breaths were deepening while the bright colors from the TV were flashing across the darkness of the bedroom. At this hour, I normally felt most active, but the prospect of holding my boy all night was far more appealing.

With my age, I didn't need to sleep nearly as much as I had when I was newly turned. Two-ish hours a day was more than enough, and though it was an adjustment to sleep during the evening, it was what I had to do to keep up with business hours.

But tonight, I'd probably stay up watching him sleep. It was almost disgusting how far this Wolf had me wrapped around his finger. This morning, I'd gone to the grocery store for the first time since the early aughts.

I lifted Delaney into my arms, and he just tucked his face into my neck while I turned down the bed the rest of the way. I gingerly settled him onto the sheets and tucked the comforter up and around him. "Whereyougoin'," he mumbled and looked up at me with drowsy eyes.

"Nowhere."

With a few taps on my phone, I made sure that the home alarm system was on. It was only a few seconds more before I was sliding into the bed beside Delaney, and like a magnet, he immediately found my body and clung to me.

The cartoons still played, and though he made valiant efforts to glance kind of in the direction of the show, he was snoring softly before the cut to the next scene.

His head was on my chest, my arms around his back and fingers threaded in his hair. I didn't dare turn to a different show, just starting it back from episode one so that I'd be better able to keep up when we inevitably watched more together.

Hours passed by, the pool of drool between my pecs growing larger and larger, and I found myself completely sucked into the children's program and the little shifts in my boy's sweet expression while he dreamed.

Until his phone rang. It was already past two in the morning, so I just let his cheery ringtone peter out as the spam caller gave up. At least, until they called again. The phone was trapped somewhere in his backpack, and I didn't want to get up from the cocoon of sheets and my boy.

The fourth time his phone rang, though, I couldn't take it anymore. Delaney remained asleep, so I tried my best not to jostle him. I rifled through his change of clothes for tomorrow and found the vibrating, older phone with a spider of cracks in the lower righthand corner.

The name 'Charlie' flashed on the screen, and I watched this person hang up and try calling *again*.

My fangs itched and my face went from mild, sleepy irritation to a full-on scowl. I pressed the green button on the screen and put the phone to my ear.

Who *the fuck* was Charlie?

The curtains still covered the windows, but the blanket of fatigue over my mind signaled the rising of the day.

After talking to *Charlie*, I hadn't gotten any sleep, so it was probably that too.

"And who the hell are you?" A voice I immediately hated drawled from the other end after I demanded to know who he was.

"Delaney's boyfriend. Who the fuck are you?" It was still a bit strange to call myself that, but on the phone with that asshole, I wore the title proudly.

The line had gone dead after that, and after finding my boy still asleep and clutching a pillow to replace me in his arms, I paced the house before slithering back into bed with him. He'd made his way back onto my chest, sensing in sleep that I was beside him once more.

I raced through the possibilities—Delaney having someone else, someone threatening him, a stalker—but at the end of it all, he was keeping something from me. I leaned down and inhaled his sunny smell. Was this what being committed to someone led to? Feeling out of your fucking mind about a late night phone call?

"G'mornin," Delaney rumbled into my skin. His voice cracked a bit as he shrugged off sleep and cuddled even more tightly into me. My phone was too far away to check the time without dislodging him, but it had to have been early.

"Good morning." I kissed the top of his head, trying to figure out how to approach this. Did I just flat out ask? What if this was the thing that led to me being without him again?

"Gotta pee." He squirmed a little, so I untwined my arms from around him. Delaney shuffled out of the bed with eyes still half-shut and walked toward the bathroom.

Last night, I'd also worried I fucked up. He'd been in the bathroom for an hour, mumbling to himself so much that I'd almost burst in there multiple times.

But comforting people wasn't my strong suit, so how was I supposed to help someone who was so incredibly sensitive? When my go-to was to break ties or drain someone if they got too irritating. What if I messed it up?

Would Delaney be upset if I killed this Charlie?

I watched him patter toward the bathroom, his god-like body naked and on display for my eyes. But was it for mine only? Had we really discussed exclusivity?

I carded my fingers through my hair while Delaney took care of his morning needs. When he came back out, he was wearing a pair of pajama pants and a sleepy smile.

He hopped onto the bed, crawling on hands and knees like he had last night, and like last time, he stopped and waited for me to give him direction. Kneeling in front of me while his fingers made little circles on the rumpled comforter.

And I watched his expression change as we sat in silence. The hopeful smile, probably excited for our day together, dimmed to a twist of his lips. His shoulders curled further in, almost shrinking him in half.

"Did I do something wrong, Sir?"

I wrestled with the side of me that wanted to toy with and hurt. No, I wouldn't do that to him.

"Who is Charlie?"

Delaney froze, blinking down at his fingers for a while. But his heart rate stayed the same cadence. "Um…well, the only Charlie I know is the one from my old pack. Why?" His large, uncertain eyes looked back at me.

"Okay. Why would he be calling at two o-clock in the morning? Multiple times."

There it was. His heart began hammering hard in his chest, and his gaze slid away from mine. But not with innocent thought —no, he was trying to avoid me.

"Uh." He wiped a hand on his cheek, as if petting himself. "I'm not sure." Really, he was a terrible liar, but I couldn't even be amused by it. The main directive I continued to give him was to be honest with me, and here he was. Breaking that in my face.

I'd expected to be angry, but I didn't expect the deep ache. "You're not sure." He shook his head, still avoiding my eyes while I stayed propped up by the pillows against the headboard. "So, all the texts between you two mean nothing?"

He flinched, heart picking up even more as he stared at me in shock. Fear. "You went through my phone?"

My jaw clenched so hard that I had to actively relax it or crack a tooth. "No. I thought about it but decided to give you the opportunity to explain what's going on. And instead, I know now that you're lying to me." To think, I patted myself on the back when I ignored the urge to check his texts and instead stuffed his phone back into his bag.

Delaney curled even further into himself, and I watched a tear fall onto the black bedding, form a shallow puddle, and seep into the fabric. "I-I'm sorry, Sir. I'll tell you everything."

Did I really want to hear about how my boy was letting someone else fuck him? How many others were there? I'd no problem with sharing before, but something about Delaney was… different. The way I showed up for him was different.

When I didn't say anything, he cringed and started, "Ch-Charlie and me…we were the only non-shifters in my old p-pack. And, and, after I started school here, he reached out. I have my scholarship and some grants and stuff, b-but he has a ha-ha-hard time, s-so I he-help him out with-with money sometimes. But, I haven't b-been a-able t-t-to, and—" Delaney's speech descended to near-incoherent, and I couldn't take it anymore. I'd been steeling myself to order him a car to leave, and my thoughts were scrambling with the harsh pivot.

I reached forward with my eyes prickling for the first time in decades. Maybe not since I'd been human. "Boy." Delaney sniffed, shoulders shaking. "Is he harassing you?"

His lips wobbled, but he accepted my hands closing around his. "He-he just keeps asking. I d-don't know how to," his breathing hitched for a moment before smoothing back out, "to tell him that I-I just c-can't right now." This boy.

"Delaney." He stiffened, and I brushed his jaw with my finger. "Listen to me. I know that you want to help him, but you cannot keep giving him money. I'm ordering you to stop. Do you understand?" He was struggling on his student-budget as it was. And he was proud, too. He stammered and squirmed whenever I bought him anything and thanked me profusely afterward.

"I...I understand."

"I know how hard it is to care about someone who needs help. But it's not on you, okay? We'll deal with this."

He nodded again, this time much more fervently. William's addiction started around the time I turned, and if I could keep Delaney from going through what me and my family had, I'd do it.

But there was also something else I had to deal with. "But first, I have to punish you, pet." He gasped, and his hand clenched at the same time my stomach did.

Delaney didn't fight me on it, though. "I understand, Sir." His bottom lip poked out, and his head bowed, resigned to his fate.

When had I gone to being a hair away from giving in to a regretful sub? In the past, I'd felt nothing but excitement to take a cane to the soft and fleshy part of the one who disobeyed me. In fact, there was a room at the back of the house that used to hold all the instruments I needed to punish Delaney in that way.

But now? I couldn't bear any touch from me resulting in that sort of pain for my boy.

What the fuck.

"Before we talk more about this, I want you to go stand in that corner." I pointed to the one between the windows and the bathroom. He followed my finger with a warily relieved expression. "You'll face the wall and think about why you lied to me when I explicitly asked for your honesty."

"For how long?" he whispered.

"Until I tell you to come back to bed. Your actions made me question my trust in you. You can always safe-word out if it's unbearable."

The air felt heavy, melancholy, but it had to be done. What kind of Sir would I be if I let my boy get away with things like that? What kind of foundation would we have if lies weren't addressed? Even when he lied out of what seemed like panic.

"Yes, Sir." I let his hands go, and Delaney slunk toward the edge of the bed. "I'm sorry, Sir."

My stomach twisted again as I watched him take up his post in the corner, facing away from me. The boy craved praise and touch, so this seemed like the most effective way to deter him from lying to me again.

I didn't move at first, watching him fidget and still. He found a comfortable position to stand in, his shoulders relaxing a bit, but it wasn't long in the silence of my bedroom until he began moving again. This time, the broad muscles in his back tightened. The scent of salty tears filled the room, calling to the ones threatening to spill down my own face.

I took a steadying breath, standing and busying myself to make the bed. And I caught myself before I could reach out and touch him as I was walking to the bathroom to brush my teeth.

After some time on my phone and dressing in my own sweatpants and t-shirt, I sat on the edge of the bed and watched him some more. It'd been twenty minutes at most, but after cresting while I dressed, his sobs had calmed to little hiccups now.

Voice thick, I called quietly to him. "Come here, boy."

Delaney shot over to me and collapsed at my feet. His large arms wrapped around my calves, and he buried his face between my thighs.

I covertly dried my own eyes and gave him the touch he needed. His hair was soft and messy between my fingers while I sat as his anchor. The sure and steady that he could depend on.

But watching him fall apart nearly had me doing it with him. When had someone cared about my opinion that badly? Or the fact that my trust had been wounded?

His crying took longer to subside this time—maybe the punishment broke the dam, or maybe it was having to explain the bit of his past that had to do with Charlie.

Whichever, it was my responsibility to help him calm once again. I took his face in hand. "Pet. Look at me." His poor, swollen face and snotty nose—I clenched the inside of my cheek so hard that I drew my own blood. "I want to be clear with you. I told you before that I didn't date, and that was the truth. What we have is new for me, and I don't take it lightly. We will be honest with each other because it's important to build trust. And if you are mine, you are *mine*. I'm exclusive to you, and that's what I'm asking of you in return if you want to be my boy. Do you understand all of that?"

He nodded before I could even finish, clinging to me so much that if I were human, I'd be wearing bruises for weeks. "I understand, Sir. I want all of that. I'm s-sorry I lied."

Honesty. "I...I don't like punishing you, Delaney. But I will if I have to."

He cracked a little smile and sniffed. "I never liked being put in time out. Thought I grew out of it."

Just like that, the tears stopped coming, though there was still evidence of them everywhere. On his skin, my pants. The sting in my mouth that was slowly abating. "Well, hopefully there won't be much corner time in the future."

Some birds trilled outside of the window, and I found myself actually being excited for the daylight hours. That was another new thing that'd become a regular occurrence with him. My boy.

Delaney straightened back onto his knees, but he kept one arm wrapped around my legs. He still held on tightly, but he released his left hand to reach toward my face. He hesitated for a second, lips parted slightly as if he was preparing to speak.

I didn't move, waiting, and the light brush of his thumb on my cheekbone made me jump. But I let him touch me, caress me how I always did him, and when he pulled his finger away so that we could both see, it was glistening.

For a split second, I wanted to snatch it away, erase the evidence that he affected me this much. That I couldn't handle the responsibility of being his Dom.

Before I could give into it, though, Delaney popped his finger into his mouth and sucked my tear off of his skin. He watched me beneath his long lashes, but it wasn't a seductive gesture. Something softer.

Delaney reached out to touch me again, and I found myself leaning forward, actively accepting him taking what he needed from me in that moment. His palm rested on the back of my neck, and he pulled me into a tender kiss.

I opened my thighs so that we could be even closer, and Delaney scooted between them until we were pressed together, sharing slow and lazy kisses. My scent was still on him, and I'd purposely skipped the shower so that his was on me. How could I dislike warm sun rays anymore when they wafted off of this boy?

Fuck, I was going to find a way to keep him.

CHAPTER NINE

DELANEY

In the large, sprawling mirror, I brushed my teeth beside Tyler while fighting to keep my smile from letting dribbles of toothpaste fall from my mouth. I failed.

He was doing the same, smirking and watching me in the glass reflection. He reached out and trailed his hands up and down my bare back while we both finished and placed our toothbrushes back on their chargers. And after quickly watering the vining plant I brought to sit in the window above the spa-sized bathtub, I followed him back into the bedroom.

A few weeks of this, staying more and more evenings with my Sir, and I was straight up addicted. Waking up next to him, getting ready beside him. Even the sillier rituals like buttoning his shirt for work.

He stood between my thighs as I sat at the edge of the bed, now an expert at getting the small buttons situated. My clothes were much easier to put on—t-shirts, slightly more professional versions for when I was going into my internship. Jeans that pulled on and buttoned in a jiffy.

I looked up at him now, just as I reached the end of the row of buttons. Instead of dropping my hands, I rested them on his chest. "Can I have a hug?" He'd gotten more and more lenient with me. Letting me take opportunities for physical affection, even when he hadn't offered them first. But I did try to be good when I remembered!

"Of course." He smiled down at me and moved even closer. I wound my arms around his waist and nuzzled into his chest. He never put on cologne—the scent would be too overstimulating for both of us. But he *always* smelled good. Like the best kind of rain.

"What are you doing today, pet?" Tyler rubbed my back again, and I wished the fabric of my shirt wasn't separating us. Even though we'd spent our morning shower with him behind me, rimming then fucking me to start the day, I almost asked for another round. I would never get enough of him—it was something I knew down to my bones, along with the fact that he was it for me.

Instead, I spoke into his shirt, "Got a morning shift before my half day at the Montessori school. If I can make it work, I've got homework and studying for my test that I need to get ahead on. Really, I'm behind, but I'm hoping if I push myself this weekend, I can get back on track. It's just a whole lot to juggle, ya know?"

That rotten part of me whispered, grateful that I hadn't heard from Charlie since he'd called. Tyler had helped me draft a text to send him next time he asked for money, but it remained in my notes app, unsent. Unfortunately, I was getting a tingle in the back of my mind that he'd turn up soon.

"Am I taking up too much of your time?"

I flinched back enough to look up at him again. "*No, Sir.*"

He pursed his lips, looking me over and swiping a thumb over my chin. "I think I am, but maybe we hadn't realized it until now. I'm sorry for that."

The pout on my lips wasn't on purpose, I swear. But pout, I did. "I'm not. You're the best thing that's ever happened to me."

Tyler huffed a laugh and dropped a kiss to my lips. The pout faded into a smile, and he kissed my cheeks, on those stupid dimples that he was kind of obsessed with. Almost as obsessed as I was with him. "Sweet boy." But when he pulled back again, his smirk faded into a serious face that I now knew all too well. The kind that came with words I needed to listen closely to. "Is there anything else you need to do today?"

I shook my head, eyes wide. "No, Sir."

"All right. First, you're going to wear these today." He reached in his pocket and pulled out a pair of blue, silk panties. When had he done that! "Then, we're going to straighten this room before you're going to do thirty minutes of homework while I make you breakfast. You'll go to your shift, then internship and do your best to focus on the things you have to do. Nothing else. There're a few services today, so I won't be able to pick you up this time. We'll meet back here, and I'll sit with you while you finish your home-work. We'll study until dinnertime and after if we have to."

The pout was back. None of that, besides the underwear, sounded fun. "But what if it takes me all night?"

He shrugged. "Then it takes all night. But I'll make sure you take breaks, and then it won't be hanging over your head anymore. Your weekend will be yours to enjoy."

"And what do I get if I do everything?" I blinked up at him.

"Brat." But he said it lightly and with affection. "You do every-thing I just told you to, and I'll show you what else I got for us besides the panties." Now we were talking. I grinned and nodded. "I'll put the list into a shared note on our phones in case you forget. You understand everything?"

I hugged him tighter. He never got frustrated when I needed him to repeat something, or when my head got so jumbled up that I had to ask him for clarification. Tyler always made sure that I understood, always helped me. And I hadn't missed all the 'we's' he dropped when giving me my tasks. After these weeks of dating, I knew that he meant every single one.

"I do, Sir." Heat flashed my face and body when I imagined saying those words in a different context. But I held *that* one to myself.

He kissed the top of my head. "Okay. Let's clean up in here." The bed was still unmade, the hamper in the walk-in closet full with his dirty clothes and mine that I'd shucked off last night and brought over from my house. My apartment with Alex, that I was staying at less and less, didn't have a washer/dryer, so Tyler let me use his whenever I needed.

He made the bed while I hefted the basket in my arms, padding out into the hallway on bare feet and with the panties slipping against the fabric of my jeans.

Tyler had once showed me where the laundry room was—well, gestured to it with a wave of his hand—but this was the first time I was going there on my own. His house was really big with more rooms and hallways that I was still getting used to the layout of. However, the smell of detergent helped me the rest of the way, and I slowly worked through the many buttons on the washing machine. It was way fancier than those in any laundromat or place I'd lived, but laundry duty was one of my many jobs at Howl's Fury.

Really, Sir was too sweet to have done all the laundry up until this point when I was more than capable.

Eventually, I got it started and did a happy wiggle when the machine gave a little trill and started filling with water.

On my way back, a room that he hadn't shown me before, the door the same dark wood as the others, caught my attention. He had a few guest rooms, the practice room for his band, closets, and the like, but this one held the faint smell of wood and paint. Curiosity getting the better of me, I tried the knob, only to find it locked.

A little niggle in the back of my mind wondered why he'd close it off when he'd been so open about everything else with me. But what right did I have to his house? To every single thing about him?

I shook off those thoughts and met Tyler in the kitchen, refocusing on the list he gave me for the day. It was the only thing I had to worry about.

He'd already set my things on the table in the area beside the kitchen, and I kissed him on the way before settling in for my thirty minutes of homework.

Even though it was about the last thing I wanted to do, I opened my notebook and smiled over at him as he concentrated very hard on cracking eggs into a bowl. When he tossed the shells and caught me staring, we shared a long look, me giving a grin while he returned it with a smirk that quirked his lip ring.

———

I guided my class through the short transition time before snacks. The first-graders I was assigned to this year were sweeter than pie, and they did such a good job lining up to wash their hands, lathering the soap with hungry giggles and excitement for the day.

Even with the clouds churning outside, their spirits were sunny, and it was pretty infectious! We all lined up again to go to the lunch room to get our snacks, which was my cue to switch off with Yasmine who'd been observing me during the first activities this morning. The imaginary world lesson had been a big hit, and my mind was already jumping and leaping with new ways to get them to integrate all we were learning.

Since I had a moment to myself while Yasmine took over the class, I used the restroom that was decorated in bright colors, and after washing my hands, took out my phone to see if I had any texts from Tyler. He sometimes sent me encouraging messages, and sure enough, there was one at the top of my screen.

Under that, though, was one from Charlie.

CHARLIE

You got another 200?

My heart automatically jumped into my throat, and I did my best to force an exhale by exaggerating the pucker of my lips. I inhaled through my nose, how Tyler had told me one night when a nightmare had frightened me awake.

In through my nose, out through my mouth.

It wasn't on the list for today, but Tyler and I also shared another note with overall reminders. And when I frantically opened it, right there for me to use as a lifeline was:

• If Charlie contacts you for more money, send him the text we drafted.

Another few taps of my phone, and I had it copied and pasted into my text thread with Charlie. I took myself through another round of breaths, and on the exhale, clicked 'send.'

And I felt relieved and accomplished for all of five seconds before my phone started vibrating with a call from him.

My fingers fumbled, and I dropped my phone, facedown on the bathroom floor. I grimaced, trying not to imagine what was invisible but lingering there, and it only deepened as I watched him hang up then start calling again.

As I wiped down my phone with one of the disinfectant wipes from the supply closet, praying he wouldn't make me block him, Charlie sent a long, long text that I quickly swiped away for later.

Tyler hadn't told me to respond to any of his texts, and I clung onto that missing instruction. I didn't have to, and with the way my mind was scrambling to get back in school mode, I was in no shape to read what he had to say.

That didn't stop his calling, though. And even when I put my phone in my backpack, it burned a hole in the back of my thoughts. What had he written in that message?

As I walked around the classroom, helping anyone struggling with the math lesson Yasmine was teaching, I snuck glances toward the cabinet where my bag was hung, probably shaking with the force of Charlie's responses.

And my curiosity, something Tyler had told me more than once that he admired about me, got the better of me while I was left to further straighten the room during pick-up time. The students spent the last few minutes of the day doing it themselves, but there was always some additional tidying I did or setting things up for the next day.

When I tucked my head into the cabinet so that I could sneak a peak of my phone, it was filled with texts and calls from Charlie. So many that my eyes were swimming as I scrolled through, and then he was calling *again*.

The panic that had been boiling in my stomach all day started to roll faster and faster, and I scampered out of the side door that led to the gardens to take the call. The clouds that hung in the sky all morning were now releasing a light sprinkling, and I tried my best to stay under the awning and not get too wet. Maybe I could reason with him, further explain the text and—

"What the fuck is the matter with you? You said you'd help me out!" I winced and swallowed at Charlie's biting words.

"I...I told you that I was on a tight—"

"Bullshit. You got all that handout money, a cushy job, and a fucking sugar daddy to boot. You've got the fucking money."

None of what he was saying was making any sense. Some of it might've been true, but the way he said it twisted reality. Reduced my relationship with Tyler to something that wasn't the tenderness and emotional support I knew that it was. "That's not tr—"

"What the fuck do you mean it's not true? You were always a stupid fuckup. You know all the shit with Howl's Fury could be traced back to *you*? Stressing your pa out to the point that he was fighting with Leader and his brothers. Eating all the food so that they had to take loans from them monsters! *You.* Just an ungrateful, worthless slut. All those years I helped your ass out, and *this* is what you fuckin' do?"

Blame it on the shaking of my fingers, but my thumb pressed firmly on the screen to end the call. And I stood outside, fighting back Charlie's words while I covered my sobs with the back of my wrist. The rain was falling in harder, fatter drops, and the joyfully labeled vegetables and herbs out back were bobbing along to the storm.

I didn't dare look at my phone, but remembering all I could

from the list made me feel a bit better. The next thing to do was go to Tyler's house, but when would he get home? Would I just be left to pace those big rooms and long hallways by myself? Alone with the cyclone of my thoughts? Another rough cry scraped the inside of my throat.

I needed him. Just his hands on me, and I'd have that extra boost to calm down. Maybe he'd be mad that I was kinda going against what he said, but this was one of those emergency situations, right? At this point, even if I had to stand in a corner, at least it would be in his office or in his bedroom.

I took a few more minutes outside, watching the rain come down harder as I stopped my crying as best I could. Yasmine would surely try to ask me what was wrong, and that would only reduce me to a weeping pile of nothing that only one person knew how to scoop up.

As I slunk back into the classroom, slightly damp just from the proximity to the rain, I made a beeline to my backpack and toward the door with one thing on my mind. Getting to my Sir.

CHAPTER TEN

DELANEY

I pulled up to the funeral home with uncertainty and the need for Tyler making it almost hard to breathe. Even the full parking lot only gave me pause before I pulled into one of the spots near the back and bolted out of my car.

Rain pelted down on me as I ran, and somehow that made it easier to not cry. It felt like a release anyway, even if it wasn't the one I truly needed.

Luckily for me, barely anyone was in the lobby to see me stumbling in like a wet dog, and that's what I felt like at this point. Charlie's nasty texts and the nightmare phone call weren't that much, but for some reason, it felt like they were.

A person was coming out of the restroom, their dark suit showing them as one of the guests of the service going on. I gave them a smile, because I knew what it was like to lose someone, and they returned it with a smaller version before heading back where the service was going on.

Another thing I hadn't considered when I showed up—where would I even go? What was I supposed to do now?

I stood for a long time, wet hair and clothes dripping onto the carpet, until I finally realized that I could just text Tyler, and he would tell me where to go. If he wasn't upset that I'd gone against the plan he told me to follow.

ME

I'm here at the funeral home. I'm sorry.

What if he was mad with me? At this point, it would be a relief to be punished.

Whistling made me perk up for a second before I caught the distinct scent of his nephew. Sure enough, Robin emerged from a different room, suit jacket off and sleeves pushed up. "Oh, hey, Delaney." He was so nice, and I could see that his happiness to see me took over first before the confusion set in. "Uh…what are you doing here? Are you…" He gestured to the funeral service room.

I shook my head. "No, I'm here to see your uncle. Is he here?" Another thing I forgot. Tyler said he had to go into work today, but I didn't even confirm that he was here. Was he leading the service? Oh no, I'd messed up again, hadn't I?

Robin's face scrunched in confusion, and I was ready to just turn around and leave. "Uh, he's in his office, but. Why?" Tyler kept things in his work and family life separate from his personal one, and I didn't want to disrespect his trust in me by spilling the beans.

"Ah, it's okay, I'll just—"

But it was too late for me to scrape together my pride and avoid Robin's questions. A door opened, and Tyler's sure stride was audible, even with the muffling of the carpet. I was rooted in place with indecision. I wanted his comfort so much, but I'd also disobeyed him. No, he never told me *not* to come here, but he'd been pretty explicit in what he told me to do after I was done with school.

Seeing his face, though, when he rounded the corner, made the tears that'd been collecting finally fall and join the raindrops on my face. His eyes shifted into concern as soon as they met mine, and then he was right there, not even hesitating.

The hitching sob got stuck in my chest, leaving only a pathetic snort, but his arms still went around me. I dropped my bag at our feet as he drew me in and wrapped me in a hug that was so strong, something to cling to.

I curled into him, rubbing my cheek against the sturdy slope of his shoulder while I let the tears flow into his pressed shirt.

"What's wrong, pet? What happened?" I loved that. How he was hard with everyone else, but with me, his deep voice was delicate, as were his hands that held me to him. My fingers clenched the back of his shirt, getting him all wet. I really hoped that he was mostly doing work in his office today. He never made me feel like a burden, but the fear of being one still remained.

I couldn't get the words out, couldn't do anything but cry because I was—"Petal. You did the right thing coming to me." The new endearment made it hard to breathe, and really, what happened today wasn't that big of a deal. I'd just wanted reassurance. To be in his presence. "Look at me." The command was gentle, but it was a command nonetheless. And I knew to follow those.

My nose was all stuffy, my eyes getting swollen already, but I'd no trouble crying in front of others. Especially not him.

"That's my good boy. You're safe. I'll take care of it, whatever it is." My bottom lip trembled, more tears trailed down my cheeks, and I could taste the salt as some of them made their way to my mouth.

His brown and silver eyes were like the moon over the trees on a clear night, and that beacon had been what I was searching for, right?

"Let's warm you up, love." Tyler's hand on the back of my neck pulled me down for a brief kiss that I couldn't help exhaling into. He would make it better. He would tell me what to do.

"Um…do you want me to get you some coffee from the kitchen?" I stilled in Tyler's arms, having completely forgotten about Robin. Did he not want his nephew to know about us? Oh no, what if I messed something up? Had he told me whether he was out to his family? Surely he was, if they knew that he was a vampire, but maybe not? What if I made things difficult for him and Robin?

Tyler answered his nephew while keeping his eyes on me, running his thumb against the side of my face. "Just some tea and honey, Robin. Thank you." The panic dissolved as he pulled me into another reassuring kiss.

I heard his nephew turn and leave, and Tyler took my hand to lead me down a series of hallways, the patron-friendly decorations falling away as we got closer to where Tyler and the rest of the staff worked.

Any other day, I would take in his office, drink up everything I could learn about him, but as soon as he closed the door, he was directing me out of my clothes and into the ones I'd packed in my overnight bag. I was too big for any of his, and at least the sweatpants and old t-shirt I folded up this morning were dry.

His touch wasn't sexual, but the brush of his fingertips was gentle. The tears had been falling silently while I changed, but as soon as he settled on a small sofa opposite his desk and pulled me into his lap, I clung to him and wept.

He undid the first few buttons on his shirt, and I greedily accepted that gift, nuzzling into his skin even more. My breaths felt easier, my heart fuller, and that's why it slipped out. Sometimes when I got like this, my words flew out faster than I was able to truly think them through.

"Daddy."

His calming caresses stopped, and then I caught up to what I just said. The embarrassing truth as to why he'd broken things off with me before. Once he was well and able to physically take charge again, the title had slipped out then, too. He'd paused, just like now, and the next day, he was telling me that it was over. After reflecting and wondering again and again, I'd been scared to admit to myself that it actually *was* my fault.

"I-I'm s-s-sorry, Sir—" I gasped to get my words out, but he shushed me and added a tug with the hand that was buried in my hair, forcing me to look at him.

His face wasn't blank, more perplexed, his brow bunched low and his lips pursed. But he didn't let me go—actually, it felt like he was holding me even tighter. His hair had gotten a little rustled with me rubbing up on him the way I had been, and it was more like how he looked when we were alone at his house. So handsome.

"Don't be sorry, petal. Okay? I want you to come to me when you need me, and that's what you did." I smushed my face in his neck again, inhaling his scent and rubbing my cheek to get as much of my skin on his as possible. His natural cologne was already making my muscles feel looser. Like clouds and rain.

After a while, and my sobbing calmed down to quiet little gasps every now and then, he kissed my temple and said, "Tell me what happened."

I tightened my hands in his shirt. It was so embarrassing. "I did what you said. Texted Charlie that I wouldn't be giving him money anymore."

"That's good, pet. You did well."

I gave a sad smile into his neck. "Thank you, Daddy. But he sent me a long message back and tried to call. I was scared to look. And then…"

"Then?" He gave another rub on my back, encouraging me to continue.

I'd snuck in the title again, and he hadn't said anything. Knowing Tyler up until this point, I figured that he didn't say anything about it because he knew that I was having a bad day. He was so good to me.

I sighed. "And then, I snuck out to answer 'cause he kept calling. And, and he said that I was ungrateful for all he did for me. That I was the reason everyone from our pack left or died. That I was a worthless slut." I whispered the last part, voice dying with embarrassment.

That got him stopping again, and this was why I was scared to tell him. For him to see me in this light that I'd been so determined to shake.

"Did he say anything else to you, pet?" Tyler's voice was lower, almost like the growly way he sang in the band.

I shrunk even further into his hold, hoping that he wouldn't throw me out now. "No. I hung up," I whispered.

Two big, fat tears slipped out of my lids and down my cheeks, and he took a deep breath. I heard it against my ears like the roar inside of a big seashell. "Listen to me, Delaney." My stomach dropped. He barely used my name, and that made me scared. "You did nothing wrong. You were living through a horrible situation. And you survived. You persisted and pulled yourself back up. He was just mad that his life hasn't turned out like yours. And I'll take care of it. Of you. Okay?"

I somehow sank even closer, but he still wasn't pushing me away. "I just want it to be over now. And I feel so much better with you. It's okay."

"No, petal. It's not okay. No one will talk to you like that, especially not at one of the places you love. I'll handle it."

My heart thump-thumped hard in my chest. He made me so happy. I knew that my friends and the pack would defend me if I was ever in trouble, but that didn't even compare to how protected Tyler made me feel. How he didn't hesitate to give me the affection or praise that I needed.

I was humming and whimpering into his chest, just enjoying being here, somewhere safe and warm, when there was a knock at the door. My scenting wasn't the best, but it was sharp enough for me to recognize Robin again.

I started to pull away and sit next to Tyler instead of in his lap, but I didn't get far. I may have been taller, but he was strong, and he didn't let me go, keeping me firmly against him.

"Come in," he said loud enough to be heard through the door, and I just closed my eyes, let him feel my smile against his skin.

The clink of ceramic against wood reached my ears, as did the shuffling of fabric as Robin took a seat in front of us. The warm and herbal smell of the tea Tyler asked for reached my nostrils, but his arms were telling me to stay put. So I did.

"Uh, do you need anything else?"

Tyler slipped his fingers just under the hem of my t-shirt, and the extra skin contact made me start humming quietly again.

"No."

"Ah, okay. Well, did you still want to meet now or…"

"Will you be okay while we do some work, pet?" Now I was grinning. I shifted so that I could look at him, so he could see how much his claiming of me in front of his family was making me happy. More than happy. All the hard stuff from today was forgotten.

"Yes, I promise. I can do my homework while you have your meeting. I'll be good."

He kissed me—kissed me!—and even gave me a little smirk. "I know you will be. Now," he reached for the mug on the coffee table in front of us and handed it to me, "don't forget to drink your tea."

"I won't!" Even though I scrambled off of his lap and sank to the floor, I was careful not to spill anything. With a cautious sip, I certainly felt warmer, but it was really earthy, and if I was being honest, not my favorite. But Tyler must've noticed that too, because while Robin was spreading out papers on the table between us, he plucked the mug from my hands and added a long drizzle from the bottle of honey his nephew brought. He made sure to stir it up really well while they started talking about business and scheduling stuff, so that when he handed it back to me, it tasted way better.

"Thank you." I grinned up at him again, but I made sure to whisper it quietly so that I didn't interrupt their meeting any more than I already was. He paused what he was saying to give me a little smile and weave his fingers in my hair.

I was buzzing. Safe and comforted to the point that I flew through the assignments I had to do, the weekly reflection from my internship that I had to type up. Those usually took me a long time to finish for some reason, but I just pecked away at my old laptop while Tyler continued to scratch and pet my head. The touch of his hand never left, even as he and Robin went back and forth about some important stuff that just flew right over my head. Who knew that dying involved all of that?

They were still going once I finished my work, so I just set my laptop down on the floor beside me and leaned into Tyler's legs, resting my cheek on the top of his thigh. I could take a nap right there, listening to the rumble of his words like a lullaby.

"So…" The tone of Robin's voice changed, and my eyes cracked open to see him looking between the two of us. "How long has this been going on?"

The panicked search for the right thing to say didn't even have a chance to start before Tyler cut in to answer for us. "Two months." He was even counting the time we were broken up, if you could call it that. Even then, he thought of me as his. I'd be lying if I said I hadn't felt the same.

"Oh. All right. I just—I didn't know you were gay?"

Just an hour ago, I'd be getting worried at where this conversation was heading, but Tyler stayed calm. I trusted that he would handle things, just like he promised. And Robin didn't seem angry, necessarily. Just curious.

"I am. Though I find it hard to believe William or your grandparents didn't mention it. That's the main reason I moved away after high school." I pressed my cheek further into his thigh, and he answered it with a good scratch behind my ear.

Robin nodded and sat further back into his chair. "They alluded to it a few times, but no one would confirm." A few beats of silence filled the room, and I watched Robin get almost shy. "I'm gay, too."

I clutched Tyler's leg and smiled encouragingly at Robin. Ma had been really supportive when I'd told her that I *like*-liked boys back before she passed away and things got really bad. There was a lot that I regretted or felt bad about, but being queer was never on that list.

"All right. Thanks for telling us." Tyler was less enthusiastic than I was, but that was just his personality. I could see how his words made Robin relax even more.

"Bummer he got to you first." Robin glanced at me with a smirk, which made me blanch.

Before I could fully digest whether he was just playing or not, I was pulled further against Tyler as he leaned forward. "You may be my nephew, but understand that Delaney's mine. Don't even joke about that."

I twisted my body so that I could look up at him, eyes wide with the even clearer declaration still floating in the air. "Don't worry, Daddy. I don't want anyone besides you."

It just slipped out again, evidence that my mind was feeling soupy and content. It was just the way he was taking care of me got my mind all mixed up. I'd gotten a taste of the Daddy/boy dynamic before, but it'd just been playing. A short scene here and there. With Tyler, if I were being honest, I wanted this all the time.

And he still didn't get upset. He even visibly relaxed, no longer poised to leap across the coffee table at his nephew.

Tyler swiped his thumb over my lip and quirked his eyebrow at me. I had the feeling that we'd be talking about this later, to the point that I was about to get worried, but his words calmed me yet again. "You better not."

I shifted, hiding my blush in his lap while keeping my hold tight on his leg. He never let anyone else touch him like this, but he seemed to like it with me. Enough to not push me away in front of Robin. Maybe it made him feel more comfortable, too? I could only dream.

Robin's laugh had a nervous edge, like it was a little too loud. "No problem. Wouldn't want you to uh, yeah. Anyway, point taken."

Tyler huffed, and I felt the gust of air on the back of my neck. I shivered with the memories of the past few evenings we spent together. Once he was done here, we'd get to do that again, and now that the thoughts cropped up, I had a hard time ignoring them. No matter how much I was trying to be good.

"Relax. I'm not going to eat you. Why does everyone think I'm going to eat them?"

A surprised chuckle, halfway to a giggle, erupted from my chest. Everyone thought that cause he was nearly hissing at people more often than not. But now, I was in on the secret that he could be quite the sweetheart. Plus, in my experience, him feeding from me was far from unpleasant.

"D—does he *know*?"

Tyler sighed again. "Real subtle, Robin."

If I'd been paying attention, I would've been able to track what they were saying without saying it, but I was remembering the last time Tyler drank from me while I rode him in his hot tub. It was one of my favorite memories, the bite of pain before his long swallows added to the ecstasy of him inside of me. The heat from the water, the fizziness of the bubbles. How connected to him I felt with his tongue lapping at my blood while he held me close.

I squirmed in my seat, trying to hide what this reminiscing was doing to me. "What do you mean?"

Robin looked terrified for a moment, and my arousal gave way to even more confusion—it really was the theme of the day— before Tyler clarified for me. "That I'm a vampire, love—"

"Shh, I'm sorry! I didn't mean to—ha ha, that's a good joke, you're so funny, Samchon."

Tyler pinched the bridge of his nose, but I was catching on now. I sat up straighter to reassure Robin. "Oh, I already knew that. And I'm…" I paused to glance over my shoulder, and Tyler nodded for me to keep going. "I'm a non-shifter Wolf. Like, my pa was a wolf shifter, and my mom was like me. I can't shift at all, which I used to cry about sometimes, but my mama would say that everything happens just the way it's supposed to. But I got some of the perks from it, and my pa used to say our Wolf blood is why we tend to be so big. Because we were born to be strong Wolves, which I'm not really certain is the reason because Daddy's stronger than me, I'm pretty sure. But I can run pretty fast when I try, and I really like…"

I trailed off, realizing too late that I was rambling when they probably weren't interested in my family stuff. My cheeks warmed at the shocked expression on Robin's face now that I was paying more attention to it.

"Sorry." I tried to laugh it off, but my fingers fidgeted in my lap.

A scrape of Tyler's short fingernails at the base of my neck sent heat down my spine, and then he pressed a kiss to the top of my head. "Nothing to be sorry for. Thank you for telling us that."

For some reason, more tears sprung just behind my lashes, and I used the heel of my hand to wipe them away. How quickly I went from vomiting up words to not being able to find any. I just leaned into my boyfriend and let his assurance wash over me.

"Um. I just—n-not that I don't believe you but—"

"Be grateful that he told you anything at all. We don't take divulging this lightly, particularly those of shifter descent. There's a reason I keep this part of my life separate from everything else now that I've moved back. Don't make me regret opening the both of us up to you."

"Jesus, I'm not—" Robin dragged his hand over his face. "It's just a lot to take in okay? Not being the only queer one in the family, this dynamic you guys have going on, and the fact that w-werewolves exist, ya know? I didn't mean any offense, I swear."

Oh no, my stomach turned, I didn't mean to start something. "It's okay, Tyler. I don't want—"

His hand tightened on my neck, and my back went ramrod straight with his stern whisper in my ear. "That's 'Daddy' or 'Sir'. And no one will make you feel badly for being yourself. Not even Robin. You understand that?"

My eyes lowered while my heart went a million miles an hour.

So many moments today would stay fixed in my memories, something wonderful for me to run over and over. "I do, Daddy." If he was going to give me a choice, I would pick the one that felt the best deep down inside. To me, a Daddy meant a greater level of tenderness, and whether he knew he was doing it, *that* was what Tyler—Daddy—gave me.

"Good. Get your stuff together so that we can go home. I'm going to walk Robin out so that I can ensure we've come to an understanding about all of this. I'll be back in a few minutes." With one last kiss to my head, he stood, and his nephew followed. It was silly, but even being that much apart from him tugged at me, square in my heart. I could still hear and scent them, but nothing would compare to having him close, soothing me with touch.

I chuckled to myself as I was gathering my things and wet clothes, which only took a minute or so. While I waited, now that I was feeling more settled, I took in the gray walls and leather sofa that I sat on. The large desk topped with a double computer screen and a bunch of files Daddy had probably been going through when I arrived. There was a window behind it, but with the rain still hammering down outside, it did nothing to brighten the office space. He didn't even have anything on the walls in here!

My mind started going, mentally taking note of how I would arrange and decorate the space if I had a say. Daddy obviously liked things to be dark, his house was evidence enough of that, but maybe—

"All right, are you ready to go?" He walked in, shoulders a little tense but not radiating a full rage. I rose to my feet as he tidied his desk, putting files in drawers, and shut down his computer.

He plucked his suit jacket off the back of his desk chair and started back towards me.

"Yeah, I'm ready. Is everything okay with Robin? I really don't want to mess things up between y'all."

His face noticeably softened, his mouth became less pinched. He reached up to cup the side of my cheek as he turned the light off in the office. "You're not messing anything up. We're both just not used to knowing this much about each other. It'll be fine."

"Okay, Daddy."

CHAPTER ELEVEN

DELANEY

I hustled around the classroom, straightening up desks and putting art supplies back where they belonged. As the student teacher, I got the less-fun jobs, but leading the first-graders through an art activity designed to help them identify the different emotions and recognize them within themselves had been a hoot and a half. The paint that splattered their fingers was easily washed away in the sink, something they knew how to do on their own fine enough, and I had a great deal splattered on my apron and hands as well.

Yasmine, the teacher I was assigned to, wasn't far from my age, and it'd been nice working with and learning from her. She didn't mind my frazzledness, especially with everything I had to juggle. But that had gotten easier, too, now that Tyler was in my life.

I finished setting everything back to rights, started a load of laundry with all the aprons and tablecloths we'd used, and fished out my phone.

Tyler's list for me was always simple, not too overwhelming, but it was the shot of clarity I needed when I started feeling lost or indecisive.

• Go to morning class and make sure to take notes.

• Remember to eat the lunch packed for you. Even the salad.

• Send me a photo of you wearing the new panties we picked out.

• Go to internship. Try your best.

• Come to the funeral home and do your homework in my office. We'll work at the same time.

The door of my old car creaked, and then the whole body groaned once I settled inside with a smile on my face. Just as I was pulling out, I saw Leader buckling his children into their car seats, and I made sure to give them all a wave. Leader returned it with a tight nod, but I was in such a good mood, I didn't even overthink it.

It also helped that I'd been around the pack and his family enough to learn that his flat affect and short responses weren't a sign that he was mad at me, but because his brain worked differently. It was still hard sometimes to train my body and emotions to not react strongly, like I had during the first pack meeting I attended, but I was making progress.

I now felt the safest, physically and emotionally, that I'd ever been.

Tyler blocking Charlie on my phone probably had a lot to do with that too.

Pulling up beside the sleek, black Challenger, I hopped out of my car and skipped inside. Or—I slowed myself down—maybe it was inappropriate to skip into a funeral home.

Ms. Beverly was sitting at the front desk, knitting while she was talking on the phone, and I started reaching in my backpack as she wrapped up her conversation and hung up.

"Well, hey there, sweetheart! What'd you bring me today?" She was eyeing the box in my hand more than my face, but that was okay. As soon as I found out that she had a wicked sweet tooth, I'd tried to bring her a treat every time I came by.

She was already opening it, but I explained anyway. "Lauren was testing out a new coffee cake recipe, so let me know what you think of this, and I'll tell her."

"Oh, I'm sure it'll be delicious. That woman knows how to bake." Ms. Beverly took the plastic fork in the box and started with a gigantic bite that rivaled her slight frame. She smiled in delight and continued eating as Tyler came into the lobby, looking sexier than anyone had any right to be.

His black suit jacket was buttoned, holding close the secrets that only I was privy to. His earrings glinted in the light of the lobby, as did his lip ring that twitched with his smirk at me. "Hey."

My face heated, and I ducked my head like I hadn't woken up in his bed this morning. "Hey, yourself."

Ms. Beverly waved around her fork while covering her mouth with her palm. "Now, don't you two get all flirty just yet. Mercy called, and they have a decedent ready for us."

I watched Tyler clench his eyes shut and shake his head. "Fine. I'll go. Tell Robin to get ready for when I get back."

"Ready for what?" I asked. Usually when I was here, Tyler was just doing work on his computer or meeting with Ms. Beverly, Robin, or one of the other employees that worked here.

He sighed. Loudly. "I have to go pick up a body from the hospital. You can go into my office, and hopefully I won't be long."

I felt a little twist of disappointment but then immediately got an idea. "Can I ride with you?"

Tyler blinked and furrowed his brow. "But there'll be a dead body in the car with us."

"I think he knows that, dear. Now, you two scoot." Ms. Beverly shooed us with a wave of her spindly hands.

But I wasn't moving just yet. Tyler looked me up and down, biting at his lip. If it wasn't allowed, I'd understand, but I was really hoping he'd say yes. So that I could learn even more about him.

Last week, Tyler had held my hand at the skate park while he taught me to slowly ride his skateboard along the fence. He didn't get frustrated with me at all, whispering sweet words and making sure I didn't fall while Río and Ramona raced by.

Last night, he shared with me some lyrics he was working on for the band, along with the music arrangements he was envisioning.

And all the while, I'd look over at my boyfriend, the way he eased into his hobbies and lowered the tension in his shoulders. Not all the way unless we were alone, but it had been amazing getting to know him, and him me.

Like during my most recent closing shift at the coffee shop— he was my final customer and helped me close up while I gushed to him about my day. Then he snuck me into the supply closet and bent me over a shelf, thrusting between my cheeks and coming on my back before whipping me around and dropping to his knees for *me*.

Then this past weekend, when we had another marathon of my favorite show—complete with my enthusiastic commentary and him adding his own predictions for the rest of the series. And the next morning, I caught him humming the secret tunnel song while he cooked my breakfast.

"All right, petal. Come on." He turned and walked down the hall, and I only hesitated a moment, catching up that he was agreeing to let me see this part, too. He grabbed a set of keys from his office, and it was no time at all until we were on the road to the hospital.

At first, heavy rock music filled the space, but after fiddling with the knobs and touch screen of the minivan, Tyler turned it to an upbeat playlist. I hummed along to the song I recognized and swayed in my seat up front. The back of the van was empty, save for a stretcher thing that would soon hold the person that'd recently died.

Though there was some traffic, we made it to Mercy Hospital in about twenty minutes. With a kiss on my cheek, Tyler told me to wait in the car, despite my offer to help, and he rolled the stretcher inside.

Again, I pulled up our shared note on my phone, and seeing the things I'd already checked off, I smiled and rubbed at my chest. When I was around Tyler, it pulled, like a thread that connected me to him and beat to the rhythm of my heart. When I closed my eyes as I settled into his side for the night, I imagined it as a golden, sparkly thing.

Once, while I soaked in his bathtub that was practically my favorite place in the whole house, I tried to describe it to him. He'd been sitting beside the tub, feeding me strawberries like after our second first time. Something like a deeper understanding swept over his features, in the purse of his lips and the sideways glance of his eyes, but his words were more simple. Saying that he could picture it.

As I sat and waited, now, I checked my appearance in the mirror, confirming that I didn't have a stray spinach leaf in my teeth from lunch or something. I hadn't had to put concealer under my eyes in a long while, and even though I'd had a full day, I felt pretty well-rested!

Probably because snoring into Tyler's chest gave me the best sleep of my life. My bed at the apartment was sorely neglected, and my side of Tyler's had my scent all over it, even when he washed the sheets.

The metal clang of a door opening caught my attention, and I watched Tyler push the bagged body toward the van and juggle a cooler bag on his shoulder. Finding the button he'd pressed earlier, I opened the trunk door for him and scampered outside. "Do you need help, Daddy?"

He smiled tightly at me but shook his head. "No, thank you, pet. I have to be the one to handle the body." While that made sense, I still pouted. What good was I just sitting in the van like a bump on a log?

Seeing the expression on my face, he handed me the bag while he pushed the body inside the van. The legs of the gurney folded up, and he secured the body in the back. I wondered what the person looked like, if they were satisfied with the answers of life that they had now received. Whether there was something to experience or just black.

I'd grown up fearing hell while living it every day. And though I never said it, there was small chance that, if there was a heaven, any person in Howl's Fury was making it to the pearly gates, including myself.

Tyler reached up, pressed the button to lower the trunk door, and walked me back to the passenger seat. His hand rested on my lower back, giving my heart little flutters and bringing a smile to my face.

I sat on the leather seat, but before he could close the door, I twisted for a kiss.

Until I saw the frown on his lips. "What's the matter?" I asked and settled the cooler bag down between my legs.

Tyler glanced toward the back of the van, then at my feet. Half of me expected him to just say that it was nothing, but as serious as he was about me being honest, he took it to heart as well. Even when it made him uncomfortable.

"Death can be uncomfortable for a lot of people. I don't like you seeing this side of things." Now, if he was telling me the whole truth of his emotions, I didn't know. Sometimes I wondered.

I didn't say it, but his worry was a bit silly since I was more than happy to be dating a vampire. Didn't he know that? "Daddy, death doesn't bother me. It can be sad, sure, but we'll all go some-time." I shrugged. Was I supposed to have more thoughts about it than that? I'd known and been witness to many gruesome ends, and though it wasn't his favorite thing, I was glad there were people like my boyfriend and his nephew to help people's lives end with dignity.

Instead of kicking bodies into shallow holes in the ground like Charlie and I had done to our pack members before we parted ways. It was all the respect for them that we could muster.

Tyler thumbed the dimple in my chin that I'd always been insecure about. Under his touch, though, I was starting to think of it as desirable. He'd also told me that if I called it a 'butt chin' again, he'd give me corner time for at least *an hour*.

"Are you sure, petal?"

I darted forward and snuck a kiss on the inside of his wrist. "A hundred percent, Daddy."

His smirk in return wasn't as light as it normally was, so maybe he didn't totally believe me, but he didn't press. We drove back to the funeral home, me chatting about the activity I led at the Montessori school. At a stop light, he brushed the skin above my eyebrow, saying there was a little splatter of pink paint.

Quiet and a little embarrassed, I admitted that the color reminded me of the night he decorated the room in pink flower petals for me. That it was the one I chose for happiness.

My embarrassment was totally worth it, though, as I watched a blush bloom across his cheeks.

When we pulled up at the home, Robin was already waiting at the back, leaned against the wall and scrolling through his phone. Tyler cut the car off, and the two of them jumped into action, bringing the dead person inside the back while I followed behind.

Cooler bag slung on my shoulder, I took in a medical-looking room that had a whole bunch of tools and chemicals neatly laid out. But before I could ask to stay and watch, Tyler was pulling me toward his office.

Robin looked in his element, white lab coat zipped up and bandana over his hair. "Good to see you, Delaney!" He called as we left, and I said the same back.

Tyler still seemed a little off, not as free with me as he usually was, but we still took up our usual routine when we made it back to his office. I plopped down on the sofa, pulling out all my school work, and after placing a kiss on the top of my head, he sat behind his desk.

By helping me study most nights, we found that I worked best when he was also doing other things, whether that be for his job or the band. Or looking up cooking videos and taking notes in his phone when he thought I wasn't looking.

Luckily, I didn't have so much to do today, and with the motivation his presence gave me, I flew through writing the reference section for a research paper for my childhood development course, as well as the start of my weekly reflection for my internship. Papers were always the worst, barely keeping my attention for more than fifteen minutes at a time, but Tyler typing away and giving me a stern look whenever I tried to pull out my phone kept me on task.

I signaled the end of my work with a snap of my laptop shutting and tapping the little checkbox on the note Tyler made at the beginning of the day.

His phone buzzed on his desk, but he didn't look at it. Instead, he glanced up and chuckled when he saw my grinning state.

"Come here, boy."

I scrambled over my feet and kneeled on the floor behind his desk. It was becoming my designated spot when his work went longer than mine. He even had a little pillow down there, now, and I settled on my knees where it was most comfortable and rested my head in his lap.

Tyler threaded his fingers through my hair, and I closed my eyes, letting the scent of calm rain wash over my mind. My cock perked up, but it was easy to ignore for this other sort of pleasure. "You did such a good job today. I'm proud of you, my good boy." Tyler's thumb traced the outer curve of my ear, and I hummed with his praise. The words and touch lit me up on the inside, while also calming me into a state that was like a cozy Sunday morning. With hot tea and giggles under warm blankets and movie marathons with not a care in the world.

Now, I got to have days like that *and* the reassurance from my boyfriend. I was so, so lucky to have him.

Time went by, minutes or hours, I wasn't sure. It was almost hypnotic, the state I reached while on my knees for Tyler. Sleep didn't fully close in, but the current of sweet goodness, happy memories with him, and echoes of his praise was better than any dream.

A knock on the door inched me a little closer into the here and now, but it didn't fully pierce the bubble. Nor did I stir when Robin let Tyler know that he was leaving for the day.

It was Tyler cupping my cheek, gently kneading my freckled skin that got my eyes to flutter open. "It's time to go, petal. I just need to lock up, and then we can head home."

Tyler continued to pet my face and neck, coaxing me back down to earth, and my humming started up again. Soon, I was able to get my body to work, to shift and move until I slowly stood with the help of Tyler pulling me to my feet.

He kept his hand in mine while he shut down everything in his office, and I rubbed at my heavy eyes as he turned off lights in the hallway and in all the open rooms we passed. Finally, as we made it to the front, he made a *tsk* noise and started toward the illuminated service room.

Evidently, someone left on the light up at the front of the large space, giving it a low, yellow glow. Pews of a pretty, dark wood bordered a central walkway and contrasted with the pearly color of the walls. The main doors were bordered by large peace lilies in pretty golden pots. "Wow. It's so pretty in here," I breathed. These doors were always closed, or the room was occupied by an ongoing service, every time I stopped by.

Tyler grunted, as if he didn't agree or disagree with me, but he did stop and glance around, probably trying to see it with new eyes. The carpet muffled my steps as I walked us down the central aisle, and when we made it to the front, I sat on the cushioned seat of the front row.

It made me think of Ma's funeral. The memories of it were ripply, like trying to see underneath the surface of a river. And filled with a pain that made my throat threaten to close.

The old church that held her service hadn't been nearly as nice as this place. The sermons had felt hollow, but maybe that was because, at thirteen, I doubted that anything positive would be waiting for me with my father.

Looking around the service room here, though, I could imagine that she would have received the service she deserved. And that she would be happy for me, wherever she was.

Tyler's palm rested on my thigh, squeezing slightly. "Delaney?"

Now, my eyes had grown watery, too, and I realized then that I'd been starting to cry when, really, I was far from sad. "Hm?"

"Are you all right?"

That. The concern in his tone that I knew would be followed by him bending doubly backwards to make me feel better. That was really what filled my heart with such emotion.

I'd made it here. To be with him.

"Yeah." I grinned. "Just thinking about how grateful I am to be with you." His pale face was still scrunched in concern, the corners of his lips turned down. But his suit jacket was now open, and the top buttons of his shirt were undone. He often did that to get comfortable while he settled in at his desk, but now, the milky column of his throat and top of his chest was doing something to me. "And how sexy you are."

That got a rise out of him. He chuckled and brought his arm to rest behind me on the pew. "Is that so, sweet boy?"

I dropped my head onto his shoulder, nuzzling into his neck. Even though his presence always wrapped me in a cocoon of safety and content, we'd barely touched this afternoon. Now, taking what he so readily offered fanned the low burn under my skin.

Tyler pulled me even closer and inhaled deeply into my hair. "Tell me more about what you're thinking," he commanded, now holding the back of my head to keep me still.

The pressure of his grip stirred hotter emotions up and down my spine. Lust. Excitement. Beginnings of frustration. More lust.

So, I let it spill. Let the safety of my boyfriend lead my words. "That I'm lucky to have you. That you always look so good in a suit and sometimes when I'm supposed to be doing my school-work, I look over at you and wanna lick you up and down."

Tyler laughed again, syrupy and smokey. The woven threads holding me together were unraveling under his touch, one by one. "Naughty boy." He trailed the pad of his pointer finger down the line between my pecs, threatening to sear my shirt right off. It was one of my favorites, with green and white stripes, but it could go. I wouldn't miss it at all.

His lips tickled the border of my hairline, which was an odd sensation that jolted down into my lap. The crotch of my jeans tightened, but Tyler somehow always knew what I needed. "Take your dick out."

My hands were clumsy, acting like I hadn't worn these pants a hundred times. But when I finally got the zipper down, the need was even worse. The panties had been a secret reminder all day that my vampire was always with me, that whatever he was doing, he was thinking about me too. And now, the sight of purple silk and pink bows was almost too much.

When I pulled out my hard cock, squeezing the base to stop myself from getting too excited too fast, I released a shaky, pathetic breath. My mouth moved over the line of his collarbone, not quite a kiss, not quite forming words. More like the gasping of a fish, but that wasn't my fault!

"Stroke it, petal." Tyler's voice was steel, hard and steady.

My fist moved slowly, and even the dry friction was enough to make me cry out. My precum slicked some of the way, but it was more than I needed. Just one pump, and I squeezed the base again. I didn't have the permission to come.

"Again," he said, and I obeyed, even if I was closer and closer to all my threads dropping into a heap for him to put back together again.

"D-Daddy, don't make me come yet," I begged before he could tell me to do it again.

He was circling one of my nipples with a featherlight touch, and I had no warning before he traded that for a sharp pinch.

Pops of electricity exploded on the edges of my vision, my back arched like the drawing of a bowstring. I groaned into his neck, and by sheer force of will, kept my orgasm at bay.

"You don't tell me what to do, petal." Tyler reminded me with a low growl and kiss. "Lay over my lap."

It took a second, for my heart and breathing to calm enough to process what he said, and while I did, he was already maneuvering my body to his liking. There were few people I'd met that were stronger than me, and the fact that this male who was already so perfect for me was able to move my large body without any assistance wasn't helping my predicament at all.

My cock was trapped between my hips and Tyler's lap, and like this, I couldn't see him. Just my hands curled into fists and the charcoal-colored cushion of the pew seat.

Tyler shoved down my slacks even more, exposing my silk-covered bottom to the air of the funeral service room and for his scrutiny. "You'll say 'red' if this becomes too much," he directed while softly rubbing over the panties and the skin of my cheeks.

The world was already melting away from his commands earlier and in anticipation of this, but the first slap threw gasoline on the fire he'd started when he first walked into the lobby this afternoon.

He did it again, making impact on a slightly different area while I tried to squirm away from and closer to the pain. "This ass is mine, boy. And so pretty all red like this." Tyler continued, spanking and praising while a wet spot formed on the cushion beneath my face. Sweat, tears, drool—it was all for him and the gifts he gave me time and time again.

"You know, there are cameras in here. What do you think about someone seeing you like this, petal? Sobbing over my knee with your pretty panties on." I raised my hips, fingernails digging into the pew. Tyler laughed darkly and gave me the few more that I was now loudly begging for.

How he managed to pull off my pants and flip me around to

straddle his lap, I had trouble tracking, but the sensation of his suit pants on my burning cheeks made me jump.

Tyler ripped through the purple silk and tossed it onto the floor, leaving me naked from the waist down. He massaged my skin, rubbing in the burn.

I struggled to stay upright, slumping over him and using the wood of the pew and hard slopes of his shoulders for support. Tyler kissed me slow and hard while I tried my best to drag my cock against his stomach. Even though I was pretty much gone at this point, the physical demand for release was still a coiled spring that was way past being wound tight.

"Fuck me, please," I drawled. There was no way he'd do this and just stop, right? Right?

Tyler nipped at my neck and tightened his control of my hips until I couldn't move them at all. His fingernails made landmarks of sweet pain, and I whined over him. Frustration was a nasty, orange and red emotion that was tinting my tears. I cycled through hating and loving it.

"As much as you like a little bit of hurt, I'm not fucking you dry, petal. And we don't have lube here."

The 'I'm not fucking you' part of the sentence snapped my mind to attention, and I was able to gasp the solution I was so relieved I could supply. "Inmybag. S'new." I pressed my chest to his, settling for that bit of stimulation.

When dropping by my apartment for another change of clothes, the unused bottle had caught my eye, and I'd shrugged, judging that we could never had too much with the rate we went through it.

One of Tyler's hands left, allowing a biting absence that was quickly replaced with the sound of rustling in my backpack, the snick of a lid, and then two of his fingers in my hole. Just like that.

It was an awkward angle for him to prep me, but I was past impatient, and he must've been too, because he undid his pants lightning fast while giving me a third finger just in case. My shouts of, "Pleasefuckmewreckmyassownme," probably didn't help. The stretch just spurred me on, chest tight and loose to the point of cracking and spilling open.

And he was cruel. So, so cruel when he slowly slid me down over his thick cock, slicked over with lube. Try as I did to bounce into the clouds, Tyler kept our pace slow, of sensual purples and deep reds.

His hair was soft between my fingertips, and the silver of his earrings was cool against my skin. "You are so perfect, petal. This ass," he let me drop until our naked hips met, "your beautiful spirit, your laugh, *everything.*"

As the one who typically couldn't *stop* talking, I was at a loss in the face of Tyler's sweet words and the bubble of pleasure ready to burst. It grew agonizingly slowly, but it was strong, the press of Tyler's cock on my prostate making me jolt and moan each time.

So, all I could do was bring our brows together, fight my heavy lids to watch him see how good I felt with him.

And he smiled. Big and true as we shared breaths.

"You can come, petal. Show me how pretty you are when you do." He lifted me, squeezing where he may very well have left heavy prints of his hands, and I felt every inch, knowing that this was the one to take me. My left hand fisted my cock while my eyes rolled all the way back in my head, my whole body lighting up with neon pink and yellow, ecstasy and relief.

My pleasure spilled onto his shirt, but by his praising words, that was what he wanted. "*Look at you.* Fuck, how did I get so lucky?" Tyler's hold on me got unsteady, but now, I was fully content to ride the wave of his last few thrusts as he mumbled frantically in Korean before coming inside of me.

"Mmmm." I held him through his orgasm, kissing up and down his neck. "Thank you, Daddy," I whispered.

And Tyler took my face, forcing our gazes to collide while we panted and came back down. I wanted to lick his fangs, but I also couldn't move too much without feeling like my body would spill through his lap, right down to the floor. "Thank *you,* sweet boy."

His thumbs rested in my dimples, and that golden feeling in my chest grew a little bit more. Now, it rested between the two of us, always there and bright. "I don't think I'll be able to walk outta here."

Tyler huffed with a smirk. "Oh, I intend to take care of you from here until we're in the bed at home. And we'll watch more episodes while I feed you dinner and some ice cream."

I brought my cheek to his, rubbing our faces together. "Okay, but you gotta carry me." Sue me for wanting to take advantage of it every opportunity I could.

And just like that, Tyler swept me up into his arms to take me home.

CHAPTER TWELVE

TYLER

The phantom punch of a bullet ached in my chest, right where the actual one had grazed my heart, as I made my way up the gravel drive. The heavy canopy of trees bracketed my way before breaking to reveal the home of the Wolf Pack Leader.

Just like my body, my car was fixed after that shifter shot my headlight out before almost killing me.

Good times.

Now, though, the sun cut through the area with a golden glow like Delaney's hair, and the dark memories cleared as quickly as they'd descended. Because when I thought I was meeting my second death, my boy who'd only known me for two days held me close and begged me to drink.

I was still biding my time, slowly dropping hints to warm Delaney to the idea of me buying him a car, but for now, I told him that I'd pick him up from his day of gardening and spending time with his friends.

Mostly, I interacted with humans or other vampires like myself, but since moving to Antler Pointe, I was collecting shifter acquaintances like in those video games Delaney liked to play when he would wait for me to get work done.

Now, he spent most nights at my house, and when he didn't, he regularly carried a change of clothes with him to class, always requesting we go to mine after I picked him up from school or his internship.

And if I had work to do and he was finished with his homework, he'd taken to sitting quietly or pulling out his old video games and giving a little cheer every time he trapped a new one in the little ball at the end of a fight.

I walked around the side of the cabin, just as Delaney had instructed me to, and the sound of enthusiastic conversation grew louder. His voice was one of the loudest, laughing and so bright. After asking Río for some guidance, I had the newest console waiting for Delaney when we got back to my house.

"Bruh, you're like a sugar daddy. You're making me look bad."

Over the years, I'd purchased numerous commercial properties and made other investments that more than supported my lifestyle. And with decades of saving and no need for human food, my expenses were more than manageable.

Taxes were a bitch, though.

"Excuse me, who bought their mate a house *as a surprise gift?"* He'd teased me like he didn't spoil his own Wolf mate as well.

My feet stuttered, but I collected myself before I tripped over a tree root.

Would Delaney want to be my mate? "Fuck." The thought had been swimming around in the back of my mind for these weeks we'd been back together, but *that* topic hadn't been broached by either of us.

Though it could be undone for both Wolves and vampires, for my kind, that sort of commitment—on both sides—was more than terrifying.

Before I could start panicking about the notion that had my heart racing, the witch's garden came fully into view. Ever since the other one burnt down, she and the Wolves had made it their mission to build this one up. The pulse of magic was so strong that I tasted cherries and blackberries on my tongue.

But I must've been on some invisible list as an acceptable visitor. Just as I felt the resistance, I was able to cross a barrier and enter the jungle of flowers, vegetables, and fruits.

Little trails cut through the sections that probably had some organizational purpose, but I knew next to nothing about plants and their care. The colors were making my head hurt, but I could also admire the feat it was to keep this many living things growing and thriving.

Unfortunately, as I followed Delaney's voice, the assault of perfumes itched my nostrils to the point that an explosion coursed up my throat and sinuses, and I hunched over as it wracked my body.

"Did you just sneeze?" Río's mate called over, and I cracked open my wet eyes to glare over at her. It was the first time she'd said anything substantial to me in months, and of course, her comment had everyone turning to stare.

Just as I straightened to retort, another two crashed through my nose, and I had to snuffle back *mucous* that threatened to spill down my face.

My eyes were screwed shut, now, too busy trying to get a rein on myself to pay attention to the laughs and downright giggles at my pitiful state. So, I didn't see Delaney coming until he pulled me into his chest.

"Are you okay?" His cheek landed on the top of my head, and I sneezed a few more times into his shirt. He smelled like dirt, but in a good way, and beneath that was the clearing orange and lemon and goodness of his scent. I did my best to focus on that to get my bearings.

"Did you have allergies before you were turned?" A musical voice called over, and I tilted my head from being totally hidden in Delaney's chest.

I circled my arm around his waist while he wrapped his around my neck and continued to nuzzle into my hair. The witch had a messy topknot that was barely containing her tight, black curls, and despite the chill earlier today, she was wearing a bikini top and cutoff shorts.

"Yes." I sniffed and then frowned at having to do it at all. "Why?"

She tapped a long, blood-red fingernail on her lip in thought. "We enhance everything to make sure it can withstand the harsher weather and any other attacks. Maybe the magic allows it to transcend your supernatural immune system." She turned to another witch that had a deep blue buzzcut, and they began to discuss spells back and forth while glancing at me.

Then, a small Wolf with brown skin and braided red hair ran up to us. "Uncle Delaney, is this your boyfriend?" she practically yelled her question. Seemed like we would be the center of attention for a little while longer.

Delaney pulled me a little tighter. "Yes! Isn't he the most handsome male you've ever *seen*? Daddy, this is Dahlia, and over there with Ramona is baby Ollie. You know Sylvie, and that's Josie!"

Heat flooded my face at Delaney's compliment and the eyes of the Wolves and witches on me. The two witches smiled and welcomed me to the garden, but the Pack Leader's sister and I were already acquainted.

"Are you blushing?" Ramona raised a challenging brow while holding the witch's son in her arms.

"Bradley at school is handsomer, I think," the pup answered Delaney's rhetorical question with a determined set to her lips. "Uncle Delaney said you have fangs. Can I see?"

I glanced at the girl's mother who just shrugged. This child wasn't too annoying, and I was already used to dealing with curious souls, what with the boy hanging onto me.

My fangs dropped, and I opened my mouth for her to see. What a weird interaction this was.

Her brow furrowed in all serious observation. Just then, I noticed a large spider that crawled up the back of her overalls and settled on her shoulder. She paid it no mind. "Why do you only have two? Daddy, Uncle Río, and Titi Juno have four." She raised three fingers at first, but caught herself and showed the right number.

Who the hell was Juno? I was assuming that was another shifter. "Because I'm a vampire, and we're different than shifters."

She thought about that for a minute, eyes on my teeth, before nodding. "I think four is better than two. I'm sorry you don't have more." And she scampered off with her pet spider in tow.

I turned to Delaney. "Should I be offended?"

"No, Daddy. I wouldn't want you any other way." He bent to kiss me sweetly, though it was a little too chaste for what I truly wanted in that moment. And once again, the new honorific didn't strike fear or discomfort.

If anything, it felt right.

When we pulled away, he made a point to kiss the tips of my fangs. He whispered in my ear, "I love the way they feel when you drink from me."

We probably still had an audience, but I didn't give a shit. Lust roared within me, the thought of tasting my boy again tonight. It'd been a while since I fed from him, preferring to reserve it for more special moments and not treat him like food.

And if I did it too much, we'd form a bond that neither of us had expressed wanting.

But, I realized, I *wanted*.

That was insane, right? Thirty-eight years of immortality, not a single person had sparked my interest to settle. They were all passing flings, food sources, or scene partners.

Could a Wolf boy that I'd known for three months truly be my mate? Would he want to sign on for an immortal life tethered to me?

Just then, a few clouds parted and revealed a brighter cut of the sun through the trees. It shone on Delaney, his honey hair and skin alight and almost sparkling. Too bright. Too bright for me.

I caressed the sculpted line of his jaw. Maybe he could be mine just a little while longer.

"Is that so, boy?" His cheeks flamed, and my cock stirred in my pants. I pulled him down for another kiss, this time giving him a little slip of my tongue against his lip. "I think you've been good enough for a reward."

His eyes went wide, and I heard his heart thump in his chest. "I have? Like what?" Images of him in the room I hadn't showed him yet sent a smirk pulling at my lips. Delaney swallowed, and I had to catch myself from cupping his cock and using it to lead him to my car. "You'll see. Are you ready to go?"

Delaney nodded again, and we bid his friends goodbye. Ramona still gave me a harsh side-eye while Delaney gave her and the others hugs, but she kept her comments to herself. Whether that was for the sake of keeping the peace in the presence of children or for her best friend's benefit, I had no idea.

The witch garden forced a few more sneezes out of me as we made our way back to the front of the house, but that wasn't going to pull down my good mood now that me and my boy were on our way home.

Hm.

We pulled away from the dark green cabin and made our way onto the main road. Luckily, we weren't but ten minutes away from my house. I squeezed my hand that rested on Delaney's thigh and took advantage of the beat between his recounting of all he'd done today. "Tomorrow morning, we'll go to your apartment and gather some things that you can keep at my house. So you don't have to pack a bag all of the time. What do you think about that?"

He froze, and again, his heart rate picked up. Delaney squeezed my hand hard. "Are you..." He twisted in his seat to fully face me. "Are you asking me to move in with you?"

Was I? Making room for some of his things and presenting it as a convenience-driven directive seemed like the easiest way to get him to agree. But the thought of not just having him sleep every night in my bed, but *living* in my house, sent a thrill up my spine. A fearful thought screamed that this could only end poorly, but it was easier to ignore. Living together wasn't taking him as a mate. This was fine.

"Is that what you want?"

Out of the corner of my eye, I watched Delaney worry at his lip as he most certainly weighed the pros and cons in his mind. Decisions remained a constant challenge for him, but I let him work through the question. There was a time for me to make the decisions for him, but I wanted this one to be confirmed by him first.

"Is that what *you* want?" he finally asked as we neared the turnoff for my driveway.

The desperation in his voice made me smile. Something about his uncertainty made me feel firmer in choices I would've questioned otherwise. I hadn't gone into today intending to ask him to live with me, but what the hell? He basically did anyway. "I'll admit, I hadn't meant that when I mentioned us getting some of your things tomorrow." He deflated and tried to pull his hand away. I used my strength and kept it. "*But,* I do. Want you to move in with me. But I also need to know that it's something you'd enjoy as well."

He was uncharacteristically silent as my driveway came into view. Until, a quiet whisper. "Okay. Yes."

The grin on my face felt foreign and familiar at the same time —something I hadn't done much ever in my life, but it came easily with Delaney by my side. I brought the back of his hand to my lips and kissed his knuckles. "I'll hire movers to get your things. You won't lift a finger."

"Um." He cleared his throat. "Do you think I could have time to tell Alex? I don't wanna leave him hanging with rent."

Alex. He was my drummer's best friend, and of course, he'd been wasting his time with a crush on me that I tried my best to ignore. Another reason we spent little to no time at their apartment. Delaney could feel the awkwardness too, and I couldn't have that impeding our time together.

But I could understand his concerns. I kissed his hand again.

"All right, petal. I'll give you a week to talk to him. After that, you're mine, one way or another. I'll pay your rent until he finds someone to take over your room if I have to."

My house came to view, and Delaney leaned over the console to rest his head on my shoulder. He nuzzled and inhaled against my neck. "Okay. Thank you, Daddy…Um—" Before he could finish his thought, I let loose a string of curses as my house and a familiar car came into view.

And my brother who was sitting on my front steps. He was supposed to be a the sober living home we'd sent him to.

"Who's that?"

I sighed and continued us around the house and into the garage, all while my brother watched my car with tired eyes. At least he didn't appear high.

"My brother, William. Robin's father."

I cut the car off and unbuckled both of our seat belts. Delaney's backpack was in the backseat, and I snagged it before rounding the car and opening the door for him. "Go inside, shower, and get comfortable. I'm going to talk to him." I reached in my back pocket and gave him my phone. "Use it to order yourself something to eat as well."

"Okay, but is there anything I can do to help?" He trailed after me into the house, but I stopped us in the hallway that split to lead to the bedrooms in one direction and toward the front door in the other.

"No, sweet boy, but thank you. I have to go see what he needs. Just do what I said, maybe see what I have waiting for you in the living room if I end up talking to him for a while."

Delaney clutched his bag to his chest, eyeing where I was headed before nodding. He leaned down expectantly, and I granted him the requested kiss.

We parted ways, my boy to wash the day of gardening off of him while I resigned myself to step in to help William *again*. I cared about him, even after all these years and the things we'd been through. After all he'd put Robin through.

But god, I was tired of this, and I knew that he was too.

My little brother was still there when I pushed open my front door and stepped out into the late afternoon. The breeze had picked up since leaving the Pack Leader's land, and some of the trees that overlooked my property were already changing shades with fall approaching.

Sitting on the porch in the cool autumn sunsets would be so nice with my boy.

I took comfort in the fact that he was inside, moving through the list of tasks that I'd given him, and sat beside William. For a few years, I could see my bygone future in his features as he'd aged. My family cut me off, finding out about my vampirism and declaring me an abomination, along with my 'lifestyle' that they'd already denounced when I was human.

And William had for a while, though he always came to me for money. Raging at me when I refused. The drugs and hard living were etched in the wrinkles on his face. He looked fifteen years older than he should, his cheeks still recovering from their hollowed state while he'd been actively using.

Robin was basically the twin of William at that age, but instead of glazed-over or incensed, the kid was full of excitement and weariness at the responsibility imposed on him, by my parents and himself.

"Who's the boy toy?" My brother raised a cigarette to his lips, and I saw the discarded butts of three more that were lying next to him.

I ignored his attempt at getting a rise out of me. "Why are you here, Will?"

"I talked to Appa and Eomma. They seem happy." Now that I was here, they were finally able to retire. Truly. "They said they forgive me."

I grunted. Retirement must've softened them somewhat. But maybe I'd be more willing to forgive when I was living my final years on a beautiful island, away from a business I'd toiled away at most of my life. Thrusting that responsibility on the children they'd neglected for this 'legacy'. "And? Isn't that a good thing?"

"Yeah. But then I called Robin, and he told me to go fuck myself." William's hair was a salt and pepper now, and he ran his cigarette-free hand through it. His flannel and jeans hung loosely on him, but I could tell he'd put on some weight since last I'd seen him.

He reached in his pack, offering me a cigarette, and I accepted. After he lit it, I raised it to my lips and inhaled. Hopefully my boy didn't mind the smell of it on my breath.

"Well, he's been through this before."

"It's gonna stick this time, Ty. I know it."

Also something I'd heard before. Tendrils of smoke wound around us as the sun continued its descent and painted my yard in long shadows. "How are you so sure? You were all the other times too."

He scrubbed a hand over his scruffy face. "I'm too old for this shit. Missed out on Rob's childhood. Lost my place at the funeral home. Fucked up my whole life, but I'm *trying*."

I ground my jaw, hearing my brother's voice thick with tears. It was hard not to blame him when he'd put us all through a roller coaster time and time again. And I'd had enough space to process and recognize the resentment I felt. Eomma always welcomed him back in, even if it came with a booming lecture from Appa.

I'd only been called when they had no other choice, too old to keep running this and the other funeral homes scattered across the region. The others had full-time directors to run the daily operations, but the Antler Pointe location had a special place in Appa's heart, and he'd remained director until our mother finally convinced him that it was time to retire. In their eighties, she argued, they barely had enough time to enjoy their work-free years.

They'd have had more if William and I had chosen different lives. Maybe it was that guilt that brought me back. And my nephew.

"I know you're trying. You still clean?" My scenting confirmed it, but I wanted to hear it from him.

"Yeah. Ninety-seven days."

I nodded and took another drag from the cigarette. We smoked for a while, looking out on the manicured lawn, until a tentative knock had us both turning toward the door. Delaney slipped through, hair wet and pulled back with a pink headband. He wore a pair of sweatpants and a hoodie. "Um, I was gonna order the food but didn't want to order for just me?"

His eyes begged, worried he'd crossed some boundary, but I wasn't upset. While I wasn't too keen on my brother possibly picking at Delaney, I wasn't ashamed of my boy, neither was I of my brother.

"You're fine. Come here, petal." I patted next to me, and Delaney walked over with head bowed and silent steps. His feet were swallowed by a pair of flying bison slippers I'd found online for him, and the childish footwear made him look all the sweeter.

Delaney curled into my side, clutching my shirt with one hand and tapping away on my phone with the other.

"Will, this is Delaney. Delaney, my brother, William."

"Robin's dad." My boy smiled over at my brother. "Nice to meet you."

"Don't know how much of a father I've been, but yeah. Nice to meet you." William's brown eyes swept over Delaney and me, but I didn't fidget.

"Are you going to stay for dinner? I was gonna get pizza, if that's okay?" I finished my cigarette and stubbed it out on the stretch of porch between William and I. And made a mental note to get the smudges pressure washed out later.

"Not sure if I'm invited. I really just came to see if you'd talk to Robin for me," he directed his words my way before looking at my boy with a quirk of his brow. "So, what's your deal?"

"Deal?" Delaney's faced scrunched in confusion, and I rolled my eyes. How naive of me to hope William would behave.

"Don't mind him, pet. Order your food and enough for leftovers. *If* Will stays, he can have a few slices." I turned back to my brother. "Watch what you say. I won't hesitate to kick your ass out if you disrespect him."

William chuckled, and Delaney tapped away, sneaking uncertain glances at my brother. I rubbed up and down my boy's back for both our sakes.

"Just curious. Never met one of your boy toys before."

Before I could react, a low, canine growl erupted into the air, and we both jolted. Delaney was glaring at William. "I'm his *boyfriend*. And I'll be *living* here." More to himself, he grumbled, "Robin is way nicer than you." I barely kept my jaw from dropping, and I shifted in my seat. Yes, I believed that I rather liked this possessive side of him. "Can I go, Daddy? The food will be here soon, and I need to set the table."

I looked Delaney up and down, visualizing again what I planned to do with him tonight. "Yes." But I pulled his face to mine for a hard kiss first. In his ear, I spoke low enough so that William couldn't hear. "And prep yourself while you're at it." No telling how much patience I'd have later.

He kissed my cheek, and I took a deep draw of his scent. "I already did." And with that, he gave one last withering look at William before standing. Even still, he mumbled that it was nice to meet him and that he'd set a place for him just in case.

I watched my boy retreat into the house—*our* house—and the way his tight ass shifted in the soft pants he wore.

"He one of you?"

William's gruff question was a bucket of ice water that splashed against my tracking of Delaney's advance into the house. We were separated by doors, walls, and many feet of space at this point, but the hold he had on me was as strong as ever. And now that I knew he was liable to get *possessive*?

First, I had to deal with my brother. "What?"

"Your boyfriend." The way he spat the word, like it was nothing but a passing infatuation had the edges of my vision flashing red. "He one of your kind?"

I squinted a glare at him. Smoking was an activity we often bonded over, but these moments emphasized the chasm between us now. The one that'd been there nearly forty years and some beforehand as well.

"No. But he knows what I am, obviously." I began to stand and gather the discarded cigarette butts to properly dispose of them. "I'm not calling Robin for you. Or talking to him about your recovery unprovoked. You said it yourself that your struggles have taken a toll on his entire life. You need to let him come around in his own time."

William extinguished his cigarette and handed me his trash. His last smoke-filled exhale was weak and lowered to the ground. "Am I still invited to dinner? Don't have much, and it's a long drive back to the home."

He looked up with uncertainty coloring his watery eyes. The crow's feet and gray hair were another sign of the distance between us. When had my little brother gotten so *old*?

I swallowed the stone that formed in my throat, but it only settled in the pit of my stomach instead. With a huffing sigh, I turned back toward the house. "Fine. But if you step foot in this house, know that you'll be kicked out if you upset my boy again. This is his space too."

"Yeah, yeah," he ground out and followed me inside. "I got it."

CHAPTER THIRTEEN

DELANEY

As soon as Tyler and I agreed to me moving in, some switch in my brain flipped, and a raw part of myself saw this space as *mine*. Even more so than my apartment that had been my home for the past few months.

The dark floorboards, white candles, furniture, and vampire that lived here were *mine* to care for and protect in my own way.

With that, anyone that entered was my responsibility to host. Keeping a space tidy and pleasant for visiting guests wasn't foreign to me—one of my main tasks as the ward of the Pack Leader of Howl's Fury was to keep his and the elders' homes in tip-top shape.

Leader Orion said that this wasn't necessary every time I offered in return for his mate allowing me access to the garden and teaching me, so maybe I had some pent up energy.

Either way, as soon as I retreated into the house, I began to race back and forth in a flurry of movements. There was no time to thoroughly clean, but I tidied all of my things that I'd left here and there in Tyler's house.

Plant clippings that I had propagating on the kitchen counter, a new botanical Lego set that I'd been working on in the living room that had taken over the floor and coffee table. My textbooks and laptop that were sprawled all over the dining area.

I clutched my things in my arms, having to double back into a room because something else caught my eye then forgetting where I'd been going in the first place. It all took way longer than it should've, and my jaw began grinding with frustration at myself and the words Tyler's brother had used. How he'd looked at me.

Boy toys. Plural.

There was no one else—right? No way could I fault Tyler for meeting and sleeping with others during his long life—lord knew that I wasn't a saint. But I wasn't kidding when I told him the other day that I was so into him that I'd drink his bathwater.

He'd laughed a raspy, hissing sound that was unhindered, playfulness filling his expression with the wrinkle of his nose. While I tried to explain it, we both descended into a fit of laughter at how funny the saying was.

Maybe I wouldn't drink *all* of his bathwater, but I wouldn't mind a few gulps.

I stuffed my school things into my backpack and ran it back to the bedroom—our bedroom. This was my house. Well, it was Tyler's house, and I was going to be living with him. And I couldn't even fully get excited about it yet.

Instead, I bolted around the dining area, kitchen, and living room—because that's where William would most likely be during his visit—and turned some calm music on using the fancy speaker system. I lit a few candles and turned on the lamps that made the space seem the coziest.

Tyler was really intentional about remembering things like food, and thank goodness we'd made a grocery pickup order the day before. The pitcher of iced tea I made came in handy as I pulled it out and set it on the counter.

He'd bought a set of dinnerware and pots and pans when I'd mentioned enjoying cooking, too. Now, the blender, food processor, and espresso maker were a little overboard, but he wouldn't hear of it when I'd told him to just return all that stuff. Spam and eggs in a ten-dollar pan from Walmart was just as fine as crepes and a fancy latte.

I was setting out the flatware—what if William was the type to cut up his pizza instead?—when Tyler and his brother came back inside.

"Bet none of his *boy toys* could make him smile like I can," I muttered to myself and immediately felt rotten. I would bet they'd been nice guys, getting drawn into Tyler like I had.

"What we have is new for me, and I don't take it lightly. We will be honest with each other because it's important to build trust. And if you are mine, you are mine.*"* Another snapshot moment that I played and rewound in my mind again and again. But now that the insecurity was there, it was hard to ignore without his reassurance.

They both settled in the living room, like I predicted they would, and I followed the sound of their voices, trying my best to erase the ugly green that was tinting my thoughts. Or was it red? I wasn't really accustomed to being *angry*, but angry I was.

Tyler and William were standing, and I waited with my hands at my front while the former talked a little bit about designing the house. William added that he'd always been fond of the sunken living room feature in the house they'd grown up in.

Tyler had already turned toward me when I entered the room, like he couldn't help doing so, but after a moment, his full attention turned to me as well. "Come here, pet."

My body slotted perfectly into his side, but William's scrutinizing up and down made me squint pointedly at my slippers before clearing my throat. "I made some sweet tea if you'd like a glass? I know that's not the norm up here, so I wanted to check first." Tyler snuck his hand underneath my hoodie and traced circles along my lower back.

I stood up a little straighter, and William met my gaze. "Um, sure. That sounds nice."

I nodded and turned to Tyler. "Can I start your supper for you too?" He'd shown me how to work the warmer thing, and his contacts at the local hospital allowed him to save some bags of blood for when he couldn't go out to feed. Come to think of it, he hadn't gone out to hunt since we'd been together, pretty sure. He'd mentioned that it was an option once or twice, but as far as I knew, he spent his time at work, with the band, or with me.

I hoped that he wasn't just eating the refrigerated stuff on my account. Seemed a little like eating a frozen meal, to me, but what did I know? He didn't need to eat every day, he told me, but multiple times a week or else his body would weaken. Couldn't have that!

"Sure. Thank you." He smiled at me, just a little quirk of the corner of his mouth, but I drank it up all the same.

Unwrapping from him was hard to do, but I needed to be welcoming, so I got to work on refreshments for everyone by starting up the warmer on the kitchen counter by the stove and pouring the iced teas. By the time I made it back to the living room, they were seated on the sofas, and William was talking more about the sober home he was staying at.

And I felt even more terrible for being irritated with him earlier. Tyler told me that his brother had been in a bad way, and though he didn't look awful, the years on his face spoke of some hard living. I sure as sugar knew what that could be like.

"Here you go." I handed William his drink first, then presented Tyler with the mug of some blood that'd been labeled as B positive. I'd have to ask him if that type had a particular taste or if that didn't matter as much.

"Where's yours, petal?" Tyler accepted his supper but raised a brow in question.

I blushed for some reason. "I didn't wanna drop anything, but I'll be—"

"No. Sit here, and I'll go get it for you." He patted the cushion beside him, and I couldn't argue.

In all fairness, I could move quickly, but vampires were faster, and he was back with my iced tea before my butt settled in the seat. William jumped and almost spilled his drink when Tyler appeared with mine.

"Thank you, Daddy." I smiled up at him, which earned me a kiss on the forehead before he plopped down next to me and opposite his brother.

I'd been testing out calling him that, after he'd given the okay in front of Robin a few weeks ago. There was always a little flutter in my heart when he let it slide, especially to chase away the clench of anxiety in my stomach that he'd tell me it wasn't okay.

And now, in front of his brother that seemed on the fence about us for whatever reason, Tyler just took his seat beside me and extended his arm around the back of the couch cushion. I leaned into his embrace.

"This is so weird," William muttered to himself. Weird? What was odd about us sitting together? Was the tea bad?

"Which part?" Tyler rolled his eyes and took a sip from his mug. "You being in my house for the first time, you meeting my boyfriend, or me drinking blood?"

William's eyes stuck on the mug in Tyler's hands. His throat struggled to swallow, and he set his glass on the coffee table instead of taking another drink. Must've put too much sugar in the tea. These northern tastes were so confusing.

"A-all of it, I guess."

Tyler shrugged and took another long pull from his mug. "If it's too much, you can leave." His brow raised in challenge at his brother.

He hadn't divulged a ton of detail about how he felt about William, more just about what he was doing to help out his parents and coordinating his brother's care, but I noticed the bites of sour. I pictured my boyfriend, looking exactly as he did now but with clothes from decades past, wanting so badly to be himself that he had to leave people behind to do it.

How his brother's illness hurt his family time and time again, and they always welcomed him back. But they treated Tyler's choices as if they were unforgivable. Only tolerable when he gave them things. He was always giving and giving.

I loved him so much.

Now I was the one coughing, sputtering on my iced tea that was the *perfect sweetness*, might I add. Tyler put his mug on the table and used his free hand to rub soothingly at my chest. "Are you okay?"

Those hard brown and silver eyes were always so open and gooey with me. How could I not feel lucky that he was mine? That I was his?

I tried my best to communicate that with my own eyes, but they were currently tearing up as I tried to get a handle on myself, so the concern on his face remained. "I—I'm fine. Sorry." No, just freaking out that I was in love with him. Probably had been for a while.

Tyler took the glass from me and put it by his mug. The kiss he gave me on my cheek, the tender press of his fingers on my neck as he caressed me. It was all that I'd ever dreamed of.

Letting my mind drift away, I let Daddy and his brother pick back up talking while I slithered onto the floor. I needed my worries to calm, and since we weren't alone, sitting at Tyler's feet, with my face in his lap, was the quickest way I could get it.

Even William's appalled look didn't bother me. My Daddy had his hands in my hair, his fingernails scraping along my scalp. Warmth trickled down my spine, over my shoulders, and spilled down my entire body. Of course, being intimate with him, either with sex or full-on cuddles, was the best. But there was something about this position that did it for me too. I closed my eyes, feeling the rumble of Daddy's words that were a low, steady pitch.

When the doorbell rang, I didn't even flinch, just reacted with a flutter of my lashes. I propped my chin on his thigh to gaze up at him.

As a little boy, I dreamed of one day finding my mate. Of wearing his teethmarks on my neck proudly, having someone to snuggle and talk to and be with forever. Would Tyler let me kneel for him the rest of my life? How would being mates differ since he was a vampire? Did they do that sort of thing?

Dagnabbit, there were my worries tiptoeing back in again. "I'll get it," I volunteered, and the darkening of Daddy's eyes, what with my face being in his lap, made heat sweep my own.

I bit my lip, wanting him to know that I felt it too, and if his smack on my behind as I stood and went to the door was partly to goad his brother, it didn't bother me none. Let William be mad.

Did that make me a bad host?

I shrugged and opened the front door, accepting the pizza and breadsticks from Vinny's Pizza with a grin. My stomach gave a hearty grumble, and I was grateful I ordered that fourth pizza at the last second. With all the gardening today, I hadn't eaten since breakfast!

Tyler and his brother drifted over to the dining table while I was setting everything out, and the three of us sat in a squirming silence as William and I loaded our plates. Well, he went with two slices, and I piled mine with five.

Despite having more than a healthy appetite, I took steady bites and made sure to wipe away any grease or sauce that collected on my lips. The pepperoni crackled between my teeth, the cheese pulled with salty goodness as I gobbled it down.

Once my plate was empty, I came up for air, grabbed the last slice from the first box, and started reaching for the second when I caught Tyler's stare. William's too. He still had one slice on his plate and the other only halfway gone.

Maybe I wasn't being as demure as I'd hoped.

I pulled my hands back to my lap, the hot sensation on my face surely resulting in a deep red.

Tyler stood from his seat and rounded the corner of the table that separated us. He reached across me to take my empty glass, and on the way, he whispered in my ear, "I love watching you enjoy things. Don't ever be embarrassed."

Well, that just made me blush more, and I stared after him as he went to the kitchen and poured me another glass of tea. I was supposed to be doing that! But wow, he made my insides flutter something fierce.

Ma would've loved him.

I fought back my tears and thanked him for my drink when he came back. This time, I didn't hesitate to fill my plate again.

After more silence filled with William's and my chewing, it was broken by William clearing his throat and directing his gaze at me. "Um. So, how did you and my brother meet?"

I patted my face with my napkin while the biggest smile pulled at my lips. Now I was the one with a romantic story, and I realized that I hadn't felt the loneliness that I'd been so accustomed to since that night. Because of Tyler.

Lord have mercy, I was so in love with him.

Tyler blinked a few times, looking surprised for a second before his own light blush colored his skin, and he smirked my way. Goodness.

I tilted my head a little, silently asking if he wanted to tell the story, but he just shook his head, encouraging me to continue.

And continue I did, starting from arriving at the bar by myself, seeing my best friend and swooning over her own love story, then thinking that Tyler had been hitting on her instead.

At that, he chuckled beside me. "As if I saw anyone but you. I fucked up multiple times during the set because I couldn't keep my eyes off the most beautiful male I'd ever seen."

Wait— "Really?" He'd never told me that!

"Yes, really. As soon as our last song ended, I jumped off the stage and made a beeline to you. How did you think I got to your table so fast?"

I was for real about to blurt that I loved him. Right then and there and maybe take Tyler's hand, apologize to his brother, and drag him into the bedroom. Would I then be punished for not asking permission first?

It'd be worth it.

Before I could, though, the doorbell rang again, and it broke the moment. "Did you order more food?" Tyler asked, but not like he was mad, only curious.

I shook my head and stood. "No, but I'll go see who it is so you can keep visiting with your brother." *See*, I reasoned with myself, *I* am *a good host*. I was *not* going to cut their visit short so that I could jump Tyler's bones. Not at all.

But maybe I made sure to swish my hips a little to keep my boyfriend's eyes on me a little longer. Another responsibility of a good host, actually.

Wait until he saw what I was hiding underneath my pajamas this time.

Opening the door and seeing Robin had my thoughts scrambling, though. His hair was a mess, and this was the first time I saw him in a casual t-shirt and jeans instead of a suit for work. His eyes were red, and I could smell the salt of shed tears. "Is my uncle here? I need to talk to him."

Uh oh.

I chewed at my lip, not sure how to play this. "Um. Yeah, but we're—"

"Great. Sorry, but I didn't know who else to talk to, and I won't stay for long, and—" Robin pushed past me instead, and I remembered that he couldn't sense that it wasn't just Tyler and I in the house. Hadn't William said his conversation with his son hadn't gone well?

Oh no. I caught up with Robin, trying to interrupt his angry murmuring and warn him that his dad was here, but he wasn't listening. When we reached the archway of the dining area, he skidded to a stop and boomed, "What the fuck is *he* doing here?"

My hands on my cheeks, I silently apologized to Tyler with wide eyes, and William stood with a similar expression. Tyler just sighed and ran a hand down his face, but he got to his feet as well.

"I just..." William looked uncertain and heartbroken, while Robin seemed betrayed. What a mess.

"You're taking his side? Accepting his bullshit excuses? What the fuck, Uncle Tyler!"

"I'll—I was just going." William's eyes got shimmery, looking at his son whose words were filled with pain.

Tyler stepped closer and kept his voice steady. "Robin. You need to calm down—"

Oh, Daddy, no. I winced right before Robin started shouting again. About how William abandoned him and his mom for drugs. How Tyler was choosing sides by having William here. It was hard on my ears, but more so on my heart because I knew how much Tyler loved his nephew, even if he hadn't said those words specifically. His was an active sort of love, one that he gave to his brother and friends, too.

Robin's words hurt, I could tell by the twist of Tyler's features, the thunder of his yell as they argued, and when William joined in, trying to explain himself, it reached a deafening pitch for my sensitive ears.

My skin was too warm, the pressure in the air making me sweat. "Hey. Hey—*hey!*" I hollered, trying to force some sense into the three of them that were going back and forth, arms waving and insults flying. If there was one thing I hated, it was fighting, and if this was my home, I wouldn't tolerate it.

They all looked like dragons, faces red and breathing hard, but at least my outburst startled them enough. I sniffed and swept the cuff of my hoodie across my eyes. "Th-this ain't gonna happen here, okay?" My accent and improper grammar pushed through worse than usual, but I didn't bother thinking through my words. "I can't take it. Y'all are *family*. It's okay to be mad, but this's too much."

"Petal, it's—" Tyler took a step toward me, and as much as I wanted his comfort, it wouldn't solve anything because Robin's burning glare at him and William said he was ready to go again.

"Naw, Daddy, it-it's fine. Just need y'all to stop fighting, all right? Matter of fact, Robin, come with me." I grabbed his wrist and for once, used my strength to pull him along toward the patio. He dug in his heels, shouting at me and everyone else, but I kept us moving easily. Over my shoulder, I called, "Y'all figure some of this mess out while I talk to him."

CHAPTER FOURTEEN

DELANEY

"What the fuck, man! You're on their side too? The fuck is with everyone just letting that junkie waltz back into—"

The moon was out now, the dying rays of the sun keeping the sky from being a total black, but it was only a matter of time. The pool still wasn't covered yet, so the blue lights cast us in a watery, wavy glow.

Thankfully, Robin kept moving with me—or else I would've had to pick him up—as I brought us to the pool lounges. I shoved him a little meanly onto one of the wooden seats and took the one opposite. He collapsed like the weight of the universe was on his back, and from what he said earlier, it was at least partway true.

"I'm—*we're* not on any side."

"Sure as shit seems like it." Robin ground his jaw, ran his fingers through his hair before roughly wiping at his eyes that were even redder, now. "That douchebag tried to call me, bragging about his newest attempt at getting sober like I haven't heard this shit all my life, man." His chin wobbled, despite how hard he was trying to calm it, but his ragged, sob-filled sigh was what made me cross the distance.

I sat next to Robin and put my arm around his shoulder as he curled over his lap. And we sat, him crying loudly and me silently, while I watched the night fully take over. We might've been the same age, but in that moment, I so clearly saw the little boy that just wanted his dad to get better. That kind of sadness wasn't one I'd experienced, but I used to have more sad days than happy.

And oftentimes, words did nothing and were more for the person speaking them.

When Ma died, leaving me to the pack to care for but only to be given a glorified closet to live in and told to serve the leaders in every way. When I'd return to my lumpy mattress on the floor, the whispers of their hands on me and the filth they spewed still ringing in my ears.

How often had I just wanted someone to hold me instead of Charlie's disgruntled rants in camaraderie?

Now, I could give that to Robin, let him feel the warmth of someone that was willing to witness this kind of emotion.

He was still hunched over, but his heart and breaths were slowing back down. The gust of rage come and gone. "I can't forgive him. I *can't*," he whispered into the chilling air.

Had I forgiven my uncles and father and all those that took part in those dark days? Immediately, a little voice in my head whispered with a convicted, *No*. Had I ever truly admitted to anyone, or myself, that when their own greed resulted in partnering with much smarter monsters and getting burned to ash in the process, I'd been relieved? That only the memory of Ma kept me from spitting on their graves?

"You don't have to. No matter what he says, what he does, that's *your* decision."

Robin looked toward the house, where I could hear remnants of Tyler's conversation with his brother. "So, why's he here? So that he can beg his case to Samchon like he did with everyone else?"

I sighed, the memories of the past and trying to work through what was happening in the present causing a jumble of old fear, frustration, betrayal, and more that I couldn't even name. But this wasn't about me. "I don't know all the ins and outs, but William and your uncle have their own relationship. Their own stuff to get through. I know for a fact that Tyler wouldn't try to upset you on purpose. A few minutes ago, I heard him refuse to be the go-between or try to convince you of anything. He *loves* you. He says that he came back for his parents, but I think he moved back for *you*, Robin. He knew that the funeral home would be too much to put on your shoulders."

He gave a watery chuckle and wiped at his face with the back of his arm. "I know that he hated having to come back here. That I mess up, and it annoys him."

I pinched the point of his shoulder and unwound my arm from around his back. "I think Daddy being annoyed is his default with most people, but it's not the whole truth."

Robin shook his head, ran some fingers through his artsy hair-cut. Without the suit, he really looked like some of the art students I saw on campus. Not someone that strove to work with the dead and grieving all day.

"That is so weird, dude. You calling him that. He looks our age!"

All right, he was definitely feeling better. I scoffed with a fraction of the irritation I felt when William said something similar. "But he's not. And even if he was, he'd still be 'Daddy' to me. Don't knock it till you try it."

He pursed his lips and shook his head hard. Further away, I heard the sound of a car stutter and struggle to start before the engine finally caught. "No. Nope, if what I've seen is evidence enough, I do *not* want to know." But he was laughing a little too, and it brought a smile to my own face. Irritated was definitely my boyfriend's base emotion with everyone else, but it wasn't

Robin's. He started standing first, and I followed, towering over him to the point that his chin tipped up to keep talking to me. "You're good for him, though. He was such a storm cloud before you. At least, most of the time."

Tyler suddenly appeared in the doorway, drawing my gaze, but Robin's observation stuck in my tired mind. "What's he like now?"

He shrugged and rolled his shoulders. "Still rainy. But the kind that feels good. Like it's helping you grow."

Tyler stomped over to us, and his petrichor scent indeed filled my senses. I grinned down to Robin to let him know that I liked his description, that it made sense to me, but Tyler cut in as he wrapped his arm around my lower back. "What are you talking about? Did you smoke before you got here or something?"

The disagreement between them didn't rise, just shuddered in the awkward pause of conversation. "No, but getting stoned and eating takeout sounds like just what I need." Tyler opened his mouth, but Robin raised a hand to stop him. "Don't even try to lecture me, I saw your stash once. And we can talk about everything later. I'm beat."

Tyler deflated in relief, nodding, and for a second, I felt like I was the one holding him upright. "Fine. And...um," he cleared his throat, "we're doing one last performance before taking a pause while our guitarist is on vacation. If you want to check out the band."

Robin's eyes went wide before he shoved his hands into his pockets and bobbed his head. "Yeah—yeah, I could check it out. Totally."

Oh, these two were definitely related. I kissed Daddy on the top of his head, and I could feel his body warming.

We walked Robin back through the house, but I stopped at the door to give them a moment while Tyler went with him the rest of the way to his car. They shared a few more hesitant words, not at all addressing the blowup that'd just happened, but when Tyler sauntered back to me, he looked weary and lighter at the same time.

I followed him back inside, and we walked the halls that were much darker, now. The bits of outside that were visible through the windows held the glow from the moon and the few lights on the exterior of the house.

Eventually, we were in his—our bedroom. Disappointment reared up my throat when he didn't throw me onto the bed, either to cuddle or tear my clothes off, but I didn't move.

"Are you okay, Daddy?"

He used the front of my hoodie to pull me down into a hard kiss. One that I opened automatically for. His hands and skin on me. The comfort of our bodies together. I whimpered, begged with the submission of my tongue.

He continued to use his control of me to pull us apart. His fangs were out, two pearly points. "I have something to show you, but the scent of Robin on you is pissing me off. And then I'm annoyed at myself for being irritated." Honesty. Tyler examined my face while my breath tickled the frontmost strands of his hair. "Thank you. For talking to him."

My hand settled on his chest, over his thumping heart that was a slow, strong rhythm. It was a lullaby that carried me into my dreams, and now I got to do that every night.

The words just slipped out, okay? The time between realization then confession was way shorter than I'd wanted, but with the sharpness of his fangs and the tenderness in his marbletextured eyes, I was helpless to it. "I love you, Daddy. I would do anything for you."

He blinked, long and slow. Then blinked again before pulling me close to whisper onto my lips. "On your knees, boy."

Had I been expecting him to say the words back? Maybe a little, but he also hadn't turned me away or broken things off the last time I made a leap that he hadn't decided on first.

I swooped to my knees, doing as he said, and looked up at him. "You're going to take off these clothes and put them in the hamper. Take a shower if you have to, but I don't want to smell anyone besides me on your skin when you leave this room. Then meet me at the back of the house. Down the hallway, the last room on the right. Do you understand?"

My belly fluttered while frustration made me squirm, already wanting relief from the tightness of the lingerie I was wearing underneath my pajamas. "Yes."

Tyler gripped my chin roughly, and a moan escaped my lips. "Yes, what?"

Mouth dry and thoughts slipping away, I responded, "Yes, Daddy."

"Good boy. Now, hurry."

He let me go, disappearing probably to the room where he told me to meet him. The one that I stumbled upon being closed off and locked when I'd been doing laundry on one of my first few mornings staying here.

It took me a few more moments to remember how to stand, but once I did, I followed his directives, shedding my clothes and tossing them in the hamper in the walk-in closet.

It was almost torture to peel off the surprise, my own touch igniting the fire under my skin, but I succeeded in denying myself. In the shower as I hastily scrubbed Robin's scent off of me. In the steam of the bathroom as I put the lace set back on and tucked my hard dick into the fabric.

Low, pounding music sounded from the direction I was headed, and I followed it, almost in a trance already. My feet fell in heavy footsteps while floating at the same time until I was hesitating at the threshold. What did he have in this room?

"Come in, boy," he called from the other side, and it was the push I needed to open the door and step inside.

The music wasn't much louder now that I was in the room, the sound more something to seep into your skin and soften your muscles, but my curious eyes fought with the need to relax.

The mellow scent of Tyler permeated the space, as it did with every room in this house. And almost rivaling his scent was the hint of new leather and paint.

The walls were a deep, dusky pink, and on one was a rack of instruments. Some I recognized like a paddle and flogger, some I didn't. There was a curved lounge chair that looked to be the perfect shape for things other than sitting. A wardrobe in the corner implied even more supplies, but my eyes landed on the middle of the floor, on top of the green and pink patterned rug. Bundles of rope waited, as well as the male I was in love with.

He wore a pair of black, loose pants and no shirt, showing off the lines of his arms and chest.

"Come here."

I might not have even closed the door. At first, I was standing in the doorway, then I was on my knees, looking up at him. The one I trusted more than anyone. Maybe even myself because I knew that he would protect me even when I couldn't do it on my own.

"You're so beautiful, sweet boy. Thought you'd surprise me, did you?" He spoke quietly, but it reverberated against my mind even more than the music playing from the set of speakers in the corner. He fiddled with the delicate strap of the cream-colored bra secured on my chest.

Another thing I bought for myself, long ago when I was feeling wistful and romantic but had no one to wear it for. Though, this set, I didn't even dare to wear underneath my clothes as I did with my other things. It had actually never seen the outside of my bedroom, where I'd put it on to feel the caress of the fabric and imagine before packing it away again.

My cheeks flamed. "I wanted to…celebrate. Me moving in."

He continued exploring, tracing his finger along the detail running the edges of the lace that covered my chest. It was almost the color of my skin, leaving more than one suggestion of nudity, and by the dilation of Daddy's pupils, he liked it very much.

"I can see that, petal. We'll get you even more pretty things like this. Would that make you happy?"

I shuddered at his words and the feel of his fingers against my face. "Yes, Daddy. It would."

He nodded. "Do you know what kind of room this is?"

I bit my lip, glancing quickly from side to side before landing on him again. "A sex room."

Tyler smirked, continued to pet my face while my lids threatened to go lower and lower. "Very good. I redid this room for us. If you'd enjoy it, we can make use of it now."

"Okay, Daddy."

"Have you ever been tied up with rope before?" I shook my head and mumbled my answer, heart beating a little bit faster. "Would you like to try it?"

I thought about it a second, lashes blinking up at him. "I don't know how I'll like it, but I wanna try. With you."

Tyler bent slightly to kiss my brow. "We'll stop if you decide you don't enjoy it. I'll check in about what color you're feeling along the way. All right?"

I smiled up at him. "Yes, Daddy."

Tyler crouched fully, now, and pulled me in for a proper kiss. One that brought the tease of his fangs and the slip of his tongue against mine. It was slow, to the beat of the music around us, but my heart pounded against my chest all the same.

Because he hadn't said I could touch him, I kept my hands in my lap, squeezing my knees to make sure they stayed put.

And the kiss went on. On and on with my love's mouth on mine, his strong hands cradling my face so gently, like I was to be treasured. Even when they trailed down my neck, to my chest, his touch turned my skin molten, my muscles into goo.

My cock was hard and throbbing in my lap, and the urgency to have him was at once there and not. I was happy to ride on this current of Tyler. Let him do whatever he wanted to me because I knew that he'd take care of both of us.

The first brush of rope against my skin pushed a moan from my lips into his. Tyler broke the kiss then and locked eyes with me. While mine were already glazing over, his were intense, searching.

He wrapped the line of rope around the top of my chest so that it pressed into my pecs and back. The compression, the sensation of it, made my mouth drop open.

Tyler kept on, tying the rope around me before coming around to my back. The hold on me tightened. "Color," he whispered in my ear.

It was hard to get my tongue to work, what with my mind in warm, fuzzy clouds. "G-green," I managed just before a few shudders of rope and a tug on my back. My spine arched, my hips thrusting in a lazy circle.

Soon, he moved to my arms, binding them behind me in a set of intricate knots that ended at my wrists. And with each loop, Tyler made sure to also caress my skin. To lock eyes with me when I could manage to keep them open, but it got harder and harder to do as he led us through this meditation of pleasure and connection. I'd never had an experience like this before. Had never been with someone like Tyler before. My perfect storm.

"Look at you, petal." My own hold on the moment was shaky, but I could've sworn I heard his voice tremble. Heard the heaving of his breaths. "You are so stunning, sweet boy. So good for me."

I cracked my eyes open, looked at him over my shoulder as he ran his fingers over the knots he made. His face was cast in darkness in the already dim room, but the silver in his eyes shined in the light of the candles. The cords of his neck were tense.

And then he pulled on the rope, stretching my spine. My eyes rolled back in my head at the sweet strain of it. Not a stinging pain, but not comfortable either.

Tyler ran his palm over my chest and thighs while he kept me arched and whimpering. "Color."

"*Green,*" I rejoiced to the dark ceiling, and underneath that, I heard him curse under his breath.

My legs were next, Tyler moving me to his liking until I had to rest on my hip while my thighs and calves were stuck together.

"Fuck, fuck, fuck," he whispered against the soft flesh of my throat while he pulled on the rope, emphasizing the constricting bind. I groaned, panties completely soaked through. "You're amazing, petal. So beautiful and good for your Daddy."

The praise and rope and his touch unclasped the last hold my mind had on this world. Like when I kneeled for him with his fingers in my hair, I slipped away until there was just the physical sensation and need for more. For it to never end.

A string of pleas left my mouth in incoherent babbles. It was probably utter nonsense, but Daddy understood. Suddenly, the press of the rug and floor were gone, and I was in his arms. I writhed against the slip of silk, lace, and the fiber of the rope. The warmth of his skin.

Until it was replaced by the cool leather of a seat. He adjusted my body, using the harness of knots so that my head hung over the edge and my hips were raised. The ties he made allowed for my knees to bend, and with my hands behind my back, I felt him settle behind me and press his hands against my cheeks that were separated by the thong strap of the panties.

"*Oohhhmygooooddd.*" Tyler moved the strap aside and swiped his tongue against my crack and around the jewel plug I wore.

But I couldn't move but for pathetic little wiggles that were stunted by the binds. The pleasure of his tongue on me was amplified more than it ever had been before. So much so that tears collected and fell from my eyes.

He asked for my color again, and I shouted with another pass and swirl of his tongue, greener than green.

It was a little tough, with my legs locked together, but he managed to pull out the plug and continue licking outside and inside of me before adding two of his slender fingers.

Beads of sweat mixed with my tears while tingles of my release began to collect at the base of my spine. Tyler's tongue retracted a moment, and he cracked his palm against my cheeks while he continued to finger me. "Gonnacomegonnacome," I sobbed, wanting so much to be good but also for him not to stop.

And he didn't. In fact, he descended again, eating me out even harder and pushing a third finger against his tongue that was inside of me. The pleasure that'd been building through all of our time in this room collected, becoming a rolling explosion that was painfully wonderful. I wept as my release swept through me, filled the delicate fabric of my panties while Tyler continued to press on my prostate until I shook with oversensitivity.

But he didn't stop. Instead, he replaced his tongue and fingers with the slick head of his cock that pressed just against my opening. "Color," he gritted and grabbed the rope between my shoulder blades.

"Green." I sniffled and trembled with aftershocks but wanting —needing—still.

Tyler pushed into me and released a growl that rivaled any Wolf's. He used the rope to hold me to his liking while he pounded into me, just how I liked. Hard to the point that the slapping of our skin was far louder than the music in the room.

With his other hand, Tyler held my hip, driving into me and nailing my prostate again and again. My cock hardened once more, and another orgasm closed in around me.

From my lips, more babbling words escaped, *"IloveyouDaddypleasepleaseohmygodgodgod,"*

From his, "So beautiful. So good, so tight, my sweet. Mine mine mine mine." And then, he gave me those blessed words as his rhythm turned unsteady and almost frantic, "Come, baby." He sank his fangs into my neck, completing the connection between us. Where I could give to him.

And I blacked out.

CHAPTER FIFTEEN

TYLER

I leaned over my boy, lapping up his blood and fighting to catch my breath after the best sex of my life.

I could say that definitively, after decades of experiences and partners that *this*, with my boy's trust and sweet, sweet submission, was it. That it was mine.

I kissed the back of his neck, tasted the sheen of his sweat and the sunshine of his blood. His heart was still beating heavily. And as much as I wanted to stay inside of him, my desire to care for him was stronger. What I just put him through was to bring both of us pleasure, yes, but it was overwhelming, too.

Slowly, I slid out of him and earned a low moan that shook his frame. For a beat, I watched my cum seep out of his body, and instead of grabbing the plug, I let it be.

It was a testament to how far into subspace my boy went because he didn't request to keep it as he often did. So, I let the sinfully thin strip of fabric settle between his cheeks again, and got to work on untying.

I stayed focused on releasing the pressure slowly, giving him praises for taking the rope and me so well. For coming untouched *twice.*

I'd never seen anything like him, his beauty inside and out.

And he loved me.

My hands fumbled a bit as I released his arms first, but once they were freed, I collected myself and caressed his skin. Delaney groaned again but didn't try to move. His chest and legs were next until a heap of rope was piled on the floor beneath us.

Delaney's admission ran in my head over and over as I picked him up again and walked out of the room I'd remodeled for us. To erase the trace of all others before him.

But when he'd said the words so sweetly and earnestly, then again when he was lost to the pleasure we shared, I couldn't say them back.

I stood back in our bathroom, watching the moon as I waited for the bathtub to fill. Juggling my pet in my arms, I dropped his favorite bath oils into the water until the gentle aroma of lavender filled the space. Once the water was at a good level, I sat him on the bench beside the tub and against the wall.

His eyes were still glazed over, but a melty, dreamy smile was spread across his face. And he remained pliant while I unclasped the bra and maneuvered him out of the soaked panties. The scent of our releases twined with that of the bath, and I inhaled it down before kissing Delaney's cheeks and my fang marks that were already closing up. I picked him up again, and like the sweet pet he was, he wrapped his arms around my neck and held on. I nuzzled against him as I tested the temperature of the water one more time before lowering him into the bathtub.

He gasped before releasing a moan that stirred my body and heart again. I leaned him back against the cushion I'd gotten for him, and once again, thanked everything there was that I'd furnished the space with this large of a tub. Never had I known someone that enjoyed soaking in a warm bath as much as him, and it was just as satisfying to watch his body relax even more into the water.

He blinked up at me, now with skin slightly flushed from the heat. "Thank you." The dimples on his cheeks popped out, and I stood dumbstruck again by his beauty. "Are you gonna get in with me, Daddy?"

I shook myself and cleared my throat. "Yeah, just one second." I raced from the room and grabbed the snacks and water from the fridge that I kept stocked for him and occasions such as this.

This time, I bought an assortment of different fruits, along with a box of the pizza in case he was hungrier than I was estimating. That went on the counter while everything else went on the wooden bathtub tray so that I could easily grab it.

Delaney watched me with sleepy eyes as I prepared everything, but when I finally lifted a leg to step in the bath with him, he floated to one side to make room and stared, biting his lip.

I settled into the tub, careful not to bump the tray or slosh any water on the floor, and he immediately found home in the crook of my neck. My boy was tall and broad, but we somehow fit perfectly, just like this.

"I love you so much, Daddy," he said in a cross between a contented grumble and a whimper.

How could such simple words make my heart flip, my breath stop? It wasn't as if I hadn't been told the words before. Never from my family, but from affectionate friends that were long dead, a few overenthusiastic lovers here and there.

After searching my mind, I realized that I'd never uttered them back. At least, not that I could recall or truly felt. But if I loved this boy, then I would have to ask him to be my mate. To intertwine our lives so that our fates would forever be locked together.

If he were my mate, if I died, he would immediately follow. If fatal harm came upon him, it would kill me too. The part where his blood would become some magical elixir that could save me from the brink of death, and mine him, seemed like a consolation prize to the monumental commitment we'd be making to each other.

I looked down at him, only to find him already staring. The tub was big enough to accommodate his long legs that were cuddled between mine. His blond locks looked brown under the weight of the water, but it was just another beautiful side of him.

Water sluiced down my arm as I settled my thumb in the dimple on his cheek, beneath the dusting of freckles and pink blush.

Tell him, my heart urged. *Ask him.*

And maybe he'd say yes. Start jumping and fawning over me like the excitable Wolf he was and request a party, outfits, and whatever else that I would surely give him and more.

I opened my mouth, but he beat me, eyes widening and brows raising like he just remembered something. "Oh! Daddy, remember how the pack was voting to officially let me in?"

My mind scrambled for a second, trying to follow this new train of thought. Plucking out the day he'd mentioned it, I nodded.

"It's coming up, and I was wonderin' if you'd wanna be there with me? I was gonna ask Leader if it was all right, but wanted to check with you first." He waited with excited nerves, fingers twisting against my chest.

The pack. The family he'd scraped and searched so hard to find. There was no doubt in my mind that they'd let him in, and *if* they let a vampire be part of such a moment, how would my boy handle watching them all die?

If he were tied to me, unless a fucking shifter mob tried to shoot at me again, we would both outlive them all and then some. The witch, her mate, their children, my guitarist, his mate—*all* of them.

Though the thought of outliving Delaney, my sweet boy, made me feel as though that bullet had met its intended purpose, asking him to make that sacrifice for me felt like I would be killing him, in a way. Snuffing out his light.

I swept my thumb across his cheek once again, peering down

at my boy through the hazy steam of our bath. "Of course I'll be there, petal. Whatever you need." And I hugged him closer.

———

Our final rehearsal before Río's hiatus came quickly, and with it, Delaney cementing his place in my house.

His scent twined with mine, opposite but complementary, but as I emerged into the living room, where he'd been earlier, he was nowhere to be found. The rehearsal room was all ready to go, and my band members required little fanfare, which I tried to tell my boy multiple times.

The hanging plants near the window and the bouquet of flowers on the coffee table were pops of green, red, and fuchsia amidst the dark colors I'd chosen when I was single. Everywhere there was natural light, Delaney had stuck some overflowing pot or herb or cutting. I'd cleared multiple shelves in the study to display his Lego creations that were also often floral themed as well.

A more concentrated hit of his scent was scampering toward me, and I smiled over my shoulder. "Oh, Daddy! Okay, I was thinking about the snacks and realized that I just assumed everyone ate meat! I know that we got fruit and stuff, but I was wondering if I should whip up something else right quick." He scratched his head and glanced toward the kitchen. "Or do you think that'd be too much? I could order something and maybe it'd get here in time? I just don't wanna leave anyone out—"

I grabbed his cheeks and forced his focus on me. "Breathe, petal."

He panted a few quick breaths then glanced around the space. "Do you think I should go over in here with the vacuum a little bit more?"

This boy. I pulled him down to kiss, and it only took a few seconds for his lips to melt into mine. My tongue slipped between his lips, moving his to my liking.

Delaney moaned, then louder when I pushed him to his knees. He sat back, hands on his thighs, but I could still see some of his worries filling his gaze.

"Take my cock out, boy." He whimpered, not even hesitating to do what I said. In this room where our relationship had started those months ago, I commanded Delaney through sucking my cock. Emptying his mind and letting him have some peace from his worries.

While I held his face and snapped my hips, I stared into his glazed-over eyes before I spilled down his throat.

He smacked his lips, tasting me, and I kissed the top of his head. "Everything you've done is perfect, petal. Every single thing."

Delaney's pupils were still expanded, but more consciousness was reaching his face. He flashed his dimples at me. "Thank you, Daddy." And then he ducked his head, going shy on me while twisting his fingers in his lap. "I just want your friends to like me," he whispered.

I crouched until we were eye-level. "They better not like you too much because you belong to me." I'd started the sentence with the intention of joking, but a hissing growl reached the last few words. Every day I spent with him, now that he'd officially moved in, a voice in the back of my mind was counting down until I had to let him go.

Delaney's brows furrowed and returned my moment of possessiveness with a canine growl of his own. "I do, Daddy. And you're *mine*. Forever and always."

I couldn't be. Not forever. But I didn't tell him that, wanting so badly to pretend. So, I grabbed him around the throat. "Is that so? And what if someone else wanted me? What would you do, sweet boy?"

His nostrils flared in a way I hadn't seen since the moment he thought I was hitting on his best friend instead of him. Had a small part of my boy been wanting to stake his claim even then?

Delaney bared his teeth and glared beneath his feathery lashes. "Anything to keep them away from you."

I tackled my boy to the floor and trapped his hands above his head in the cage of one of mine. Our kisses were rough, my bare cock hard again and rubbing against the steel rod of his. The panties I picked out for him today were red, and just the thought of them underneath his jeans ratcheted my need even higher.

The front door slammed open and shut, and purposefully heavy steps struck the floor in the hallway. "Yo! Make yourselves decent unless you want us to see somethin' we probably shouldn't."

Delaney grumbled beneath me, and I pulled away from his lips to hiss at the intrusion, just as Río and his mate came into view. In one hand, he held his guitar case, and he had a backpack slung on his shoulder.

"Hey, hey, don't look at me like that." My guitarist pointed a finger, and I hissed again at both of them. He had a mate now, who was also my boy's best friend, but he was also pansexual, so the sliver of threat was still there. "We're here right on time, so if you couldn't keep your dick in your pants—literally—that's not my fault."

His mate, who'd remained silent up until now, rolled her eyes and crossed her arms. "We could've stayed outside, though."

"And not give this douchebag a hard time?" He scoffed while also smirking at me.

I started to pull away from Delaney so that we could get up, but he pulled me back down against him with another growl. His head was craned at an odd angle so that he could glare at our friends. "Don't look at him! He's *mine*."

It wasn't like Río hadn't seen my dick before, but I wasn't about to tell my boy that. We'd never fucked, but with the possessive state I'd egged Delaney into, he probably wouldn't understand if I tried to explain that.

Ramona huffed. "No one's trying to take your vampire."

At the same time, Río whistled and grabbed his mate's hand.

"You Wolves are something else. We'll just christen the practice room for you while y'all get busy out here."

"Shut the fuck up," I snapped lightly at Río's teasing. Delaney was still clinging to me, and I breathed to clear my annoyance so that I could reason with him. "Petal," I said softly. "I'm getting up now."

His grip tightened even more, and he growled, "*No.*"

My head jerked back, not used to insolence from my boy. After I collected myself and he still wasn't letting go, I bent to whisper in his ear. "You keep on the way you're going, and you'll be punished. Is that what you want?" Ramona and Río's steps retreated toward the rehearsal room, but I was focused all on my disobedient boy. "If you really need me, use your safe word, and I'll take care of you. If not, you're going to let me get up." I was strong enough to break his hold, but we both knew that.

Delaney dropped his hands from my waist, and his face fell, too. Now with the threat of someone else seeing me exposed gone, he smacked his hands to his cheeks.

"Oh-oh my god, Daddy. I'm sorry."

His eyes glistened, tugging on my heart while it was still beating with the need to put him in his place. He was already on edge with hosting my bandmates, so I didn't want a punishment hanging over his head all night. I ground my jaw, trying to find a reasonable solution of what to do.

"You were out of line, petal."

He nodded, and his lip trembled. Oh, fuck.

I gave in to the urge to kiss him. "I know that you're anxious, so I'll let it slide. Don't make me regret that." I stood, and he didn't fight me.

I tucked my dick in my jeans before offering him a hand. Delaney gave me all the reprimanded puppy looks as I pulled him to his feet and used a hand on his back to lead him through the house.

"Now, we're going to apologize for our rudeness." Because I

wasn't blameless in what happened just now, but Río had better fucking apologize first.

When we came upon the practice room, thankfully, my guitarist and his mate were fully clothed and keeping their hands to themselves. He was checking the tuning of his guitar while his mate watched his fingers like they were the most magical thing.

I rolled my eyes and cleared my throat. They both looked up at us, and I stared daggers at that asshole. But it took his mate nudging him with an elbow for him to clear his throat and attempt to look contrite. "All right, that's my bad for poking fun at you guys."

My jaw unclenched a tick. "And I'm sorry for my reaction."

Delaney's back was tense, I could feel the strain of his muscles beneath my fingers while his were twisting at his front. He sniffed, and his shoulders were curled inwards. "I'm sorry y'all. I don't—I don't know what came over me."

Ramona fidgeted in her seat beside Río, looking between the two of us. The scent of shifter times three was wild and almost overwhelming, but I breathed through it. Focused on the grounding, summer note of my boy.

"You needed to stake your claim. Even if you logically know we'd never make a move on your ma—vampire. It's fine, Delaney." She even offered a little smile at him, something I only saw her give her family or mate.

And my boy left my embrace to collapse on the sofa beside her and put his head on her shoulder.

The Jaguar rumble and vampiric hiss their proximity incited earned Río and me barely a side-eye. The two of them just went on, Ramona even mussing Delaney's hair in a friendly gesture that, irrationally, didn't look so fucking friendly to me.

Río and I glanced at each other, and I watched in real time as he tucked away the violence in his eyes, letting the jokester persona come forth once again. I called on myself to fight back my own territoriality as well, especially when my time with Delaney had resulted in him seeing his friends less. They were now chatting back and forth, gently tapping and twisting their fingers together as they spoke, heads close.

Wolves.

And I was in love with one.

I focused back on Río, who was now grinning at me like a loon. "So what's been going on, man? You've been MIA from the skate spot. Barely texted the band—you've turned into a recluse." I rolled my eyes and plopped down on one of the stools nearby while Río set his guitar to the side.

"I have a funeral home to run, family shit, and settling Delaney in to think about." Skateboarding had been another thing to pass the endless time I had in Antler Pointe, and meeting Río during an evening skate resulted in me finding a replacement for a very mediocre guitarist. He was better than good, and his company usually didn't piss me off.

He shrugged. "Just sayin'. You're never around anymore."

"And who's going on a months-long road trip?" I spat back. Delaney and I had recently agreed to apartment-sit for them while covertly moving items to the house Río bought for Ramona. He planned to surprise her when they returned to town.

Now, he was impervious to any venom I tried to get him with. "Whatever, man. I'm gonna piss before we get started." With a kiss to his mate's neck—which put him too close to mine for comfort—he left.

And the two Wolves turned to stare at me.

Ramona was the one to whisper first, brow raised. "Quit being an asshole."

I scowled her way, but the expression was wiped from my face when my boy leaned forward and turned his big, innocent gaze on me. "Daddy, he misses hanging out with you."

I twisted in my seat, glancing toward the direction my guitarist had headed. "But we're hanging out right now."

Delaney rose and kneeled in front of me, settling back on his shins. "But y'all used to hang out all the time. He brought that stuff up because it's bothering him. *I've* been taking up all your time."

My hand grabbed his chin, making sure to put my scent atop Ramona's that now clung to him. Truthfully, though, his now held a lingering hint of mine, which only fed my possessiveness. "You don't take up all my time."

And he rolled his eyes at *me*. "Yeah, right, Daddy. How 'bout Ramona and I catch up somewhere else while y'all do bro things?"

"Brat." I kissed him and swept my thumb against the freckles on his right cheek. He had them on his chest, too. And dusted on his back and on the tops of his asscheeks. "Okay, petal. Go show her what all you've done with the house. Brody and Jess should be here any minute."

Delaney leaned in for another kiss, this one as soft as the pet name I'd given him. "Yes, Daddy." He flashed his dimples at me right before turning to his friend and leading her out into the house.

DELANEY

I gave Ramona a quick, formal tour of the house since she said Tyler hadn't given her one before. It was still something to get used to, living somewhere big with nice things, but I fought through my excited stammering to make sure I showed her all the cool stuff! Like the rooms with the best lighting for my plants or my favorite corner to work on my Legos in the fancy office space.

"You seem...happy," she said as we made our way back toward the kitchen.

"Did I not seem happy before?" No telling why the rest of the bandmates weren't here yet, but I myself was starting to feel hungry, so I started serving up the buffalo chicken dip that was staying warm in the slow cooker. Ma's family cookbook still served me well, so of course I had to make one of my childhood favorites for our guests.

Ramona leaned against the counter while I brought the pretty serving dish between us. It was some fancy French brand that Tyler insisted on when we went to a kitchen supply store downtown. The robin's egg color made me smile before I saw the price, but he was already putting it in the cart and wouldn't change his mind. "I mean. You *did*. Sometimes. Like bigger dips into sad that you'd shake yourself out of pretty quick. But now, the dip to sad isn't nearly as big. Your happy seems steadier."

I waited for her to have the first bite while I thought that one over. It was hard noticing changes within myself, but maybe she was right.

She dipped a tortilla chip into the steaming orange, cheesy goodness. "After Tyler hurt you, I was prepared to beat the shit out of him." A low warning growl rumbled my chest, and her amber eyes lifted to lock with mine. "Now I think you'd actually fight me off if I tried." She took her first bite and moaned, nodding and already reaching for another chip.

I didn't like thinking about hurting my friend, so I swallowed down the protectiveness that surged inside of me. Tyler and I had been together only a few months, but my inner Wolf had already made up his mind.

I cleared my throat, swirling my chip in the dip and watching the cheese pull. My voice was quiet so that our words stayed between us. "What's it like to be mated?" I whispered.

Ramona's lips curled upward, giving her face a light, airy appearance. "Amazing. Safe and grounded on a completely other level. Like I always have someone beside me to help figure out the puzzle of life." My chest ached, wanting so badly to complete that connection with Tyler.

But he hadn't asked me.

I continued to tell him that I loved him, and he'd smile, tell me I was his petal or his sweet, perfect boy. But never did he repeat the words back.

Ramona hesitated until deciding to put her hand on my shoulder, rubbing up and down. The contact of my pack sister's touch gave me enough gumption to ask the next question. The one that I'd spent too many of my work and school hours wondering. "Do you think he wants to mate me?"

Her rubbing stopped for a moment as she thought through my question. Then, she leaned closer and whispered even lower. "Río thinks he's scared."

I frowned. Scared? Scared of *me*? Before I could ask, the doorbell and a few jolly knocks hit our ears.

"I got it!" I hollered and smoothed my hands over my thighs. Ramona gave me a funny look, but I rolled back my shoulders and proceeded to answer the door.

The scents of Tyler's bandmates weren't completely unfamiliar—they lingered in the rehearsal room enough that it wasn't hard for me to identify Brody and Jess. He had on a happy smile that was shadowed by a full beard, and her hair was a pretty, fading magenta color.

My grin dipped a little at the stony expression she was giving me, but I was going to do my best. After talking with Alex and him admitting that he'd been pining after Tyler for some time, the flash of smug satisfaction had caught me off guard.

The dip into rotten was swift during that moment, and pieces of it were coming up now in front of my former roommate's childhood best friend.

"Hey y'all, come on in." I gathered myself. "You must be Brody and Jess!"

He kept his shoes on, darting past me after giving my back a few good-natured slaps. "Yeah, hey, what's that smell? You guys get us food?"

"I made some stuff for everyone. I'll dish it out now that you're here!" He was already halfway to the kitchen, and I shook my head, chuckling.

Until Jess gave a meaner laugh, toeing out of her shoes and

leaving them by Río's and Ramona's. I swallowed and tried to straighten my spine. This was my house too.

"Do you need help with your stuff?" Her big tote bag looked heavy, and I was gonna try anything to get her to like me. Brody seemed like the food would be enough to win him over, but I could tell already that Jess wasn't moved.

She raised her head, spreading her lips in a smile that didn't meet her eyes, singsonged a, "No, thanks," and clutched her bag tighter to her side. She swept past me toward the rehearsal room.

A little sob, or the beginnings of one, crackled up my throat, but I forced it down.

"So, I'll be moving out. Thank you so much for letting me sublease these past few months." I was laying it on a little thick, since I knew I was leaving Alex in a bind, but I just needed this conversation to go smoothly. Then I could be at my new home. In my boyfriend's arms.

"Oh." Alex wound a hand in his long hair, frown starting and already making me feel so bad. "Where are you going?"

Was I mistaking the deep breath he took? Like he was preparing himself for my answer? "Um…well, I'm moving in with my boyfriend." I couldn't keep the cringe out of the last word. When Tyler admitted to me yesterday that he knew Alex had had a crush on him, I'd been a mix of emotions.

And then I hadn't been able to really look at or talk to my roommate. Not that I had much since I started dating Tyler. But still, Alex was the reason we met — the invitation to the metal show started all of this. For that, I'd always be grateful and continue to be kind to him.

And for that reason, I was going to try and not take Jess's attitude personally. Hopefully. Would they all notice if I snuck to the bedroom to cry?

Rolling my shoulders back, I made my way into the kitchen and found Brody hunched over the serving dish Ramona and I had been snacking on. Or, rather, he had it cradled in his arms with a blissful expression on his face.

That got me grinning and my belly warm. The house was Tyler's doing, but the cooking was all me.

"Wait until you try the meatballs I made." I opened the lid of the second slow cooker, this one borrowed from Leader and Sylvie because I refused to have Tyler buy another.

"Holy shit, dude, please get married so that we never go hungry during rehearsal again." I blushed as I started to put the meatballs on a platter.

If he said yes, would Tyler want a wedding *and* a mating? One ceremony for our friends and then another private one for us? Who would walk me down the aisle?

"God, Brody, leave some food for the rest of us," Ramona snipped back, only to have Brody shake his head and load up another chip. I smiled wider, looking at my friend.

"Brody, I swear to god, stop eating and get in here." Tyler was walking slowly up the hall, more slowly than I was used to now that I was accustomed to him in the comfort of our home. His natural movements were faster than a human's, and I wondered if his crankiness had to do with constantly tempering himself. "My boy made that food for *everyone*."

He stopped beside me, and my body automatically found the contact of his. Tyler snuck his hand beneath my t-shirt, and I relaxed into his side. My head tilted to rest on top of his.

"Nah, this is the best thing I've ever tasted. It was made for me, obviously. I already told him you guys need to get married." Brody scooped more dip into the dish still in his arms, then started carrying that and the bowl of chips back toward the rehearsal room.

Ramona looked between Tyler and me, arms crossed, and pushed off of the counter. "I can't believe I'm saying this, but I agree. With the first and last things he said, anyway."

My mind started scrambling a little, trying to remember exactly the order of things Brody said, but Tyler must've realized, because his fingers tightened on my skin. I pulled my head off of his and put my hand on his chest.

"Come on, boy," he said quietly. "You can watch us play, then we can soak in the bath together. How does that sound?"

He sounded sad.

I reached up to cradle his face, feel the hard line of his jaw. At least he didn't try to hide from me. He met my stare head-on, brown and silver eyes so open but also not. There was something there that I didn't think I was meant to see.

"Río thinks he's scared."

Well, I would make him un-scared. I'd be brave for both of us.

I dropped a kiss on Tyler's lips. Nothing too hot. Just a reminder.

"I love you, Daddy."

And he smiled, like he always did when I said that, and kissed me again. "I know, baby boy. I know."

CHAPTER SIXTEEN

DELANEY

After classes on Friday, I hustled into Tyler's car when he picked me up, and instead of heading home, we went deeper into downtown Antler Pointe. The traffic was terrible, but Tyler had a bunch of stuff for the show tonight that was packed away in his car. This one was bigger, a black SUV that he drove less often and still smelled new.

But everything was really in the background, because my eyes were glued to my male. My vampire.

When I left home that morning, he'd been in his pajamas, prepared to work from home so that he could also be getting stuff ready for the show. Now, though, he was in a black shirt with the sleeves torn off. His jeans were ripped in a bunch of places, too, flashing his pale skin.

His eyes were lined with smudgy liner, and his hair was slicked back with a few messy strands dangling in front of his face. Really, it was a fairly simple outfit, but the way he carried himself, even sitting, was different.

The piercings laddered up his ears and in his lip all made for a picture that was dark and light, like his eyes.

"You're drooling, petal." I startled and glanced down at my own metal show attire, trying to find the wet spot but seeing none.

I glared weakly at him and huffed, but I couldn't even be annoyed at him. He just looked so good! "Am not."

"Well. If I didn't have to keep my eyes on the road, I certainly would be. You look gorgeous. As always."

I preened, now that I knew getting ready in one of the cramped bathrooms at school had been worth it. Luckily, it was a single-stall that I holed myself up in after all my classmates left in a mob to start their weekend. Tyler had tried to insist that he could pick me up, take me home to get ready, and still make it to the venue in time, but that was just silly.

Based on his reaction now, my cropped Concrete Executioners shirt and black jeans were the right choice. The top was a little tight, but after some twirls in the mirror, I decided that I looked all right.

We pulled into the employee lot behind a row of bars, and I saw Brody walking inside with his bass guitar case in his hand. He up-nodded us, and I waved.

I was still working on Jess, who was luckily nowhere to be seen.

"If Jessica continues to give you a hard time, and I'm not around, let me know. It's disrespectful."

How did he read my mind like that! Tyler pulled us into a spot that wasn't really marked, and I turned a little in my seat to look at him. "It's all right. Well, I understand. She's just taking up for her friend."

He wasn't having it though. "It's not okay. Alex and I were never anything. Neither of us is responsible for an unrequited crush. Now. Did you make sure to do everything on the list I gave you today?"

I wasn't the smartest, but I could tell when someone was trying to change the subject. Tyler and I got out of his car and began to gather the merch, amps, and a bunch of other band things I wasn't familiar with.

"Daddy…do you think it'd be helpful if you talked to him? Alex?"

Tyler scoffed and hoisted several bags onto his shoulders, only handing me a stack of t-shirts to carry. "Why? He'd come by rehearsals and shows, make puppy-dog eyes at me, and now he's talking shit to his friend like I cheated on him. I'm more likely to curse him out."

The back door was propped open already, so we headed inside the bar that was dark and bustling with other band members who were also performing in the show. The lineup had three other metal bands, and one was already on stage doing their sound check.

Someone with a really scary t-shirt walked past, but they must've known Tyler because they exchanged a nod, and I said hello. Once they were gone, I sighed and continued, "It would be nice of you. Maybe he thought y'all were more than you actually were." Being a romantic could do that to you—I just got lucky and found my prince charming. But if I hadn't? I didn't feel annoyed by Alex, just sad.

Tyler still wasn't convinced, though. "You're too sweet for this world, pet. What happened to you wanting to keep away anyone who was interested in me?" We walked into a room with lime-green paint, and Tyler dropped the bags in a free-ish corner. There was a lot of stuff in here already, as well as posters from previous shows and some couches that looked worse-for-wear.

I set the stack of t-shirts on top of the bags and wrapped my arms around Tyler's shoulders. He pulled me in by the waist until our fronts were pressed together. My voice went deeper. "Well if he tried to kiss you, that'd be a different story." I shivered, not wanting to think about what I'd do. If the churn in my muscles and clench of my teeth was any indication, it'd be some sort of bodily harm that I probably wouldn't regret.

"Mmm, there's my possessive Wolf. I wondered for a moment

if you didn't care." Tyler brushed his finger across my lip, and I licked at it with a little flick of my tongue. His eyes darkened as he tracked the movement, pupils expanding.

"'Course I care. I was just trying to be nice." And then, being brave, I licked his finger again and whispered, "Even if we were mated, I'd still get jealous over you. Always." Tyler stiffened, but unless he commanded, I wasn't letting him go. Not with my intention hanging in the air. "If you'd have me."

He swallowed and glanced around, as if—as if looking for an escape route. Now *that* didn't seem like my Daddy at all. When we'd faced down those monsters from my past, he'd stood tall and thrown himself in front of a bullet to save my best friend. But now? When I made it known I wanted to mate him? *That* was the thing he wanted to run away from?

Hurt, blue and damp, had my face falling. I started to untwine my arms from his, planning on running to the car so I could sit by myself for a bit, but he squeezed me even closer. His heartbeat pulsed hard enough for me to feel it against my chest, faster than it normally was. "I...if we mated, Delaney. You would be tied to me."

I blinked. "I know that." Did he think I was that unaware?

"No—no, for my kind, our lives would be joined. You die, I die. I live, you live. You wouldn't be turned, but you would live for as long as I do. Looking the same way you do now."

Oh.

Well, that *was* different from shifters. But—was *that* why he hadn't asked me? That would be odd, living so long, but there was no being without Tyler. I'd already decided that much without this conversation.

Tyler was the one to let go, this time, but he didn't run. He just sighed, looking more tired than I'd ever seen him. He ran his palms over my exposed stomach, softly caressing the hair that trailed toward and past my navel. "We'll talk about it later, petal." Again, my boyfriend—that word was starting to feel less accurate and not enough—looked sad.

Was I afraid of his answer? Or so trusting of his will that I didn't fight it? Probably the first one, because I'd disagreed with him before. Gone against his directives. He talked a big game, but I knew that he hated punishing me as much as I hated corner time.

No, what if he *didn't* want to mate me? What if having me tied to him that long was what he was avoiding?

Tyler held my hand once again, and we finished bringing everything inside. The brush of his arm against mine, his boyish features turned hard and severe, his words of thanks for all my help. It helped keep my mood from totally plummeting, but there was definitely a darker cloud that hung over us that hadn't been there before.

Why had I opened my big mouth?

"Hey, little dude!" Ramona's mate came through the back door, purple electric guitar out of its case and ready to go. He was dressed similarly to Tyler, though his long hair was in a braid that matched Ramona's.

Seeing the two of them together made the cloud grow heavier, threatening to spill, but the smile and hug she brought me into helped some. Like a shiver of warmth to hold off the torrential downpour.

Río and Tyler went up to the stage for their band's turn at soundcheck, so Ramona and I selected a perch to watch from.

It felt like the night I met Tyler all over again. Sitting with Ramona, listening to her mating story. How had it been so easy for them? She'd told me that they made the decision in the moment, following the current that was already sweeping them under, and that it'd been the best decision they ever made.

What was I doing wrong?

"Are you ready for tomorrow?"

I stared at her, thoughts a runaway train that I was struggling to get back on track. Thankfully, she asked me again, and I remembered what exactly *was* happening tomorrow. The pack initiation.

My stomach twisted with nerves and excitement, and I clung to those emotions, even if they made me feel jittery. And despite whatever was happening with us, Leader agreed for Tyler to come to the ceremony.

I sat on my hands and hunched over the high-top table. "Happy. Nervous." She kept looking at me, waiting for me to continue, but I didn't have much else.

Unfortunately for me, my friend was super smart and had a talent for reading feelings. Both of us had pretty good senses of smell, what with our Wolf heritage. She, though, had taught herself to read feelings since, apparently, they all had slightly different aromas. I still wasn't any good at it, but I saw her purposeful sniffs of the air.

Her features twisted in anger, but after watching me longer, they fell. Ramona scooted her chair closer to me and brought her arms around my shoulders. We put our heads together, and that was more than I could've asked for. For her to hold space for this confusion and sadness for a little while.

TYLER

"You good?"

I'd fumbled my way through our sound check then silently convened with the band in the green room so that we could make final adjustments and settle in before the show. Río took over for me, making sure we were all good with our setlist because I was pretty much useless at this point.

The look on my boy's face. Sadness that I hadn't seen from him in so long. And it was my fault.

As many differences as Ramona and I had, seeing her hold my boy didn't spark any jealousy. Begrudgingly, I felt gratitude. That she could be there for him when I felt a chasm widening between us, and I'd been the one to take the giant chisel and make the first gouge.

Brody and Jessica went to the bar to get drinks before the place got too crowded, so with just Río and me in our claimed corner of the green room, I sighed. "Sorry. Just…"

"Everything fine with you and Delaney? He looked sad."

Fuck. Logically, I knew that I wasn't completely responsible for his emotions, but how could I not feel that way? As his Dom and also as the one that was going to have to crush his hopes?

Now *I* felt like crying. "We're good."

My guitarist's black gaze narrowed, and the universe wasn't gracious in my prayers that he'd let it go. "You're absolutely not. What's the issue?"

Groaning into my hands, I quietly recounted what'd happened, leaving it as short as possible. Still, it felt like forever, trying to convey my hesitation toward mating Delaney.

And Río listened intently, even creepily looking me in the eye the whole time, not a joke in sight. When I finally finished, feeling lighter and fatigued, he nodded a few times. "You're being an idiot."

I flinched, wanting to hiss and maybe fight, but there were humans around, so I swallowed the urge. "What the fuck—"

He held up a hand dressed in silver rings. "No. I get your logic, but I don't think you're giving little dude enough credit. He's got a good heart, and you're mistaking that for him being naive. And trying to fall on your sword for no fucking reason."

My guitarist's scathing assessment hit me like a stake to the heart. "And who the fuck asked you?"

He wasn't deterred. He just stood from the questionable couch we were sitting on and stretched his back with a feline flexibility. "Gee, not sure. Just some guy whose head is getting lost in his own ass. *I'm* gonna go see my mate for a second before the show. Later." And I watched him weave his way out of the green room.

Maybe he was right, but he also didn't understand that I was in a constant state of saying goodbye. Grieving the inevitable deaths of those around me. How could I live with myself if I inflicted the same fate on my sweet boy?

By the time my band was called to the stage, the bar was

packed, and we were first up. Normally, the roar of an intimate crowd would give me a buzz. Make me forget my worries and the cage of my life in Antler Pointe. But now, the bars just felt tighter.

The set wasn't terrible, but it wasn't the best either. Our rehearsals paid off, my choice of musicians were obviously the right ones, and even with my mind elsewhere, we made it through with little fuckups.

"We're the Concrete Executioners. And this last one," I locked gazes with my boy, "is called 'Moonflower.'"

His big, brown eyes were wide as I started the song that I'd been working on during the hours he slept. While I watched his lashes fan against his freckled cheeks. His soft smile or the sweet, sleepy grumbles he would make.

I'd tried not to look at him for too long at a time during the other songs, or else I would completely forget the words I'd written. And though a love song wasn't our usual choice, the slow, deep riffs from Río and pulsing beats from Brody and Jess held our audience's attention.

And that of my boy, who hadn't yet heard this one. I sang about delicate flowers blooming at dusk. Using the white petals to guide through the night. Gladly forgoing a sunrise since the flowers were all the light I needed.

The applause at the end, once my voice trailed off, was just background noise for my boy's thundering heart. The stage lights that normally obscured faces and details were no match for my view of Delaney. My moonflower. My petal.

And like the night we met, instead of heading back with the rest of the band, I jumped off stage and walked through the crowd that parted automatically for me. Whatever air I gave off then and now convinced people, drunk and otherwise, to not get in my way.

Tonight, instead of politely telling me to fuck off in misunderstanding, my boy swiveled in his seat, tracking me with his whole body. And when I finally reached him, I grabbed his face and brought it to mine.

I slanted my lips over his, pouring all the love I had for him, all the words I still wasn't ready to say, into the kiss.

A few people cheered, or maybe that was for the next band that was coming on stage, but it was all secondary to my boy's tongue against mine. His sweet summertime scent weaving with my own. He gasped, clutching onto my arms and letting me lead the dance of our lips.

The words still wouldn't come. They were a mix and jumble in my mind, but by Delaney's searching stare, I knew that I had to give him something. Honesty.

"Petal." My voice cracked, but I forced myself to continue, "You mean everything to me. *Everything*. I'm unsure of what that means for us down the road, but I want you to know that *you* are perfect. You've never done anything wrong."

I swiped away a tear that formed and dripped down his face, but like the happy Wolf that he was, he grinned through it. A true one with his dimples. "I love you. And I think you're fibbin' a little 'cause I do plenty wrong."

With a tug in my chest, one that felt stronger and brighter every day, I laughed. "No, you don't. You're perfect in every way." He rolled his eyes, so I pulled him into a hotter kiss, one complete with the tease of my fangs against his lips. This time, when I pulled back, he was panting, and his cheeks were beet red. "Now, let me buy you a drink." He blinked and blinked before nodding and going shy on me.

Holding tightly onto his hand, I led Delaney through the crowd to the bar. For now, I put the concerns for the future to the side. We would enjoy this night together, and many more. Whatever end we had, by death or separation, would be painful. Why couldn't we just revel in being beside one another right now?

My heartbeat harmonized with that of Delaney's which was pressed into my upper back while we waited. My arms were propped up on the bar top while his were around my waist. His chin rested on top of my head.

"Samchon!"

The bartender was making their way down the line, but I turned in the opposite direction to see my nephew waving excitedly. He'd somehow procured a Concrete Executioners t-shirt and was wearing it underneath an unbuttoned flannel.

And the sight of Robin was a welcome one. The person following him, however, had me stiffening within my boy's embrace. "That was fucking *awesome*! You definitely downplayed yourself!" He gave my arm a lighthearted punch that I barely felt.

By the tightening of Delaney's body around me, he noticed whose hand Robin was holding. Their nervous gaze darting back and forth between us.

"Thanks. I'm glad you could come." I nodded, took a bracing breath, and turned my attention to behind my nephew. "Hey, Alex."

Delaney's thumb pet softly against my stomach, as if soothing a skittish cat. But I would try to be nice for his sake.

"Oh—you two know each other?" Robin startled and looked between all of us. He ran a hand through his hair and pulled Alex even closer.

"Um." My drummer's best friend gaped and clutched Robin's arm. "Yeah."

"And Alex was nice enough to let me sublease for a while." Delaney cut in, and I could hear the kindness in his voice.

My nephew, none the wiser about the tension between the three of us, nodded along. "Oh, cool! Yeah, Alex and I met at that bar you recommended, Delaney." And then Robin looked over at Alex, eyes sparkling when his pining was returned with a nervous but equally happy smile. "They've been great."

Alex was dressed similarly to Robin and everyone else here, but his hair was in a shiny, curled ponytail. His makeup slight but noticeable. From the moment I'd met him, I saw the longing directed at me, but all I'd felt was indifference. Neutrality. As I did with most who wanted time in my bed.

Maybe because, somehow, I knew that I was waiting for my boy.

Beside Robin, though, I could see that Alex and my nephew had a spark. "So, um. How do *you* all know each other?" Alex asked.

Robin then turned to panic, and I couldn't help rolling my eyes. Better answer for him before the whole town knew about me. "We're related. Also, are you still okay with both 'he' and 'they' or has that changed?"

Alex noticed that pivot in topic but thankfully didn't press and ask *how* my nephew and I were related. That was harder to explain. "Uh, both are still perfectly fine."

An awkwardness settled upon us, where even with Robin's good-natured questions about the band, it felt like we were taking up space without truly utilizing it. Delaney continued to rub my stomach, something I normally did to him, and it was the only grounding I had with my old irritation for Alex shrinking in the back of my mind.

Admittedly, watching both them and Robin at least provided some relief that they'd moved on. And if my nephew's attachment was any indication, they were a far better fit for each other.

"I was gonna head outside for a second—you guys wanna come with?" By then, I'd ordered a Coke for Delaney and a whiskey for myself, and I looked to my boy for what he preferred.

He dropped a kiss on my cheek in agreement, and we meandered our way to the door and outside. The air was a blast of cool, washing off the hot and tight that'd been clinging from everyone else's body heat.

Out front, metal railing served as a surface to put our drinks on, and Robin snagged one of the ashtrays after settling Alex in a metal barstool. Delaney and I remained standing as I frowned, watching Robin pull a pack of cigarettes and a lighter out of his pocket.

"Don't start, Uncle. I'm an adult," he grumbled in Korean. To which I just huffed and stole one for myself from the pack. Delaney and Alex were chatting back and forth, about Alex's new

roommate who was moving to Antler Pointe next semester to transfer to the college. Some kid named Javier.

"I'm just thinking of your health. I'm sure you know how unhealthy these things are." I lit up and took an inhale while he exhaled a cloud of smoke away from Alex's face.

"And what about your *health? These really don't affect you at all?"*

"No," I shrugged, *"just an old habit at this point."*

A tap on my shoulder brought me out of my conversation with my nephew to find Delaney looking at me, head ducked as he sipped from his straw. Even with the dark clothing and liner on his face, he was a bright, pure guide through the night, just as I'd written in the song.

"Uh, Daddy…do you think you can teach me to speak Korean, too? Or is that too much?"

Oh, fuck me. This boy. I brushed a lock of his wavy hair away from his face and tucked it behind his ear. His lashes fluttered. "If you'd like me to, petal. I'd be happy to."

I hadn't even thought about it, but to bring him even closer to me would be nothing less than a treat. A privilege.

Something about that moment, the way he was looking at me with relief and excitement, cleared the path in my thoughts, leaving a free trail for the words to come. For me to give the definitive stamp that I felt about him the same way he felt about me.

But Delaney suddenly grew panicked, mouth falling into a terrified frown and his heart rate speeding exponentially. His hand began to tremble around the half-drunk soda as his attention was directed behind me.

"Well look what the fucking cat dragged in." A sneer personified, colored with a southern twang, neared us, and I had to breathe deeply through my nose so that I didn't out myself. I pulled my boy more closely into my back and twisted around to find a non-shifter Wolf that bore the slightest resemblance to mine.

"Ch-Charlie. How's it—how are you?" There were enough people milling about that the stark chill coming over our group barely earned a passing glance. Or maybe that was just coming from me.

For my boy, I felt hot rage with his fear that I could practically taste on my tongue. Within myself, though? I homed in on the pulsing within the Wolf's neck. The flush beneath his skin. I could hear the swishing of his blood as it was pumped through his veins.

He laughed, but instead, I imagined myself following him. Maybe back to wherever he was staying. Making his death last to the final drop.

Charlie gave a mean chuckle, looking between my boy and me. My head cocked, and my eyes narrowed. Or, did I want to take his throat in hand and crush his windpipe? There would be less fight that way. For me to drain him dry. The telltale itching of my gums reached an almost unbearable height.

"*This* is your big, bad boyfriend?" I took notice of the rest of him. The shirt and pants he wore were understated but probably expensive. Were they purchased using my boy's money? "Shit, I think I was right to convince your pa to let you rot in that closet. 'Least that way you could stay earning your keep."

When Delaney told me about his upbringing in small bursts, I'd exercised every meditation and calming technique I'd ever encountered so that I could remain the pillar he could lean against for support.

He'd recounted to me how Charlie was 'lucky' to be chosen by my boy's disgusting father. That he'd been grateful at the time for Charlie to have gotten out of the cycle of being used.

But lying in bed with me, Delaney wondered with a cry stuck in his throat. Why he couldn't have been chosen, too.

Over the railing that separated us, my arm shot out and wrapped around Charlie's throat. Eating him wouldn't come at the end of a satisfying hunt. But I didn't *need* to toy with my food.

To eliminate a demon from my boy's past and sate this part of myself at the same time?

Charlie's skin beat frantically beneath my fingertips, and a cold smirk shifted across my lips.

DELANEY

Charlie's admission, one that wasn't even necessary and certainly something I could've gone my whole life without knowing, pummeled against my ears and my heart.

That he'd… he'd convinced my father to let me stay in hell so that he could find comfort warming Pa's bed.

Strangely, my eyes were dry. Other than the surprise, I was mostly just… resigned? That was an emotion I'd seen on the feelings wheel I found online when planning one of my lessons.

Maybe I'd always suspected that Charlie really didn't care about me. That—that he used me, even with the bonding moments we shared when we were in the same predicament. But when he was given a chance out of it? Instead of reaching behind him to pull me along, or even just further out of the muck, he shoved me down with a kick of his boot.

Just as I was about to tell Charlie to leave us alone, Tyler, who'd gone deathly quiet and tense, moved with vampire speed to grab Charlie's throat. With no strain at all, he pulled him closer, and I could sense it. Smell it.

How the rainy scent of my boyfriend went dark, almost black, like the churning of clouds that would release a devastating storm.

Out of instinct, I put my hand on Tyler's shoulder. I'd never seen him like this. Movements almost jerky but also smooth at the same time. His side of the bond growing between us was beating a deathly slow rhythm.

If I had to bet money, I would've said that he was two seconds away from sinking his fangs into Charlie in front of all these people. And not in the sexy way he did with me.

He'd once said that he never saw me as food. That when he fed from me, it was like connecting on the deepest level possible.

Now, though, he looked like a cat with a mouse's tail trapped under its paw.

"Tyler. It's okay," I soothed, bending to whisper in his ear. "Let him go. Please." There were too many humans around, and Charlie wasn't worth it. "I wanna go home."

Tyler had brought a scrambling Charlie just a bit closer, but my words stalled his descent. Maybe months of just me and bagged blood hadn't been such a good idea.

Running my hands against his sides, I kissed his temple. "Please, Daddy? I need you." That got his hunter's gaze, intense and calculating, to shift to me. Silver and brown.

My body heated, and by the flare of Tyler's nostrils, he could sense it. He needed some sort of release, and I wanted him just as badly. I always would. "In the hot tub at home, our big bed, in our special room. Anywhere. I want you to ruin me then take care of me."

That did it. Tyler dropped his hold on Charlie without a second glance and dragged me around the side of the bar. Neither of us said anything to Robin or Alex—I'd get embarrassed about them witnessing all of this later—but we didn't make it all the way home for Tyler to make good on my request. If anyone came outside to their car, neither of us were the wiser, because after finding a packet of lube in the glove compartment, we worked through the need that ran between us.

And when we eventually made it home, band stuff halfheartedly packed in the trunk, we stumbled into the bedroom to do it all over again. That time, though, was slow and lasting with brows connected and kisses swallowing groans.

He hadn't said it, but I knew that Tyler loved me. Through his song, his instinct to protect me, his care of me—*everything*. In the way he made me weep in the best way before cleaning my body and putting me back together with heavenly tenderness.

And in the morning, he made love to me again, whispering

apologies and praises. But, I reassured him, I wasn't bothered by his actions the night before. Just worried that he would be exposed in front of humans for what he was. He may have been stronger, wiser, but I could protect him, too. In my own way.

CHAPTER SEVENTEEN

DELANEY

The next day, my pack initiation was at sunset.

Leading up to it, Tyler assured me time and time again that I'd be accepted. That they wouldn't have me come to a ceremony just to reject me. Somehow, though, I didn't fully believe it until I was lined up next to Ramona and her mate, facing Leader and the rest of the pack. Tyler stood off to the side, with the others but also separate, as a guest.

"Delaney Warner, former member of Howl's Fury. Your insight into the downfall of your old pack has been essential in protecting this one. You have proven to be kind, loyal, and brave, and we have unanimously voted to make you pack." My breaths were fast, my palms sweaty. With all that'd happened since that awful night, I hadn't thought much about those conversations with Leader. When I divulged some about my past, even though I was still a little afraid of him at the time.

Now, I'd found family in more than one form. "Do you vow to respect and honor this land and pack to the best of your ability in this life and after?"

I looked to Tyler, searching for something. Maybe it was the blur of my watery eyes, but his smile, though approving and supportive, held a twist of sadness.

"I-I do," I vowed, voice steadier than I'd anticipated.

And down the line, with Ramona then Río, Leader addressed us all, followed by the pack chanting in unison their vow to us in return. "We see you, we welcome you, and we vow to respect and honor you as pack. In this life and after." Through their promise, though, I watched Tyler. Wishing so much for the day that we'd exchange our own vows. After the mess with Charlie, we hadn't talked about our future. There hadn't been time, but we'd have it eventually.

"Uh-uhm, Leader?"

"Yes?" After pack meetings, Leader always hung around to chat with us, and, knowing from Ramona how much socializing tired him out, I was both nervous and grateful that he was taking the time to speak with me.

"Thank you again for allowing my boyfriend to come to the next meeting. I really appreciate it."

He shrugged while his daughter used his legs as a hiding place for whatever game she was playing with the other pups that were running around. "It's nothing. He saved my sister and has been good to you, as you stated."

I nodded and twisted my fingers at my front. I was taller than him, but not by too much. Even with him not looking me in the eye, his bright green gaze was intimidating all the same. "I was wonderin'...w-what would happen if he became my mate?"

Leader frowned while resting his palm on the top of Dahlia's head. When the pup that'd been chasing her got too close, she screeched and darted off in another direction. "I suppose then, should you both request it, we'll put it to a vote whether he'll be let in the pack."

I let out a gasp and then quickly deflated. Could it be that easy? "Really? I've never heard of a vampire in a pack."

He looked confused. "I haven't either, but why would we deny a mate of yours just because of his race? Sylvie isn't a shifter, but she's pack. Río isn't Wolf, but he is to be pack. It isn't just my decision, but it's a simple one."

I still hadn't told Tyler about my conversation with Leader, about my hope that he wouldn't just agree to be my mate but to also join the pack with me. Just as everyone else's mate had.

The pack bond had already been solidifying with each meeting, each pack run I attended, but with the vows exchanged on Leader's land, I felt a new grounding. One that satisfied my inner Wolf, even if he would never truly come out like the others'.

My friend understood that, and after hugging her, my pack sister *officially*, I moved through the sea of congratulations and smiles to get to my boyfriend.

He was dressed down, like everyone else here, and his hands were stuffed in the pockets of his cargo pants. The oversized hoodie just made me want to cuddle him all night, and after food and a celebratory pack run, I intended to do just that.

Tyler didn't have to say anything. He just opened his arms, and I fell into his embrace, clinging and whimpering with *almost* everything clicking into place.

"I'm so proud of you, petal. How do you feel?" My lips pressed into the curve of his neck. Where I wanted to bite and claim him as mine. Soon.

"Good. Relieved. And so happy you're here too 'cause you're my family just as much as they are."

His petting touch had wandered underneath my shirt, teasing the waistband of the panties we picked out this morning. But now, it stilled. The rest of the pack was laughing, yipping and hollering while Bill and a few others worked on grilling for everyone. The lake beside us lapped in lazy ripples.

"And you're my family," he whispered, but the crackle beneath his words sounded almost painful. "Sweet boy."

TYLER

"So, you wanna let the pan warm *before* you put the oil in," the YouTube chef remarked, and I added this tidbit to my growing list of cooking tips. Growing up, Eomma cooked everything for us, and as a young adult, I did the bare minimum when I had to fend for myself.

Now, I was making up for lost time. Though he enjoyed cooking, particularly from his mother's recipe book, sometimes my boy was too tired to want to make something for himself. And just because I didn't eat food, that didn't mean that I couldn't take care of him in this way, too.

Speaking of recipe books, I directed my attention back to my laptop where I was formatting an electronic version of Delaney's family cookbook so that he wouldn't have to flip back and forth between the old pages when he was moving in the kitchen.

With that open, my phone at the ready for notes, and the TV going, I had more than enough to occupy my mind on my day off from the funeral home. Unfortunately, my boy had his internship *and* parent-teacher conferences leading into the evening, and after *that*, I had a sneaking suspicion that he'd want to resume the conversation of our Future, with a capital 'F'.

At least I had the sight of his form swathed in dark lace as a motivator. Whatever heartbreak would come from that conversation, at least there'd be an opportunity to witness his beauty. Even if it was the last time.

We hadn't discussed it after I watched him become a fully-fledged member of the Antler Pointe Pack, and we'd still put it off when an unseasonably warm day—for fucking October, might I add—brought our friends over to send off Río and Ramona before the months-long road trip slash honeymoon. The pool party had been a great distraction, wherein I soaked up my boy at my feet, and watched him in his element when he was able to host others in our home.

Would Delaney want to move out when I told him that we

couldn't be mates? Could *I* live without him when he inevitably grew… old? And left this world?

No. The second that happened, I'd end it all to join him anyway.

The doorbell rang, and, mind churning with that depressing reality, I paused the video teaching me how to perfectly sear a steak. I scoffed when the impatient delivery person rang the bell again, grumbling all the way to the door.

But when I opened it, it wasn't the groceries I'd ordered, nor was it some forgotten package.

It was that Wolf—Charlie.

With longer hair, perhaps he'd look more like my boy, but his face was devoid of that *goodness*. There were no sweet freckles, nor the summer scent.

His was *too* sweet, like rotten fruit. "Hey there." He put a hand on his hip, twisting slightly to show off a frame that was, by his Wolf heritage, toned. The tight shirt and jeans put that on display, and he ran a hand over his hair that was shiny with product.

None of that drew me in. The vein pulsing in his neck, though?

And if he was so stupid as to show up here to… why was he here? How did he know where we lived?

I didn't say anything, calculating, waiting, but his confidence didn't shift. Instead, he pivoted. "Look, I didn't mean any offense the other night. I was just surprised to see my old buddy, ya know? We're actually cousins, and so I found out he was staying here—"

"You followed my boy?"

His blue eyes shifted, wheels and schemes turning. "Well, really," he widened his eyes, trying for some look that would convince me to his side, "I wanted to talk to you."

"About?" I toyed, keeping my voice measured while already making preparations. It'd been too long, and the night where my boy rightfully kept me from killing Charlie in front of my nephew and the rest of this fucking town had halfway cracked open the lid on this side of myself. No hunt, no kill in *months*.

Waiting for my food to come to me, indeed.

"…and really, don't you wanna find out what I have to offer? I can give you everything he can and more."

My head tilted, catching up that he'd been… trying to convince me to choose him over my boy? "And what would you have me do with Delaney?" I leaned against the doorframe, feigning nonchalance when I really wanted to rip out his fucking throat.

Charlie's shoulders lowered, and he waved a hand. "That'd be up to you. Get rid of him any way you see fit. Honestly don't know why the Serafim's didn't listen to me in the first place. They shoulda taken him out with the rest of the trash."

The dark part of me, one that I'd tried so hard to hide these months, both rejoiced and recoiled in this fool's presence. He'd likely been following my boy and assuring that he was elsewhere this evening. Or maybe he'd been watching us since the night when I almost killed him.

There was no audience here. Not even my boy's purity to raise me out of my instincts that would surely land me a front row seat in hell.

"Come on, *Daddy*, it'd be so easy to get rid of him. He's simple and will go wherever you drop him off. He knows how to find a bed, so you don't even need to feel guilty. And I'll make it all better for you. Can I come in, *please?*" He batted his eyelashes at me, and without a word, I stepped away from the doorway, letting him inside.

Even the night we'd met, Delaney had been wary of me, despite his arousal and excitement. This one, though? Either he'd never met a vampire or he grossly misjudged himself in comparison to my boy who was *everything*.

This one was nothing but dinner.

The sun was already down when he came to, but by then, I'd already cleared the coffee table from the living room. Put the plastic sheet down for easier cleanup. Though I had to do this quick, I also couldn't help myself once I started the ritual. Dragging Charlie's unconscious body into the room.

But I wouldn't desecrate our home or my boy's favorite spaces more than I already was. And when he smelled the blood? Maybe even recognizing *Charlie's* blood?

Perhaps the difficult decisions would be made for me, then.

I breathed through that despair, settling again into the excitement in my limbs. The single-minded thoughts that wanted nothing but to kill.

After all these years, did my Hippocratic oath, taken when I was bright eyed and had the best of intentions, still hold weight?

Charlie groaned in the chair I'd propped him up in, and another shot of thrill popped under my skin. Flashes of how he'd look at the end, pale and drained while his blood renewed my strength, spurred me on.

Not giving him a chance to speak, I raised his wrist to my mouth and let my fangs sink into his vein. He cried out, but even that was pathetic. Delicious.

After taking enough to leave him weak and unable to get up, I dropped his arm, going then to his other one and neck, biting and taking bit by bit. It would've been faster to just go for one of his jugular veins and suck him dry in a matter of minutes. But where was the fun in that?

I stepped away, looking at my masterpiece. At this one who'd taken so much away from my boy, reduced to a paling slump in our home. One that was decorated with signs of life, all thanks to Delaney. I ran my hands through my hair, breathing in the note of death that I preferred to the stale, chemical-laden one at the funeral home.

"Please," Charlie whispered, voice already dying out. He really should've thought better before coming here. In fact, he should've shown *half* of the kindness that Delaney just gave away for free

back when they were younger. Perhaps then, he would've had a different fate. At least, one not at my hands.

But, what could you do?

"You thought you'd come here, insult my boy and convince me to kill him, and make it out of here alive. I should kill you just for being that fucking stupid."

Charlie's eyes were heavy lidded, barely open, but they widened now. Looking over my shoulder.

"H-help, Del…"

And that was when I smelled it. Him. Vanilla and summer, citrus and warmth. And where that usually made me feel settled, more at home than I'd ever, *ever* been, I felt colder than cold.

My body froze, the grief I'd been so adamant in avoiding washing over me like thick, sticky tar. It was over.

CHAPTER EIGHTEEN

DELANEY

I checked my phone one last time, confirming once again that I was making progress through my list for the day.

•Don't worry about tidying the house. I've got it.

•Eat all of your lunch, no exceptions.

•Send me a photo of you in your new lingerie.

•Know that you are smart, you're a good teacher, and those kids love learning from you.

•Text me if you need anything.

The first three things were done, the fourth was a reminder, and, luckily, I hadn't needed anything other than reflecting on the words Tyler had already given me. I'd been through one round of parent-teacher conferences before, but this one still sent me into a small spiral of nerves. Working with kids was challenging and always kept me on my feet. But by far the hardest part was dealing with their *parents*.

I had to draw on all the manners I'd learned from my mama and the reassurance from Tyler. Luckily, though, the batch I was given to speak with were fairly easygoing. I suspected that Yasmine had done that on purpose. Part of me wanted the challenge because I knew I needed to learn, but the other, more demanding part wanted out of here as quickly as possible. The squeeze of lace beneath my dress shirt and slacks every time I moved around the classroom was more than a reminder of what waited for me at home.

Once the last of my parents left—smiling and thanking me to boot!—I checked my phone. No text from Tyler, aside from the curse words after I sent the picture he'd requested after my morning college class.

Yasmine nudged me with her elbow in between her sit-downs with parents. "You're free to head out if you'd like. I know you probably have homework and stuff to get to."

Tyler had ensured that I was all caught up on homework this morning, but I didn't try and correct her. "You sure?"

She said that she was, nicer than she really had to be. And because she was used to me by now, I hugged her briefly, tidied up the room to give her a little extra help, and headed toward the exit. I smelled Leader's and Sylvie's scents somewhere, but my drive to get home to Tyler was stronger. To have his hands and love all over me, and maybe, *finally*, get this mate thing sorted out.

The fancy SUV that Tyler drove us to the metal show in beeped when I put my fingers in the handle. At the same time, the sound of the fancy doorbell camera chimed on my phone.

Tyler set up the app once I'd moved in, and usually, I kept the notifications off. We were far out of town enough that I felt safe. Especially considering who I lived with.

But I had another surprise for Tyler, and I'd wanted to intercept the package before he could, if I was able. But based on the estimated time on the tracking email, it was hours early!

When I pulled up the footage of the front porch, though, all happiness drained from my body.

My heart was bruising the inside of my chest, my throat near burning with my harsh breaths, but I couldn't keep standing in the doorway.

As softly as I could, I set down my teacher bag by the door, toed off my shoes, and walked down the hall. The lights in the kitchen were off, as they were in the rest of the house.

"*Please*," Charlie's rasp was barely audible, even to my own ears.

The metallic scent of blood was almost overwhelming, but nothing could've prepared me for the scene in the living room. Tyler's voice was cold and amused. "You thought you'd come here, insult my boy and convince me to kill him, and make it out of here alive. I should kill you just for being that fucking stupid."

I caught his last word in the same moment that Charlie's dulling eyes met mine. Tyler's back was turned, facing Charlie. "H-help Del…" He was struggling to keep his eyes open, and underneath the chair from the dining room that he was propped up in was a sheet of plastic. Blood slowly dripped from his wrists and neck, and from the color of his skin, he wasn't far from having lost too much to survive.

More of my focus, though, was on my boyfriend. He froze for a long time while the sound of my heartbeat and drips of Charlie's blood falling like raindrops filled our home.

Tyler's shoulders rose and fell in a large sigh, and when he finally turned around, I gasped.

Trails of deep red ran down his face, onto his neck, and into his shirt. His eyes looked almost glassy, and I realized now, the true damage his extended fangs could cause.

The muscle in his jaw pulsed, and he almost said something, opening his mouth even more, before he clamped it shut. He closed his eyes tightly, shook his head, then tried again. "Delaney. I didn't realize you were home."

How I managed to speak, I had no idea. But I croaked, "My… they let me leave early. I missed you."

And Tyler drew in a hard breath, one that held such torment.

He wiped his face, but that just smeared more of the blood. In the background, Charlie tried to say something else, but neither Tyler nor I looked away from each other.

"I never—I never wanted you to see me this way. But," he closed his eyes again, as if he couldn't bear looking at me, "it's too late for that now. I'm sorry." And then he did something I'd never seen him do before.

He fought them, the tears, but I saw twin drops fall and make paths through the blood. My own started to flow, and I blurted the only word I could to get it to stop.

"Red. *Red.*"

Tyler started to cry even more, this time releasing another sobbing breath, but that wasn't what I meant!

Crossing the distance between us, I stumbled down into the sunken living room space, not even caring that my socks were now wet with Charlie's blood.

I took Tyler's face in my hands, and while he resisted at first, remaining immovable stone, he thawed with the passing of my thumbs across his cheeks. "Please don't cry," I whispered over his face. Like this, I could see the male he was and the man he'd once been. Young and scared and determined to live on his own terms.

He still wasn't opening his eyes, but he wasn't pushing me away. At the same moment I kissed his forehead, he gritted through his teeth, "I don't deserve to keep you. To have you. I'm a monster, Delaney."

And that, I was having no parts of. I refused.

"Silly, silly Daddy. You're not a monster. You're an *angel.*" I kissed the tip of his nose, the lids of his closed eyes. I planted another one on his lips, smearing blood on both our mouths. His cheek was hot and slick against the skin of mine, but the warmth beneath, of this male that I loved so much, was filling my heart. My arms wrapped around him, my body curled into his, and I hoped with everything that I had that he felt all the warmth I was trying to give him, too.

He shifted then started pulling away, and as much as I wanted him as close as possible, I also wanted to obey him. To follow his lead.

So, I went for a compromise and gave him space to breathe but kept my hands clutching his back. Like he always did me, I ran them up and down and in calming circles.

"Delaney." Tears still shimmered on the edges of his eyes, but they were harder, now. Narrowed. I wished that he wouldn't use my name. "*Look at me.* I feel bad for scaring you, but I *don't* feel bad for what I've done. I don't think you understand that." His tone got worse by the end of it, and then he was trying to pull away for real this time.

I growled, the loudest I'd ever done with him. The frustration and beginning of heartbreak gave it a rough, pleading edge. "*Red,* Daddy. *Red.* You're not listening to me!"

And he froze.

"You said that if I ever said that, you'd stop, and I need you to stop saying these things. Do I look scared to you? *Do I?*" Never mind the fact that I was crying and growling at the same time, now.

Tyler twisted in my arms a little, and I followed his gaze toward Charlie. He was slumped over in the chair, breathing shallowly and struggling to keep his eyes open.

"*Come on,* Daddy, *it'd be so easy to get rid of him. He's simple and will go wherever you drop him off. He knows how to find a bed, so you don't even need to feel guilty. And I'll make it all better for you.*"

Tyler turned back to me, brow raised and waiting, and I looked down at our feet, at the blood we stood in, the growing puddles beneath Charlie.

I slammed my lips onto Tyler's and tasted pennies and the rawness of him. My Daddy, my Sir, the love of my life. My mate, if he'd have me.

Again, he started off hesitating, stiff. But then, *then,* he reacted, moving with the kiss until it became ours. His tongue twined with mine, tasting Charlie's blood and coming back together again.

And soon, he took over, fisting the back of my hair and pulling my head in just the way he liked. The way I loved. I whimpered into him, submitting to the slides of his tongue and the pressure of his lips. His fangs were always there, too, razor sharp and gorgeous.

He separated our lips with a smack, and we both panted. Our chests swelled and brushed against one another. "I love you, Daddy. Tyler. I do," I whispered.

Tyler licked his bottom lip, tongue a pop of pink against the red that still stained the rest of his mouth. A few drops of blood were dotted near his straight, black brows, and more was streaked around his hairline and into the strands.

He was so beautiful.

"And," he swallowed, "I love you, petal. Delaney. My sweet, sweet boy."

I didn't wait for his lead when I leaned in again, sobbing against his face. It felt as if I'd waited for him to say those words for forever. But now, it was perfect.

Tyler backed up, bringing me with him as he sat on the leather couch where we'd spent many nights and mornings making memories. Love.

He sat first, and pulled on my shirt until I was straddling his lap. His strong grip cupped my cheeks, palming and squeezing them through my slacks. I held Tyler's face, melting into the kiss and confirmation that there was no more holding back. That he would go to any lengths to protect me.

And I would do the same for him, and especially when it meant protecting him from the mean thoughts within himself.

"As my mate, petal, your life would be tied to mine. I die, you die, and the other way around. Our blood would be a cure-all for each other, and you could live as long as me. Stay the way you look right now, forever."

I was already nodding, leaning in for more kisses. With long swipes of my tongue, I cleaned the blood from his cheeks and fed it back to him.

There was no life if I didn't have him, and so much to live

when he was by my side. "Yes, yes, yes, I'm all yours, Daddy. *Forever and always.*" My chest pulled tight with a surge of love and rightness. More whimpering grumbles escaped my lungs, needing my mate even though he was right here.

With his hold on my thighs, Tyler flipped me onto my back, and I groaned as he pressed his hips into mine. His hard cock met the impression of mine through my pants.

My stomach felt light and jumpy, and my eyes rolled into the back of my head as he kissed down my jaw, into my neck. More than butterflies were alight beneath my skin that was a live wire under his touch.

But he didn't bite. Tyler kissed and nibbled, giving me a tease of his fangs while I whined and writhed into him. Only for him to give a nip on my earlobe in answer. He licked around the shell of my ear while increasing the friction between our cocks.

Using the control he had with a hand in my hair, Tyler wrenched my head to the side, putting Charlie's cooling form in my line of sight. His head was lolled to the side, the flow of blood from his body slowed to a few intermittent drips.

"Do you see what I'd do for you, petal?" With his free hand, Tyler ripped through the front of my shirt, sending buttons plunking down on the couch and onto the floor.

His palm slid up and down the edge of my torso that was wrapped in the lace lingerie bodice. It was softer than soft, a gift from him that he told me to wear today and think of him. But the black, hand-woven fabric felt too tight. Like a barrier that kept me away from joining with him.

Tyler flicked his thumb over my nipple, intensifying the constriction of the lace and crashing waves of anticipating plea-sure. "He wanted to take me away from you, and I took joy in tearing into his veins. Ensuring he knew that *no one* will hurt you and live another day. I would make the whole world bleed for you, petal. Each and every person. I don't give a fuck. You're all that matters."

I moaned at his words, the pounding of my heart that was

twice as fast as his. The floating of my mind into that place I reached only with Tyler. Where I was safe and taken care of and could let everything else go.

"You like that, pet?" Tyler kissed his way even lower until he connected with the raised bud of my nipple. Over the lace teddy, he laved it with his tongue, and my back arched off of the soft leather.

I gasped, holding him while I thrust against his stomach, needing more of the good feelings he gave me. The scent of blood was a full cloak around us, as was that of our love. It was the full scope of the perfect day—rain and dark to soothe then the sun to brighten, around and around and around.

Tyler's hand closed around my throat, and he easily ripped open my pants. The first suggestion of freedom left me pushing and thrashing, needing out of my clothes so that I could have him already. "*PleaseDaddyfuckmenownowplease.*" My vision was hazy, homed in on the sensation of Tyler and only Tyler. My words were a quiet, desperate plea.

And he had mercy on me, giving into the need roaring within him that I felt as if it were my own. Intense, dangerous and caring and unconditional.

He leaned away from me, sitting back on his heels, and I blinked, trying to clear my wet eyes and watch him tear through his own clothes.

It was a clumsy fumble to get through both of our pants, but once we did and his naked body was over mine, I started begging again. My cock was trapped against my body by the lingerie, pushing more tears out of me. I needed Tyler's help—to keep denying me that level of freedom. And while he watched me, his black hair and dark eyes were wild, as were the streaks of silver around his expanded pupils.

He wielded his strength, flipping me again until I was on my knees, collapsing my face into the leather. The position felt natural, something I was always meant to do, but only for him. Until our end, whenever that would be. When we'd go together.

The crashes of Tyler's hand against my cheeks were met with my screams of, *"Green,"* before he could even ask. I arched my back further, fully presenting myself for him to take. To own.

Tyler brought my wrists behind my back and removed the plug he'd placed there before I left the house. The lingerie he bought me held an opening in the back, allowing him access without having to take it off and further my torture that was just as sweet as it was frustrating.

And though I was still slick and slippery inside, the press of his cockhead against my hole promised a bit of a burn.

A burn that I needed. "Color," Tyler panted as if he'd been running for days, weeks, and instead of answering with words, I pushed back on him while bearing down. I took him in one plunge, and it drew a loud groan from me and a gasp from him. He split me open in the best way.

Tyler pulled on my wrists even tighter. "Brat," he said before retracting his hips and thrusting forward again with a smack. I bit down on the fold of leather couch beneath me for some sort of purchase and gag, but my screams filled the room nonetheless.

Feral. I'd heard that word applied to my kind and Tyler's many times before. Usually in a mean way, like it was a bad thing to give way to the most natural parts of ourselves.

Sure, it could be violent, especially when you had more strength or speed than most, but joining with me, that was the word that came to mind. With the scent of blood in the air, stirring further my Wolf instinct to submit to my mate and bring pleasure to both of us, I was helpless to it. My hips pushed back on his, spurring the both of us on to fuck hard until there was room for absolutely nothing else.

He'd killed for me. Had been willing to do it in public before.

Tyler's vicious vampire nature was heaven and colored each of his heavy thrusts into me. His cock, thick and *mine*, impaled me while his fingers made indenting marks on my wrists and hip.

And when he changed the angle, nailing my perfect spot dead on as if he'd been sparing me before, I choked. Rejoiced.

His words, I didn't know. They were in his first language, but the communication of our bodies was more than enough. The golden glow was impossibly bright around us.

Until it exploded, sending out sparks behind my eyelids and my mind to float away in the smoke. My muscles tensed and released, even further giving way to Tyler's control. My mate, my mate, my mate.

Tyler flipped me onto my side, where I faced Charlie's body and the art Tyler made with his blood. He lifted my leg and plunged inside of me again. "You're my mate, petal. Forever. And when we decide that we're done with this life, we'll end it together. Never will we be apart. *Never*."

My Daddy's words were like butterflies fluttering against my skin, a gentle reminder of how life could be so beautiful.

The love in my heart, a rainbow of the deepest and most vibrant colors, extended to every piece of me. The pleasure that'd retreated like the rearing of a wave started churning, wanting to crest again. Cum and sweat had made a mess of my stomach and the lace covering it, and my cock was already hardening again with Tyler continuing inside of me.

His fingernails dug into the flesh of my calf and hip, while he reached an impossible speed. I'd surely need a rest after this. Maybe even a day for my body to recuperate, but now, I knew that we had all the time in the world.

And Tyler coming inside of me while our lust-covered gazes locked was the thing that sealed it. The mating ritual would be the official declaration, but the connection was already in our hearts, now.

He painted the inside of me, and with the cum and lube that had slicked the way already there, the addition and his cock made me fuller than full.

I came again. On a smaller scale after the tsunami of the first, but with my fingers twisting my nipples, I managed to release another few lines of cum into the lingerie. My muscles jolted with the triple sensations. All for him.

"I love you, Delaney. More than anything, my sweet, sweet moonflower. My light."

And I grinned, waves of Tyler having swept me up until we floated in the sea of together.

TYLER

I pressed the button, starting the cremator that held Charlie's body inside. After the roar of lust calmed between Delaney and me, we'd luxuriated even longer, limbs tangled, until the need to dispose of my latest kill took over.

Despite my urging Delaney to stay home and let me take care of everything, he continued to refuse, lip jutting out in defiance until I relented. We stripped the body, wrapped it in the plastic, and transferred him to the funeral home.

This process was familiar to me, but to my boy, it was the pulling back of a curtain. He watched with wide eyes while I talked him through all that I was doing. But he never balked in fear. Nor did he complain when we had to wait for the cremator to heat.

Now, with the cardboard box and body within drying out and being reduced to ash, I turned to my boy. "It'll take over an hour for it to be done. Maybe even longer." I shifted on my feet, a large part of me still waiting for him to turn around screaming.

"That's okay, Daddy. What should we do while we wait?" A bit shameless, Delaney eyed me up and down with a blush spreading on his face.

Surprised, I released a sudden chuckle that only had him flushing deeper. "Naughty boy." I brought him closer until my arms were completely wrapped around him. After packing Charlie in my trunk, we'd quickly showered and changed out of our blood-soaked clothes, and Delaney's Antler Pointe College sweatshirt still smelled fresh out of the dryer. "I wrecked your little hole, and you're *still* wanting more?"

He'd been trying to hide it, but I'd seen the abused state of his ass and the way he walked with an uncharacteristic tenderness. What he needed was to soak in the bath and for me to pamper him. Not to join me in getting rid of murder evidence.

Delaney canted his hips against my side, showing me the *very* explicit confirmation that, yes. He was an insatiable little sub, maybe even turned on *more* by the violent turn of events tonight.

How had I not realized until now how perfect he was for me?

"But, petal, you seem to forget that you're due a punishment."

His thrusting stopped completely, and an intoxicating mix of delight and fear swept his features. His plush lips parted as his body curled around me. "For what?"

I thumbed those perfect lips. "For coming *twice* without permission." Another thing I'd noticed as my mind settled after said wrecking.

My sweet boy pouted but didn't fight it. He knew that he wasn't supposed to come without my leave, and how he gave me that control over him was a heady privilege.

"Are you gonna give me corner time?" he whispered.

"No, petal. Just no sex until the day after tomorrow at the very soonest." After the night we'd had, I couldn't fathom a true punishment. So, I'd disguise my caring for him as his consequence.

And he whined while I led us into my office to wait out the cremator. *"But that's so long."* He sank onto the couch, bulge in his sweatpants evident. I adjusted myself before pulling up our usual streaming site on my computer. A few more clicks, and the opening monologue for our favorite show played through the speakers. I twisted around the monitor.

Feigning that I had no problem also denying myself the deep physical connection, I shrugged and sank onto the couch beside Delaney.

Even with his complaining, he cuddled up to me. "You get

brattier every day, pet. What on earth am I going to do with you?" I skimmed lightly over his Adam's apple, already a few ideas in my mind.

Delaney picked up on the sarcasm in my voice and started playfully nipping at my finger. "Keep lovin' on me while I keep lovin' on you."

"Mmm," I hummed as we turned our attention to the show. "That's right, baby boy."

EPILOGUE
TWO MONTHS LATER

TYLER

The four of us sat outside of the coffee shop, under the heated awning, though the cold didn't bother myself or my boy at all. For my nephew and his partner, though, the December chill was palpable.

Delaney was talking excitedly back and forth with Alex, and Robin watched with adoration clouding his eyes. We'd been working through two services we had today when Delaney and Alex came by with bouquets of flowers clutched to their chests.

Now, my office, with its gray walls, was dressed with plants, pictures of my boy and me, and a new bouquet every week.

Instead of our usual walk, we drove to the coffee shop and now sat outside to avoid the crowd that was packed inside.

I blew on top of my boy's hot chocolate, cooling it just that bit more so he'd be able to drink. When I handed it to him, he paused his conversation to kiss my cheek. "Thank you, Daddy."

"Watch it, man. If you make Samchon blush any harder, he might stay red forever."

I rolled my eyes and willed my face to cool. These little double dates were making Robin too comfortable.

Delaney opened his mouth, but I cut him off, threading authority and heat into my voice. "Careful, petal. Depending on what you say, I might change my plans for us tonight."

Even though that was highly unlikely. After months of putting off our mating to make sure that Delaney thought through this decision from every angle, tonight was the night. I encouraged him to talk it through with his friends and family, but each time he came back, he settled into it more and more. He didn't waver once.

Now it was his turn to blush. Did he have a feeling of what was coming? "I wasn't gonna say anything, Daddy." He threw his wide, brown eyes at me. Fanned those lashes until I was helpless. I kissed his cheek like he'd done me and gave another on his earlobe for good measure.

And I didn't miss the little shiver as he turned back to talking with Alex.

"So," I faced Robin again, "are you excited for your graduation?"

He took a large gulp of his coffee and rubbed his thumb on Alex's shoulder. "Yeah. Mom is coming in the day before if you wanna have lunch with us or something." I nodded, open to catching up with Melanie. We'd conversed here and there since my moving back, and whatever Robin told her, she didn't ask any questions about my immortal state. "And…I invited my dad."

I kept my expression calm, but just barely. "You did?"

Robin stared down at the metal table between us. He tapped his fingers on the green surface, his words quiet. "Yeah. Figured it'd be… nice. Hopefully."

William hadn't come back to Antler Pointe since the night we all argued, but he continued to inform me of his sobriety each time I called. And his intention to keep staying at the sober living home. Apparently, Robin had been keeping in communication with him as well.

"It will be."

We stayed outside long after we finished our coffees, hearing of Robin's graduation celebration plans—a vacation with Alex—and his excitement for a break before starting full time at the funeral home. His licensure still required a yearlong internship, so I'd be in Antler Pointe a little longer.

I looked to my boy, who would be graduating in the spring. And then, we'd go anywhere he wanted. Stay here, move cities, countries, come back again. Whatever his pure heart desired, I'd give him.

Feeling my eyes on him, Delaney glanced over and popped his dimples for me, the light of my life. How lucky was I to have him.

DELANEY

I was already gone when Tyler connected the rope to the hook suspended in the ceiling.

The knots along my legs held them in the air, and Tyler fastened the other end to the hold on my wrists, stretching my back and my love for him to an endless loop.

The music had been pumping against my muscles until I could feel it humming through every cell and fiber of my body. I was naked this time, with nothing but a golden headband, the patterns of ties on my skin, and the collar he'd gifted me over a fancy dinner.

The steak and vegetables were far better than the ones by the professional chef those months ago. Because, as I watched Tyler's frown of concentration while he spooned butter and thyme over the steak in the skillet, I'd known that it truly was made with love.

And when he got on one knee? Presenting the delicate, gold chain with an O-ring in the middle and pink, sparkling diamonds on either side? I'd wept and grinned like there was no tomorrow. It was simple, easily tucked into my shirt when I was at work or school, but always with me. Another sign to everyone that I was claimed.

In our special room, Tyler's touches and praises each time he wrapped another length around me were the last push into space. I was here and not, made up only of need and pleasure. Raw clay in his hands and joyous to be manipulated into whatever artwork we could create together.

The suspension, though, brought it to new heights. With my arms and legs bound, I couldn't really move aside from the swaying I'd taken up as he tied me. Now, my back arched, and the strain deepened with my weight contorting me.

The rug was as soft as my whimpers while the fabric pressed against my shoulder, my cheek.

Tyler slowly walked around me. Even with my eyes closed, I sensed his presence, the shift in the air. He'd gone without clothes too, letting me taste him here and there while we did this.

I blinked my eyes open at the brush of his lips against mine. He was crouched beside me on the floor, gently massaging my face. "Look at me, petal."

And look, I did. His hair, though dark as night, shined with faint orange and red in the face of the low lamps. His lips were crimson and dripping from the bites he'd given me as he worked the rope. From the blood I gave him.

"You said the words before we started, but I need to be certain. Are you sure?"

After he proposed, Tyler, the shyest I'd ever seen him, had opened another jewelry box. Inside, was a wide, gold ring with a rectangular pink stone set in the metal. *"If you're willing. I wanted to show that I was yours, too."*

It was a good thing that he'd waited until I was done eating to ask, because, of course, I was full-on weeping then. Nodding and crying, I let him collar me, and then I put the ring on him.

My face was wet again, lying below my mate. It was slow work, scooping my thoughts together and putting them in the right order. But I was able to breathe the words again. "I-I'm yours, Tyler Lee...Daddy. Forever and always."

Another kiss on my lips, the heat of my blood on our tongues, and Tyler whispered over me, "And I'm yours, Delaney Warner. My sweet boy. Forever and always."

Tyler completed his promise, opening up the vein in my neck once again. And, giving into the Wolf inside of me, I followed my instinct that was able to act. I craned my head and sank my teeth into Tyler's neck. It deepened my position even more, heightening the mix of hard and soft that I loved so much as I tasted my mate this way for the first time.

He was like rain, yes, but also the sweet and deep of the coziest night. I sucked on his blood, groaning with the pressure in my chest finally bursting. Tyler held me to him, arms strong and grounding. A new peace overtook me, as if the final part of my soul had slid into place.

"Like I always have someone beside me to help figure out the puzzle of life."

My pack sister's words finally rang true, and when Tyler released his fangs from my neck, and my teeth from his, we made the final joining with flesh, with him inside of me.

After slowly releasing the suspension and lowering my legs to the floor, we groaned in time with each other. Tyler's grip held me steady, and I trusted him with everything that I was to keep me cared for and safe.

"My beautiful mate. My bloom in darkness. I love you. I love you," Tyler whispered while he made love to me, slow and deep. I was beyond words now, but I communicated with my tears, with my side of the living bond in my heart where I could feel his, too.

Forever and always.

ACKNOWLEDGMENTS AND A NOTE

Thank you for reading *Bloom in Darkness*! I hope you loved Tyler, Delaney, and their story as much as I do!

Writing this book came pretty hard and fast, but, per usual, I had help from some kind people along the way.

To Darcy, thank you *as always*, for being my sounding board, my ideal reader, and continuing to provide feedback and critique that helps me polish these sweet and angsty books!

To Bojana, I'm so glad that we've been able to connect through the bookish side of the internet. Your feedback on this manuscript helped me probably more than you'll ever know. After going through a period of deep insecurity over this story, you helped lift me out of it. And without you, this story definitely wouldn't be what it is now!

To Avery, thank you for your help with the early drafts of this story.

To Jules, thank you again for always taking my panicked DM's for art in stride. You continue to bring my characters to life in the best way.

And, like every other book I've written, none of this would be possible without my husband. Thank you for being you. For always hyping up my books to others—even when I get embarrassed. For giving me space to lose myself in writing (while also reminding me to eat), and for continuing to be inspiration that I draw from again and again. I mean, there would be no Concrete Executioners if not for you!

What's next, you ask?

For now, I have my next calendar year of writing tentatively planned out, and with that I've slated the following projects: Juno/Josie's book, Shadows and Flames (book two of the Twin Blades series), and book three of the A Light in the Dark series that will be a villain x villain love story.

I'm also planning some short stories sprinkled in between all of those, so it will definitely be a busy year!

If you're interested in more content, run on over to my website to sign up for my newsletter. I've got artwork, bonus shorts, and exclusive updates for subscribers that you don't want to miss.

And, as always, please rate and review this book on all the relevant platforms. As an indie author, this is greatly appreciated and helpful in connecting my book with new readers!

Until next time!

ABOUT THE AUTHOR

Noelle Upton is an indie author and lover of fantasy, romance, and dark tales. When she's not writing or reading, Noelle enjoys dancing, chatting with friends over good food, and laughing with her husband. Her three series, *Twin Blades*, *A Light in the Dark*, and *Demons & Cryptids* are ongoing, and *Bloom in Darkness* is her fourth novel.

www.noelleupton.com

ALSO BY NOELLE UPTON

Twin Blades

The Warrior Queen, the Protector of Innocents… fights in seedy taverns and picks pockets for the highest bidder.

But her people have been rebuilding from near eradication. And after a century of running, Meline returns home at the request of the only family she has left. They've built a kingdom from ashes and connected with other leaders to give them all a fresh start, but they are still under attack with the threat of another slaughter on the rise.

So, to atone for her sins, Meline agrees to travel to faraway lands and persuade more to her family's cause. Even if the agreement demands she take a personal guard. But not all is as it seems, and her Shadow is hiding a secret of his own.

Through homecoming and redemption, Meline finds herself leaning on her companion as they face tense negotiations, assassins, and the mysterious powers of a dark Goddess. But will it be enough to confront the person she once was and conquer Death? Or will it lead to the ruin of those she loves most and the future of her people?

Shadows & Flames

He is blessed with Fire.

She is cursed with Death.

After years apart, a new contract brings Meline and Elián face to face with both each other and a mysterious new enemy, more powerful than these immortal assassins could imagine. While they travel to a new world, the spark between them burns even brighter, and back in their realm, an old foe has been stoking the flames of war.

Shadows and Flames follows two immortals with Goddess-given powers as they rebuild what was broken between them, rescue a dear friend, and shed light on secrets that could break them all over again. It is the second installment of the Twin Blades series.

In the Light of the Moon

Sylvie, a twenty-eight-year-old undergraduate student, has recently moved to Antler Pointe following the death of her father. She's committed to finally finish her degree in English and to learn her family craft under the tutelage of her grandmother. One night, while closing up at her part-time job, Sylvie stumbles upon an injured man. After helping him on his feet, and watching him shuffle off into the night, Sylvie goes into her last year of college with an enthusiasm to finally set her life back on track. What she doesn't expect, however, is to quite literally run into the man she helped, now fully healed. He's curt and suspicious of her but is committed to settle the debt of her kindness.

Orion is a literature professor who has settled in his hometown after years of trying to find his place. After a disastrous attempt, Orion has resolved himself to live a quiet life on his family's land with nature and books for companions. But once a witch with kind eyes saves him by caring for and generously gifting him with her smiles, he starts to hope that he may not need to remain alone.

However, there is something sinister happening in Antler Pointe, and while they're eager to explore a peaceful life with one another, Sylvie and Orion are quickly swept up in a string of disappearances that culminates in a bloody showdown. *In the Light of the Moon* is a paranormal romance with a fall backdrop where witches and shifters meet, fight, and love. All under the light and shadows of a living forest that calls to both groups with very different songs.

Scars of the Sun

Fresh out of the hospital, **Ramona** has left her apartment and studies to move to the small town of Antler Pointe. Being the non-shifter sister of the local pack Leader is pretty lame, but she throws herself into helping with her brother's kids and working in her sister-in-law's magical garden. Anything at all to keep the dark thoughts at bay. But it's when she locks eyes with a tattooed jaguar shifter that Ramona rethinks what it means to be seen.

Río's days in Antler Pointe have already run out. He's overstayed his usual six months maximum in the little town and should be moving on to the next. After eight years on the run, he's used to the rhythm by now, but he's already put down a few extra roots in this place. And when he keeps stumbling across the non-shifter Wolf girl with long legs and honey eyes, he feels an even stronger pull to stay.

Ramona and Río are both floating through life until they collide in a rich and passionate summer romance. So used to living with no true home, Río is unwilling to let this thing stay temporary, and Ramona is terrified to let her Jaguar go. But a greater threat is looming on the horizon. One that endangers the Antler Pointe Pack and has the potential to blow Ramona and Río apart completely. Will they put their new love before the blood ties of family? How far will they go to protect the ones they care about? And how the hell do they fight a damn shifter mafia?

Scars of the Sun is a paranormal romance standalone novel and book two of the A Light in the Dark series. Prior knowledge of the events of *In the Light of the Moon* is helpful but not required.

Love Always, From Antler Pointe

Welcome back to Antler Pointe, a town filled with humans, shifters, vampires, and faeries. This time, we catch up with Sylvie and Orion for a special moment, Río and Ramona as he tries to make up for some oversights, and Tyler and Delaney as the former showers his mate with an unexpected surprise.

After their own celebrations, the Antler Pointe couples convene for an "Intimate Palentine's Day Extravaganza." Hosted by one very excited Jaguar and his mate who would do anything to keep that goofy smile on his face.

This Valentine's Day novelette is filled with a few spicy moments, a lot of sweet ones, and a special night for this found, supernatural family.

Prior knowledge of the previous *A Light in the Dark* series books is recommended before reading this story.

Wicked is the Night

Xiomara is the head enforcer of the Serafim Group, the best shifter family business in the world. She gets called in to collect heads or make sure people get with the program, but this new assignment is different. When her father tasks her with taking down their biggest rival from the inside out, Xiomara is all too eager to sign the marriage contract. Her husband turns out to be a stupid workaholic, but the job gets harder the longer she's out from under her father's thumb.

Boone isn't new to this. At one hundred and twenty-five years old, he's been in the business since he was running moonshine in the North Georgia mountains. Benicio Serafim has been a thorn in his side for the last few decades, and when the opportunity arises to get close enough to stab him in the back, Boone doesn't hesitate. His new wife is a ball of chaos, claws, and hidden knives, but he slowly grows used to his kitten.

Will Xiomara be able to end Boone Albright when the time is right? Will Boone be able to take down the Serafim Family? And who the hell is stealing from them all?

Wicked is the Night is a paranormal romance standalone novel and is book three of the A Light in the Dark series. Prior knowledge from the previous books is helpful but not required.

How I Became a Succubus's Pet

Daniel, a college junior who somehow found his way in a History of the Occult class, is trying to keep his scholarship. With a degree he may not even want hanging in the balance, he decides to go all-out for this extra credit paper. But conducting a ritual from an old, forgotten textbook isn't one of his brightest ideas.

Not when it ends up being real.

After summoning a succubus and accidentally binding his soul to hers, Daniel is dragged to Hell where he waits for his demon to find a solution. He works in her shop, meets new friends, and builds a new life for himself while Feronia's allure grows by the day. One that asks him to submit.

www.ingramcontent.com/pod-product-compliance
Lightning Source LLC
Chambersburg PA
CBHW032254310726
48973CB00008B/2405